Bloomed to Be Messy

A SMALL TOWN SWEET ROMANTIC COMEDY

MESSY LOVE ON MANGO LANE

DINEEN MILLER

Copyright © 2023 by Dineen Miller

All rights reserved.

No part of this book may be reproduced in any form or by any electronic or mechanical means, including information storage and retrieval systems, without written permission from the author, except for the use of brief quotations in a book review.

This book is a work of fiction. Names, characters, places, and incidents are either products of the author's imagination or used fictitiously. Any similarity to actual people, organizations, and/or events is purely coincidental.

Cover design by Jillian Liota, Blue Moon Creative Studio

CHAPTER 1
Amanda

"Wait...can you read that part again?" Sitting in a lawyer's office on a Saturday afternoon is not what I call fun. And neither would my Aunt Paula. But here we are, just two weeks after her sudden departure from the living and one week after the funeral.

My aunt's lawyer, Mr. Tate, clears his throat as he shuffles papers on his desk. "You have to run the business for one year before you can sell or close it."

"From what date?" One needs to be clear on these things, right? Because, if I'm understanding things correctly, this is about to mess with my plans.

Big time.

He checks the document again. "The date of her death."

I bounce forward in my high-backed chair and slap down the top of the pages so I can see the proverbial fine print. "Well, look at that. Says from the day of her death."

"That's correct." In lawyer-y fashion, he shakes the papers back up. "Shall I continue?"

"Yes, please. Sorry." I give him a grin-like grimace and shrug.

As Mr. Tate continues to read the stipulations of the will,

sunlight streams through the bay window to my right, warming the right side of my body. I turn to gaze out at the bustle of this small Florida beach town that moves with the ebb and flow of tourism.

Mango Lane runs the entirety of downtown Sarabella and is known for its quaint shops and bistros that are mostly comprised of converted houses originally built around the turn of the twentieth century. Along with a close-knit community, the business district here shares a special camaraderie that hasn't changed much in twenty years.

By the way, mangos are to Sarabella, Florida, as garlic is to Gilroy, California.

Big.

We even have a festival in the fall that boasts foods made out of mangos that you never imagined possible, like mango wine and savory mango fries made from green mangos. And the tourists make sure to arrive in time to attend this event that draws vendors, from all over the state of Florida and beyond, who sell their wares.

Being back here brings a flood of memories. Mostly good. Some not so much.

I left several years ago to pursue my own dreams, convinced my days of living under swaying palms and my mother's brow-raising reputation were over. Yet now I'm yanked back by Aunt Paula, whom I adored, but she always had a unique gift of meddling.

Yes, I'm calling it a gift. Otherwise, I'd stomp out of the lawyer's office, refusing to take over the flower business my aunt has so *graciously* willed to me—a ready-made business that has nothing to do with my dreams of being a communications and product designer in the Big Apple, something I'd imagined since being a high school senior in art club. Plus, New York had one of the best art schools in the country.

I *could* cite Mad Men as part of what cultivated my interest in the advertising world, but it only fueled it. In reality, Aunt

Paula is to blame for that one because her father—whom I never had the pleasure to meet—was a real live Don Draper in his day. He even had the same first name!

Thus, I grew up listening to her stories about him and his life as an ad man in NYC that bordered on the scandalous at times. So in reality, she helped set the trajectory of my life, even though she would never have admitted it.

Not that I wanted to do something scandalous. I just wanted more. More adventure and excitement, to see more of this big wide world I lived in. And more distance from my mother's notoriety, which never seems to fade when you live in a place with people who have long memories and sometimes loose tongues.

And finally—the final decider—I wanted out of this beach town that hummed half of the year and slept the other.

Mr. Tate's throat clearing snaps me back to the present.

I give him a smile to reassure him I'm listening. Well, half listening. Most of what he's relaying now has to do with his law firm's involvement in the handling of the will, so I'll just go back to justifying my decision to get out of Dodge nine years ago and reminisce about how well things have worked out.

Well…mostly…

When I moved to New York to go to art college, I figured the Big Apple had room for one more designer. So did my former classmate and current roommate, Sasha, who's more of a fine artist. And since graduation, we've managed to scrape by (not starving, mind you) in a tiny two-bedroom walk-up. Not exactly ideal for creating art, let me tell you.

I'm still more of a production assistant at this point, and Sasha has to work on her paintings on the fire escape, which leaves a lot to be desired but makes cleanup very easy. As long as the downstairs neighbor doesn't happen to be outside at the moment. That's a story I relish telling at any and all opportunities.

But we've persevered, sustained mostly by the belief that our next break was just around the corner. Which one? We had no clue. We just kept turning those corners as they came. Early on, we lived mostly on ramen noodles, peanut butter and jelly sandwiches, and the fancy appetizers at the art shows I frequented with Sasha. Plus, the occasional event my boss needed me to help him schmooze old and new clients.

Over time, Sasha and I have upgraded our menu and splurge on an occasional night out on the town. Not exactly how I imagined my life would look at this point, but it is what it is, right?

"Ms. Wilde, do you have any other questions?" My aunt's lawyer blinks at me through his designer glasses as he neatens the stack of papers in front of him. He sits behind a broad desk with a stack of folders on one end, an overflowing inbox on the other, and a wall of books behind him that appears rather dusty on the upper shelves. Just like his head.

"Did I understand you correctly, her condo is mortgage free?"

He shuffles through a separate stack of papers on his desk. "That's correct. Just the property taxes due at the end of the year, and the monthly HOA fee."

Mr. Tate clears his throat before giving exact figures with his official lawyer expression of authority. I had no idea how pricy living in this beach town had become, which has sprouted and expanded quite a bit in the last five years alone. Not so sleepy anymore, it seems. I do a quick calculation in my head. Less than what I pay for my half of the rent in New York but not by as much as you'd think.

He continues reading where he left off, but my mind has flitted to yet another thought.

"Any stipulations about selling *it*?" Even I can hear the edge of desperation trying to peek its way out in my voice. Maybe Aunt Paula's meddling—I mean generosity, of course—could be used to my advantage for once.

And the way Mr. Tate raises one brow tells me he knows

exactly where I'm headed with this. "Once the transfer of ownership is complete, it's yours to do with as you wish. But if you don't mind a word of advice?"

"Yours or Aunt Paula's?"

"Mine."

I give him a nod.

"Sarabella has grown a lot in the years you've been away. Property is valued at an all-time high, but that has thrust rental prices through the roof as well. A one-bedroom apartment would cost you more than twice the HOA fees on your aunt's place."

Okay, closer to New York rates than I thought. "So, keep the condo?"

Now his other brow rises to create a uniform, fur-lined wrinkle in his brow. "You need a place to live, don't you?"

Boxed in again by my crafty aunt. She always did have an interesting sense of humor that tended to break the rules of decorum but in very subtle ways. To meet her was to be immediately enchanted by her Savannah-born and raised southern charm. The woman knew how to get people to do what she thought was best for them. All out of love, she would tell you. But despite that somewhat irritating trait (only because she was usually right), she was one of the strongest and noblest people I've ever met.

Mr. Tate clears his throat again.

Clearly, he's trained his guttural sounds and facial muscles from years of lawyering. (And yes, that's a word. I looked it up.)

"Any other questions?"

"No, just trying to figure out what my aunt is up to."

He gives me a knowing smile that tells me he knew Aunt Paula better than most. "Paula always had a mission."

"That's one way of saying it."

Mr. Tate either didn't hear my mumble or chooses to ignore me as he slides a set of keys across his desk. "These are to the store and her condo."

I hook the ring on my finger and count five keys. "That only accounts for two keys."

"Paula loved a good mystery, too."

I drop the keys into my bag as I stand and extend my hand. "Thank you, Mr. Tate. I'd like to say it's been a pleasure, but the verdict is still out on that." I smile and give him a short laugh so he'll know it's nothing personal. I know who's still pulling the strings in this scenario, even if she's watching from the heavens she so dearly loved.

After shaking my hand, Mr. Tate comes from behind his desk to walk me out. He's taller than I realized and towers a good ten inches above me. And I'm not short. Now I understand why he's seated in his family picture that sits on the shelf behind his desk. The camera would have been hard-pressed to fit his wife and kids without him looking like a giant.

"I'm here if you need anything. Paula was very special to my family, as well as the firm. Please don't hesitate to call if you need anything, Mandy."

"Amanda, please." What I don't say is that since my mother, born Josephine Wilde, hijacked my nickname to create her stage name, Mandy Wild, I preferred not to bring her up at all in this scenario. But knowing my aunt as I do—did—Mr. Tate is probably aware of our history to some degree.

He blinks and drops his gaze. "Of course. I forgot…" He clears his throat and his gray sideburns stand out against the blush darkening his cheeks. "Whatever you need, I'm happy to help…Amanda."

"Thank you, Mr. Tate. I'm sure I'll be in touch."

I leave the Law Offices of Tate and Tate, which makes me think of the expression 'tit for tat'—a phrase that aptly describes this scenario. My aunt's scheme could very well be her way of telling me moving to New York was a mistake, which at this point in my life, I could be persuaded to see it that way if she were still alive and having this conversation with me.

But she's not and now I'm a prisoner in her little scheme for the next year or more. The next task on my agenda is to let my roommate know that I'll be gone for a while. Maybe she can sublet my room.

And then?

Check out the flower shop I now own and am required to run successfully for an entire year.

As I walk up the steps and unlock the back door of the shop, I'm transported to the past and the fragrant memory of flowers and greenery. I spent most days after school helping Aunt Paula at the shop and always had a guaranteed job during the summer, which was a mixed bag of love and hate. As in, loved having money to spend at the movies or at the mall but hated being stuck at the shop, working while my friends hung out at the beach.

But as I open the door, the putrid stench of rotted flowers assaults me, making me gag. Seems things have been neglected much longer than anyone realized. And let me tell you, the smell of rotting greenery is like none other.

The culprit is a large garbage can of discarded flowers and clippings that clearly never made it to the dumpster before Aunt Paula's sudden departure. With my hand over my mouth and nose, I drag the can outside, walk a few steps away, and inhale the humid mid-morning air that carries a hint of the beach in its scent.

For a moment I'm tempted to lock the door and head in that direction—to the beach and deal with whatever else lurked in the flower shop of death tomorrow. But I've never been one to put off what I can get done today. Especially in light of the big picture. The sooner I get the place up and running again, the better my chances of making it through this next year so I can move on to my original plan. Maybe even with a financial cushion to give me more time to make NYC notice my creative talents.

I snicker out loud at my own thoughts. What does that tell you?

"Mandy?"

I whip around and see a face that brings a flood of childhood memories that includes building sand castles on the beach and hanging out at the movie theatre on Friday nights. All the wonderful memories of growing up in Sarabella.

"Zane!" A flood of warm affection launches me into his bear hug.

"How are you doing?" He steps back but hangs onto my hands, giving me that look that requires only the truth. "I wanted to stop by sooner, but I had to fly out for a conference in California right after the funeral."

Zane Albright is the quintessential surfer, who turned his childhood passion for the beach into a full-blown career. He worked as a lifeguard at Mango Key Beach straight out of high school. Not long after, he revamped the training program for the Sarabella County Lifeguards and now he's Director of Operations.

"A conference full of lifeguards? That sounds like way more fun than a funeral."

"Seriously, how are you?" Zane gives me his concerned, big brother look, which always made things seem better in high school. He's also the only one who completely supported my dream of moving to New York.

"I'm okay."

Overwhelmed by the concern I see in his eyes, I drop my chin, feeling the heavy weight of grief twisting around my neck like the string in my gym shorts caught in the dryer. I refuse to shed more tears over my aunt while I'm still wrangling the mess she's left me to clean up.

Maybe it's payback for all the years she wound up raising me while she waited for my mother—her little sister—to "hit it big" and come back to claim her daughter. "I still can't believe she's gone."

His voice rumbles up in a deep baritone. "I know."

I shield my eyes against the sun that's now peeking over Zane's sun-bleached head and blasting me with its brightness and heat. Sweat trickles down my back. Though nearing its end, summer is still very much present, as is the humidity.

"What are you doing here? Why aren't you at the beach?" I finish my words with a laugh.

"Mom figured you'd need some help. She called me when you left Mr. Tate's office."

Sally is the owner of The Pink Hibiscus, a super cute clothing boutique, and has been my Aunt Paula's best friend since they opened their shops around the same time. Supporting each other in their businesses translated into a close friendship in other areas of life, which meant Zane and I pretty much grew up together.

"How did she know when I left his office?" I know the answer to this question, but I still have to ask.

"She told him to call her when you left."

The small town grapevine was alive and well in Sarabella. I look over my shoulder at the can of putrid death oozing its noxious smell like an evil gas looking for a new victim. Who knows what else lies in store for me inside? Maybe giant cockroaches have invaded and set up shop. Or one of those ornery raccoons Aunt Paula always complained about raiding the dumpster behind her shop because she shared it with Peppery Pete's Wine and Cheese Shop.

Now there's a rank smell in the summer.

Zane glances at his watch. "I can spare a couple of hours before I go on duty. How about I help you figure things out?"

Gratitude nearly brings me to tears again. "Thanks. I can really use the help."

He winks at me before grabbing the garbage can and tipping it over into the dumpster. His face scrunches up as he turns his head away, revealing his pure disgust, which says a lot for a guy who's had to deal with red tide and rotting fish.

Therefore, I am vindicated that I nearly barfed my own putridity at my first encounter with what shall forever be referred to as 'The Can.' God only knows—Him and my Aunt Paula, that is—what else lies in wait for me in the place.

Somehow having Zane's help to navigate the unknown jungle inside boosts my lagging confidence that I might be able to handle what lies in store. In *that* store. I go back inside and scan the back room, which used to be a kitchen when the place was a residence. A plant cooler sits where a refrigerator used to go and a work counter and stool filled the place where a stove might have once stood.

At least that's what I imagined as a child when I helped my aunt. The cabinets needed some paint and small repairs—one seemed to be missing its door—and smears of green, yellow, and red stained the wood table. Evidence of who knows how many floral arrangements crafted over the thirty-plus years my aunt owned the shop.

The storefront itself is spacious and thankfully free of giant cockroaches and angry raccoons. Aunt Paula didn't have much set up display-wise, except for a rickety greeting card display near the counter, a bookshelf with various mugs and decorative pots displaying plant themes, and a table near the front door that touts several dead flower arrangements, an emaciated cactus, and a few orchids that still have blooms—the only things still living in the place.

Three glass-front coolers line the wall to the right, one unlit. The flowers and greenery in the buckets inside have either dried out or drooped over the sides. I can only imagine the stench waiting inside to greet me. Although the baby's breath seems to have persevered.

Does baby breath ever die or does it just dry out?

Zane comes alongside me, toting the can he just emptied.

"How about I empty the coolers while you water what's still living over there?"

He must have seen the look of horror on my face as I stared at the contents. "Thanks. Not sure I can handle any more of that smell."

I open the front door to create a cross breeze, giving up the air conditioning for some hot but fresh air. Outside, I turn around to look at the sign above the door.

Bloomed to Be Wilde.

If you're thinking of the Steppenwolf song, you're on target. My aunt loved that song. So much so she modeled the name of the flower shop after the title, using the spelling of our last name, which aptly describes the women in my family, it seems. Aunt Paula said it was the family motto, which my mother seemed to have lived up to in spades.

And here I stand, the new owner of her legacy.

I glance upward and sigh. Aunt Paula had to be loving this.

CHAPTER 2
Kade

"What did you expect to find out?"

I'm sitting on the sofa in my mother's small but immaculate trailer, wishing I were back in my studio, torching metal. There's a certain satisfaction in controlled destruction. That probably sounds strange, but if you knew my past, you'd understand.

But now my future is about to get way more complicated.

By a four-year-old.

"I didn't know Shannon was struggling."

"Maybe you would if you bothered to check in more often with your family. After she lost her job, she had to move in with a friend. Things got overwhelming for her."

I run my hands through my hair and let out a long exhale. "I'm sorry. Business has picked up over the last year."

What I don't say is that my reputation in Sarabella has grown. An increase in custom home builders wanting original metal work detailing for homes has doubled my orders in the last six months alone, thanks to the popularity of a couple of DIY home shows on TV and social media.

But that won't matter to my mother. She only sees the man

who left the confines of a toxic family that boasts a long line of motorcycle-riding 'bad boys.'

Cliché, I know, but we do exist.

However, I shifted gears five years ago in order to pursue a more creative and lucrative future. It's not that I don't love my family…I do, but I no longer share their perspective that life deals us what we get and we're stuck with it. Nor do I subscribe to the belief that men who are creative and artistic are somehow…unmanly.

Plus, watching a person die brings life-changing side effects. Don't ask me how I know.

Do I need therapy?

Maybe?

Probably.

Right now, all I know is I'm doing what I love and now I may have to redirect for a compact human being whose big green eyes and dimpled smile melt my every resistance.

"I'm so glad life worked out for you while the rest of us are stuck here in the muck."

Acknowledging her comment will only feed her pessimism. I learned not so long ago that you can't reason a person out of a place they didn't reason themselves into to begin with.

I also know she's still bitter. "What else did she say?"

My mother shrugs. "Just that she needed time to get back on her feet, which I was happy to give her. Elly is my granddaughter, and I want the very best for her."

We interrupt this guilt-laden dialogue to interject that this is my mother's way of reminding me of all she's done for me. She's the queen of passive-aggressive dialogue and part of the reason I had to get out of close proximity. The constant reminders of how much I've disappointed her became life-sucking.

"But then this happened," she gestures to the brace encasing her foot and ankle, "and there's no way I can keep up with a four-year-old."

I nod but say nothing because I'm trying to picture how to adjust my life to accommodate a child. Which isn't mine, by the way. Just want to be clear on that. Eliana is my niece. And the daughter of my brother Devon.

"Of course not." I rise from the couch. "Where is she now?"

"Preschool, or what we used to call daycare. My neighbor dropped her off for me. Figured it might be easier for us to figure this out without little pitchers around."

"Little pitchers?"

My mother waves me off. "An old expression. Means big ears, even though hers are small." A hoarse laugh rumbles in her chest.

"When does she get back?"

My mother looks up at me with an expression I've come to recognize as her loaded gun. "That's up to you, now isn't it? Her bag is packed on the bed, and they're expecting you by three."

Unbelievable. "You could have told me this before I drove out here."

"Why? And spoil the fun?"

"No, so I could have planned for a passenger. I rode my motorcycle." I notice her flinch as I check my watch. Maybe she cares more than she lets on. All I know is I have about an hour to get back to Sarabella, get my truck, and come back to pick up the squirt.

I push up to my feet, careful not to let my work boots bump against her coffee table.

A flash of regret moves behind her eyes so fast that I would have missed it had I not been looking for some sort of recognition. But it's gone before it can do anything to soften the hardness that's settled permanently around her mouth. "Then I guess you better figure something out quick."

And now I've clamped my jaw so tight I can only nod. I grab Eliana's bag from a makeshift cot in the corner of the tiny bedroom.

At the front door, I pause. Despite the chasm between us,

she's still my mother, and I'm a duty-bound son. "Do you need anything? Help with anything around here? I can come by this weekend."

She waves me off. "No, I've got great neighbors and people who love me nearby."

Guilt trip received. I exhale, drop my chin, and count to ten. "Bye, Mom."

My mother just stares at me. She doesn't move. Doesn't say a word.

I'm guessing she's disappointed again that I didn't allow her to manipulate me, but as I said, I can't reason someone out of a place they've chosen to be in.

I close the door and stride to where my motorcycle sits. After lashing down Eliana's small bag, I hop on, pulling my helmet over my head, and then crank the motor.

The ride home will give me some time to think and plan, as will the ride back.

Because I don't have a clue about how to take care of a four-year-old.

In a split second, Eliana recognizes me and comes running. "Uncle Kade!"

Her little pink backpack bounces behind her as she runs toward me. I scoop her up with a grunt, realizing she's grown nearly half a foot since I last saw her. And in preschool, no less.

"Hey, squirt."

Her little arms hang onto my shoulders as she stares into my eyes. "You smell funny."

"Yep. I was working."

"Why are you picking me up today?"

My gut clenches because I see Devon staring back at me through green eyes that are an exact duplicate of his, even down to the freckle in the right one. I have one too, but in the opposite

BLOOMED TO BE MESSY

eye. Mom said we got our green eyes from our father, who left town around the time Devon was born. Which left me to become the man of the house.

"Because Grandma sent me to take you on an adventure."

Her little mouth forms a circle to match her rounded eyes.

"Do I get to ride on your motorbike?"

She couldn't get the hang of the word "cycle" when she was younger because of a lisp she's mostly outgrown. Bike became her default and stuck.

"No, not yet. You're still a squirt."

She wiggles to let me know she wants to get down. When her feet hit the floor, she stands straight with her shoulders back and her chin up. She lifts her heels off the floor to look taller. "But look how big I am now."

I squat down and hold her hands. "Yes, you are, but this adventure is bigger than my motorbike."

She frowns, but her eyes are round with wonder. "Bigger than a motorbike?"

I can picture her father's proud smile right now at his daughter's awe of motorcycles. But my mother would kill me if I let Eliana anywhere near one. Shannon, too, for that matter.

"Way bigger. You get to come stay with me for a while. And you can see my metal shop."

"What's a metal shop?"

"A place where I make things out of metal with a blowtorch."

"What's a blowtorch?" Torch sounds more like *torsh* with her residual lisp peeking out.

"I'll have to show you. So, what do you think?"

She lowers her chin. "Did I do something wrong?"

I can almost hear the "r" in wrong this time. She really has grown a lot since I last saw her. As much as I don't want to admit it, my mother was right. I've been too busy and away too much.

17

I hug Eliana. "No, squirt, not at all. Why would you ask that?"

"Because Mommy said she needed a break and now Grandma does, too."

I smooth a rogue, pale brown wisp behind her ear. Even her hair has grown, judging by the Rapunzel braid she now sports. Braiding hair—another thing I'm going to have to learn.

"Grandma broke her foot, which means she can't run around and play very well right now."

"So she called you?"

"Yeah, is that okay?" I almost hold my breath because if she says 'no,' I've no idea what to do next.

The corners of her mouth lift slightly as she nods, looking at me again with Devon's eyes. "Yeah, as long as you promise I can sit on your motorbike."

I stand and tousle her bangs. "I'll think about it."

Eliana crosses her arms and pouts. "All right."

As I take her hand, the teacher walks over, holding out a slip of paper. "Mr. Maverick, can you sign this so we have it on record that you picked Eliana up?"

Nodding, I take the slip of paper and pen.

"Will Eliana be coming back?"

That's a good question. One I don't have an answer to, though. "Uh, I'm not sure, to be honest."

She gives me a sympathetic smile that makes me think she's more aware of what's been going on with Shannon than I am. "No problem. I'll just mark down on her file that she'll be away for a while."

"Thanks, I appreciate it."

She points toward an odd-looking chair near the doorway. "Don't forget her booster seat."

I scrawl my name on the blank line and hand the paper and pen back to her.

A simple slip of paper, yet somehow I feel like I've signed up for something way bigger than I can handle.

CHAPTER 3
Amanda

For the last two weeks, my days have been filled with cleaning the shop, painting cabinets and walls that haven't seen a new layer of paint in at least ten years (the initials of my first crush plus mine are still on the bathroom wall), and scrubbing a squeaky floor that I discovered used to be white when I moved a small display cabinet that I remember from when I was a kid.

And my nights? Well, party girl that I am—snort—those I spend binge-watching YouTube videos showcasing the latest trends in floral arrangements and researching the best marketing strategies for small business owners.

The sooner I can open for business, the better because the meager reserves my aunt left to me for running the place are dwindling fast and my paltry savings have gone toward food and the utilities for my new condo.

Yes, I'm now a condo owner—free and clear. My one relief in this crazy scenario. And one of the keys on that ring turned out to be for a storage area in the building's basement. I found a few pieces of small furniture and about a dozen boxes I've yet to explore. Add that to my unending to-do list.

But today's challenge is—

DUN, DUN, DUUUUUUN...

The cash register.

I'm impressed that Aunt Paula upgraded her system to something this sophisticated sometime during the last year, in which I didn't make it back for a visit. When I tried to figure out this thing yesterday, the machine locked me out. Today I found the owner's manual online and am reading the small print on my phone as I push buttons. So far, the only success I've had is unlocking the cash drawer only because I tried one of the other keys on that mysterious key ring.

That leaves one key to figure out.

As I study the cash register manual, I hear a tapping on the glass, which brings my attention to the front door. Sally is standing there, holding a drink tray with two cups and a small sack bearing The Last Bean logo. I've made *that* place my daily reward for cleaning up *this* one.

The grumbling in my stomach launches me forward. As I unlock the door, the distinct aroma of banana bread—my favorite—fills my nose. Which means she had it warmed up. Saliva has now filled my mouth so full, I'm afraid to say anything lest I drool all over my aunt's best friend in the world.

Aunt Paula may have raised me like a mother, but Sally was like the favorite aunt that played backup. Oh, the irony…

"Anything I can do to help? I brought supplies." Sally holds up the drink tray.

I push the door open wider and wave her in. "Any idea how to operate that thing?" I point to the sleek black beast sitting on the counter as I grab the sack holding my banana bread.

"As a matter of fact, I do. I have the exact same one."

"Seriously?" Banana bread crumbs spray out of my mouth as I say this.

She wags her finger. "Say don't spray, please."

"Sorry." I cover my mouth as I mumble my apology and nab one of the coffees. Once I know my mouth is clear, I dare to speak again. "How did you wind up with the same cash register?"

"Both of us needed new ones, so your aunt negotiated a deal with the vendor."

Of course she did. Aunt Paula knew how to wield her southern charm better than anyone I knew. I once watched her not only charm her way out of a speeding ticket, but then convince the police officer that we needed an escort to the hospital in order to deliver a bouquet to a patient in critical condition.

I have more stories like that one, too. Maybe I should write a memoir about her. I think I'll add that idea to my bucket list.

Sally stands in front of the cash register, her fingers tapping the screen that's illuminating her face with a soft glow. A little tune rings out and she smiles. "There. I entered you into the system with the password, born to be wild with an 'e' and no spaces."

Of course she did. That makes total sense, too.

I crumple the empty sack and mourn the end of my baked goods fix for the day. "Thank you for the banana bread. That's my favorite."

Sally glances at me as she picks up her coffee. "I know. I remember."

A sudden rush of emotion pushes tears into the corners of my eyes. The banana bread threatens to make a reappearance as well.

It's been years since I saw my mother. She didn't show up when I graduated from high school or college, so it didn't surprise me when she didn't show up for her sister's funeral. Her occasional notes or Christmas cards always mention her busy schedule. When they arrive, that is. Come to think of it, I don't think I've seen one of those in a couple of years either.

I don't know where my mother is these days, only that she lives somewhere in Hollywood and is living her dream of being an actress. Like me, when she turned eighteen, she left Sarabella in pursuit of her dream to be a movie star.

Three years later, she came back broke and pregnant.

Being the good sister that she was, Aunt Paula took her in and tried to help her figure out life as a single mother. That lasted all of three years. After which my mother fled back to Hollywood with the promise to come back for me once she hit her fame and glory.

Which she finally did around the time I entered my teenage years. By then, it just made no sense to uproot a teenager and take her to LA. That's what she told Aunt Paula on one of her sporadic visits. Plus, her life of 'glamour' didn't allow her much time to keep up with a teenager in her formative years.

Fine. She could have her life of fame. By then I had a good idea of what I wanted to do with my life and that didn't include her either.

So what did I do as soon as I graduated from high school? Left Sarabella as fast as I could to go after a dream that now seems hazy at best. Funny how many times I've wondered if this was what my mother went through in those early years of pursuing her dream.

Sally's expression turns somber as she looks at me, then over my shoulder at the sparse shop. "Paula planned to do a total makeover on the shop next year."

I hear the sadness in Sally's voice and realize I'm not the only one who lost someone close. Sally was more like a sister to Aunt Paula than my mother was. And Sally's husband, Jacob, owns the local nursery and was Aunt Paula's main supplier since she opened the flower shop.

Sally, Jacob, and Zane are the closest thing I have to a family now. They're all I have in the world. Except for my roommate and best friend, Sasha, but she's more like a porcupine when it comes to relationships. She'll tell you she loves you, but it might prick a little.

I swipe away the thought with a rogue tear. Jacob is

supposed to deliver my first order today. Once I get a feel for all of that, I can figure out what else the place needs to step business up a notch.

Or two.

Because a lot has to happen in a year...

Sally gives me a sympathetic smile. "This will get easier. I promise."

I nod and take a deep, shuddering breath. "I know. Just didn't expect to see the shop in this condition."

She blinks away the moisture that's trying to collect in her eyes, too. "I know. Paula didn't expect things to go the way they did either. None of us did."

I actually laugh, because I can imagine my aunt arguing with death that she had too much to do and needed to get back to her shop. "I can only imagine."

As I sip my mocha, Sally walks me through the system like a pro. And at each step, she backtracks and has me repeat what she showed me so that I can remember the order of functions.

Just as she finishes the last run-through about entering inventory, she scans the rest of the store and frowns. "You have so much open space. Have you thought about expanding the business to more than just plants and flowers?"

I've done little more than eat and sleep the last two weeks, but her suggestion sparks something to life in me. Could this place be more than floral arrangements, flowers, and plants?

"No, actually. I've been on overload, trying to figure out what to order and what to do with it." I finish with a pathetic laugh that borders on sounding like a sob.

Sally leans her hip against the counter. "And I can tell you are oh-so-thrilled by it, too."

"Am I that obvious?" I huddle tighter behind my coffee cup to no avail. Nothing can hide the discouragement that's lodged in my throat right now.

If the store fails, I walk away with nothing. Except for the condo. But at this rate, I may have to take a loan just to make it through the year. I'd rather not wind up in debt.

"You're an artist. You'll figure something out."

"More of a communications and product designer really."

Sally holds me by the forearms. "Then figure out how to communicate with your customers in unique ways. Use that talent of yours to expand this business into something you love. Put your skills to work and create new revenue streams with things you design. You won't succeed if you're not doing something you love. Not really."

She's right. More right than I thought possible. My vision blurs as tears build in my eyes again and drop down my cheeks as she pulls me into a hug. And it feels so good. I can't remember the last time someone hugged me.

Like I said, Sasha isn't the affectionate type.

But Aunt Paula always was, and she knew how to make me feel loved better than anyone I know. I regret not coming back for Christmas last year. Or for Easter or the Fourth of July. Then she got sick and things went sideways fast before I could even get back in time to say goodbye…

I'd give anything for one of her hugs right now.

Sally leans back. "Grab some paper and a pen and let's brainstorm some ideas. We're going to figure out how to make this business a huge success."

Two hours later, I have pages of ideas and thoughts for items I plan to research and figure out how to produce or purchase for the store. Sally was full of ideas inspired by requests she'd received at her store, and things she overheard people saying they found online but only after a lot of trial and error.

Just having a plan of action seemed to brighten my view of what the next year could look like. And you better believe I grabbed onto it with every fiber of my being. Give this girl a project, and she'll get it done. I'm like a dog with a bone, at least according to my creative director, Daniel, who made it clear I could have my old job back anytime I want it.

The back door buzzer sounds as I lock the front door and wave to Sally through the front windows. I race to the back to let Jacob in. My anticipation of filling the place with fresh flowers has kept me from sinking like the Titanic in this whole endeavor. And now that Sally has filled my head with possibilities, I feel like I can wrangle this iceberg by its metaphorical horns.

Or should I say icicles instead to keep with the metaphor of ice? The thought keeps me smiling as I swing the door open.

Jacob is standing there with a bucket dangling from each hand. "Happy flower day! I brought some help."

His familiar greeting brings back a rush of memories of working at the shop as a teenager. As does the man holding a tray of small succulents and cacti standing behind him.

I do a double-take to make sure I'm not mistaken, and I'm not.

It's him.

Kade Maverick.

My high school nemesis.

The bane of my young existence.

The one who made my freshman and sophomore years a royal pain in my—

"Root Beer?" Dark brows lift above killer green eyes that have deepened in color with age and a slanted grin that reminds me why my best friend in high school drooled over him every time he came near.

Me? I called him the Maverick Menace because of that stupid nickname he insisted on calling me. More like shouted it across the courtyard so everyone could hear him. Drove me batty.

Root Beer?

Why? Just…why?

But that was a long time ago. I can rise above this. I really can, right?

I muster all the gumption—Aunt Paula's word—that I accumulated living in NYC for the last nine years and grab the first strategy that comes to mind.

Hand on my hip, I don my best game face. "No, thank you. I prefer Diet Coke."

Kade puts down the tray he's carrying on the worktable and pats his chest like the gorilla I remember. "Kade Maverick. We went to high school together. I was two years ahead of you."

Jacob's frown is so intense that I'm certain more gray hairs have sprouted from his ample eyebrows. "You two know each other?"

I blurt a firm no as Kade says yes. He gives me a look like he's figured out my ruse, but I refuse to relent.

I put my fingernail against my cheek and pretend to think. "High school? Are you sure?"

His expression turns sheepish as he nods. "I wouldn't remember me either. And sorry, by the way, for the nickname."

At a loss for words, I just stare at him because my revenge strategy is now totally defused by his unexpected apology. That's when I notice he has crinkles by his eyes that tell me the man has seen some life and a scar above one eye that runs from his brow into his dark hairline.

"I'll, uh, take this up front." He grabs the tray and leaves me standing there with my mouth still moving but nothing coming out.

Once again, I've made a complete fool out of myself in front of the guy who always rattled me with his stupid soda nickname. But not this time. I'll show him I'm not that bumbling girl who always thought of a comeback too late.

I head to the front of the shop where Jacob is loading the coolers with the flowers he brought.

"This should hold you for most of the week. Once folks know the shop is open again, we can revisit your order." He

BLOOMED TO BE MESSY

plucks an odd-looking light bulb from one of his apron pockets. "And I brought a replacement bulb for that cooler."

Kade unloads his tray on the other side of the store.

"Thank you, Jacob. And those?" What I really want to say is, 'and him?' But I've committed to the role of the aloof woman who doesn't remember this guy from her past and plan to stand by it.

For my protection.

As I recall, Kade had a brother, and where there are two Mavericks, there is trouble. They were wild and unpredictable.

And no, the irony of calling someone else wild when I bear the name and family reputation isn't lost on me.

"Just some extra starter plants I had in stock. No charge. I thought they might help fill your front display a bit more. And if they sell well, we can make them part of your weekly order." Jacob's kindness defuses my cranky state. He's a total teddy bear.

"Thank you, Jacob. I don't know what I'd do without you."

His cheeks actually turn slightly pink. "Aww, you'll be just fine. The folks on Mango Lane look out for each other." He gestures to where Kade is standing by the rickety card display by the front counter. "I asked Mav to look at your card display. Along with the cooler light being out, Zane mentioned it needed some work and thought Mav could help."

Mav? The man has a nickname now? And a cool one. I call no fair!

"Oh. He doesn't work for you, then?" Like I said, I'm committed to the part.

"Goodness, no. He's got his own metal shop, Maverick Metal Works."

Kade—or Mav?—walks over to us. "I can repair the rack, but honestly, I don't see the point. It's rusted in so many places that it would only be a temporary fix." Now he fixes his green gaze on me. "I have a custom display I made for another customer that didn't work out for them. I'd be happy to bring it by."

He's staring at me again as he waits for my reply. One side of his mouth twitches up, almost like a dare, and the challenge is quite clear in his crystal green eyes.

My brain is making some vague argument about making a deal with the devil, but the pounding of my heart over the thought of seeing him again has drowned it out. If I didn't need it, I'd rip my heart out and call it a traitor.

"Sure. That would be great. Thank you." I even smile. See? I can be nice.

"No problem. I'll come by at six." He smiles back, flashing me with a dimple on one side that must have come with age, too, but then I realize it's a continuation of the scar.

What has this man been through?

After Jacob and Kade leave, I stand in the middle of the shop.

My shop.

The coolers are filled with a variety of colors exemplifying the fall season, as well as the standard roses and carnations. Green ferns and baby's breath fill another bucket, along with some eucalyptus leaves, spruce twigs, and chrysanthemums. Jacob set me up well. Now it's up to me to craft some arrangements and figure out what else the place needs.

Kade even did a decent job displaying the small succulents and cacti with their cute miniature clay pots that are begging for some color or a cute design.

This day has been full of unexpected surprises.

The least of which—at least, that's what I'm telling myself—is one by the name of Kade Maverick.

Or is it Mav now?

Oh, whatever!

CHAPTER 4
Kade

Should I be offended that she pretended to not recognize me?

Or embarrassed?

Seeing Mandy again brought back memories of the past—of the old me. Back then, Devon and I had quite the reputation. And sadly, the past has a way of labeling a man and not letting go. Also, part of the reason why I moved back to Sarabella five years ago was to build a new life pursuing what I loved most—metalsmithing.

But Mandy...she's part of my past that I don't mind revisiting. Even though *she* clearly took issue with it. I wanted to tell her I had an ulterior motive for giving her that nickname back then, but the right time never presented itself. And now she's back from New York, and she's...different.

More confident. Maybe even a little snarky, which I like.

I walk into the storage room at my shop and locate the display I have in mind. It's wrought iron with swirls of metal, creating a vining effect around the edges of the stand. Now that I look at it again, I see a way to add some leaves and floral finishes to customize it more for her shop. Maybe if I present it to her as a peace offering, she'll let go of her silly act of not knowing me. I shake my head to myself as I haul the display into my work area.

I don my welding helmet and gloves, then grab my torch just as my phone rings. The preschool's name floats across the top of the screen. I fumble with my gear in a rush to answer it.

"Hello?"

"Mr. Maverick?"

"Yes." My heart is pounding. In the few weeks she's been staying with me, Eliana has become the one female who can knock my life off kilter faster than a loose nut on an axle.

"This is Janet, Eliana's teacher. Any chance you can bring a fresh set of clothes for her?"

I pinch the bridge of my nose. "What happened?"

"She had a little accident…didn't make it to the bathroom, if you know what I mean."

"What about the spare outfit in her bag?" Part of the requirements for the preschool is an array of backup items, which I thought I'd done a pretty decent job of packing.

Janet sighs. "She already used it."

"Two accidents?"

"Yes, she's having a rough day. She'll need shoes, too."

"I see…" Which I don't. "I'm on my way."

After a quick stop at my place, I arrive at the preschool with what I hope will be a suitable outfit for Eliana. At four years old she already has a definitive style all her own that's more about what she won't wear than what she will.

For instance, no jeans—or pants, for that matter. No shorts, tank tops, or T-shirts. She loves dresses and skirts but not ruffles. And you'd think a pair of tights in every color of the rainbow would be enough, but the squirt collects colorful hosiery like grown women collect shoes. In the three weeks she's been with me, she's filled the small dresser and most of the closet in the second bedroom in my apartment. I guess I'm a sucker for a woman who likes to shop.

Or I'm a guy who hasn't a clue what to do with a four-year-old, so we wind up at the playground at the park, in which she destroys her tights, which then requires a trip to a clothing shop to replace them. And let me tell you, girls' tights reproduce like bunnies.

I check in at the main office, as per protocol, before making my way to Eliana's classroom. Since Eliana's birthday is the day after Christmas, she has to wait another year to start kindergarten. Maybe by then her dresses and skirts only phase will have passed, and she'll be more open to jeans and pants.

Janet spots me and rushes over, hands covered with finger paint. "She's in the little girls' room."

I hold up the bag, confused. Why is she telling me where Eliana is?

"The door is right there." She points with a red-covered index finger. "It's a single stall so no one else is in there."

I lower the bag and feel my shoulders slide down with it. This will be new territory for both of us. I approach the door that has 'girls' scrawled across it in playful letters and knock before cracking the door open.

"Elly, it's Uncle Kade. I'm coming in."

"Okay." A sniffle follows.

The bathroom has one stall with a sink next to it. In the corner, I recognize the bright tights, the multi-colored dress with Little Mermaid on the front, and Eliana's purple sneakers.

"Hey, squirt. Here you go." I hold the bag under the door.

"Thank you." I hear another sniffle, which makes my heart clench.

Doesn't seem right to have to deal with this kind of embarrassment at such a young age.

"Need some help?"

"No." This time a hiccup followed by the sound of the bag rustling.

I tuck my fingers into the top of my jeans pockets and lean against the door. "Want to tell me what happened?"

"No." Now she sounds angry.

"Why?"

"'Cuz it's stupid."

I haven't a clue what to do to help. My only experience has been adult females and only a few, to be honest. "I bet it's not as bad as you think."

The stall door opens enough for her to shove the bag back out before she closes it again.

"Are you dressed?"

"Yes." There's a slight warble in her voice.

"Are you coming out?"

"No." Bold refusal this time. Pure and simple.

I roll my eyes. Maybe I need to ask more open-ended questions. Or use the one thing I know she can't resist. "Could I interest you in a Happy Meal?"

The door flies open so fast that I have to jump out of the way.

Eliana nods at me with red eyes still full of tears. "That would be okay, I guess."

I crouch down in front of her. "Let's get your backpack and tell Miss Janet you're leaving early."

Eliana nods. And her bottom lip is protruding more than the norm. I will do whatever it takes to turn that pout into a smile.

I point to the sink for her to wash her hands as I load her wet clothes and shoes into the bag and then wash mine. What a mess. Good thing I'm proficient with washers and dryers because this little kid creates a lot of laundry.

She stays in the hallway as I retrieve her backpack from Janet, who's giving me the once over. But not in a good way. More of the skeptic who's wondering if I'm fit to take care of a four-year-old.

I'm tempted to tell her I'm not sure either.

After a stop at McDonald's, I take Eliana back to my studio to eat her lunch while I finish the display for Mandy. The squirt eats her Happy Meal in a unique fashion—fries first and no ketchup. She says the tomato taste messes with the salt. And then she takes the top bun of the hamburger off and folds the rest in half like a taco. Eliana says that makes a better bun-to-meat ratio.

She's four.

Four years old and already understands how one flavor affects another and knows how to maximize a hamburger. Either the kid is already on her way to being a connoisseur of fast food or a genius in the works. She most definitely got her picky genes from Shannon's side of the family because my side, well, we're simple folk, I guess you could say.

"How's that hamburger treating you?"

Eliana blinks at me. "That doesn't make sense, Uncle Kade."

"Oh? Why not?" I'm kind of half listening because the last flower I'm welding to the display is proving to be more complicated than I planned.

"It's a hamburger. Not a treat." Except it sounds more like she's saying 'hambugga' and 'tweet.'

I have to stop because I'm laughing too hard to keep a steady hand and my shield is fogging up. After turning off my torch, I push up the visor on my helmet with the back of my gloved hand.

Eliana has a confused look on her face.

"I meant, are you enjoying it?"

Finally, a smile breaks her frown. "Oh, yes. It's delicious!"

The kid sometimes uses words most don't, which makes me suspect she takes after her brainiac father, but that thought twists my gut because Devon won't see his daughter grow up into the amazing woman I suspect she'll become.

And that brings me to a terrifying realization—I'm the

closest thing to a father in Eliana's life. I have to take a step back from the display I'm working on because my hands are shaking.

I don't know why I'm suddenly seeing this now, but it strengthens my resolve to be more present for her, and more helpful to Shannon. I owe that to Devon.

After I finish the last touches and wipe down and polish the metal framework, I grab the keys to my truck. I consider stopping in at Sally's clothing shop to see if Eliana can hang out with her for a few minutes while I deliver the display to Mandy, but that would probably break my bank account. And Eliana's dresser is already packed to the max. She'll have to come with me.

"Okay, squirt. I have to take this to a very nice lady." Who I hope won't mind that I have a four-year-old tagging along. But first things first. "Do you need to use the bathroom before we go?"

Her face turns red, and she crosses her arms as she turns her back to me.

Seems my way of communicating annoys ladies of the smaller size as well. I'm at a complete loss, once again.

"Elly, what's wrong?"

She shakes her head, making her long braid swing back and forth. "That wasn't nice, Uncle Kade."

I sigh and crouch down by her. "Okay, can you tell me why?"

Never imagined I'd be taking social etiquette lessons from a four-year-old, but here I am. But then I notice those big crocodile tears streaming down her face again.

I tug her shoulder so she'll face me.

Her face breaks into a grimace. "I didn't have an accident. I lost the bet."

"What bet?"

She tucks her chin. "To see who could hold it the longest."

Preschoolers make bets?

My world just shifted.

"Why did you make this bet?"

She holds her hands out like her mother does when she talks. "To prove I was better at it than Allison."

No doubt about it. She's inherited her father's competitive streak as well. Hopefully, hers won't get her in trouble one day like it did her father. Devon never turned down a challenge.

"Okay, so why do you have to be better than Allison at…at that?"

She deepens her voice, which makes her sound more official. "You ask a lot of questions, Uncle Kade."

"Seriously? I ask a lot of questions?" I shake my head. Can't argue with four-year-olds either it seems. "I'm still waiting for an answer."

She crosses her arms in a huff. "Because she's always bragging about how she never has to stop and use the potty!"

Eliana gives me that look that says this should be obvious, but for a guy who's never even dated a woman longer than a few months, this is way over my head. And I'm trying so hard not to laugh because the kid is adorable, which is inadequate to describe her cuteness.

"Do me a favor?"

Her angry face turns into curiosity. "What?"

"Next time Allison brags about her iron bladder, just ignore it, okay?"

"Why?"

"Because it's not worth hurting yourself. Holding it," I gesture toward her midsection, "isn't good for you. And it's not good for Allison either."

"It isn't?"

"No, she could make herself sick."

"Oh…" She gets this look in her eyes that tells me she's lost in thought.

Maybe not a bad thing.

I give her a few more seconds. "So, are you ready to go?"

Her gaze focuses on me. "I need to go potty first."

CHAPTER 5
Amanda

The shop is mostly ready thanks to Jacob's delivery this morning. I've spent the rest of the morning setting up a display of fall decor items on a small card table I dragged out from the back room and covered with a green tablecloth I found on one of the shelves.

Dissatisfied with my result, I grabbed my purse and went on a mission. First to Aunt Paula's—or rather, my storage unit. Aunt Paula loved to decorate for every season, and I remember a fall-like table runner she spread out every Thanksgiving.

Despite living in tropical Florida, I've always loved the dazzling array of colors associated with fall best. And living in New York fed that love affair well. Taking drives out of the city into the countryside to see the change of colors became a weekend pilgrimage for my roommate, Sasha, and me.

And this table runner epitomizes it—a tapestry of mustard, orange, and red leaves detailed with gold and bronze-colored threading. Just thinking about it makes me long for the first hints of the leaves changing colors I would see as I walked past Central Park on my way to work. The telltale signs of fall that held the promise of more to come.

But, back to reality. On the upside, tropical foliage is always green.

The storage unit is compact—about eight by eight. Small boxes fill the shelves built into one wall. Aunt Paula set up gorilla shelves on the other side, which contain more boxes and some clear containers, revealing mostly Christmas decorations.

But a container appearing mostly filled with orange catches my eye. I slide it out and open the top. There're all kinds of stuff in here I could use at the shop—leaf garlands, pumpkins, and a candle that smells like a bakery. I've heard of real estate agents baking cookies in houses before an open house to boost potential sales.

If those drives to the countryside taught me anything, it's that atmosphere is key. And since I'm going to be practically living at the shop, I might as well use it to make the place more festive and cozy. Or 'hygge' as Sasha would say.

As I dig around the contents, my fingers hit something that feels smooth and satiny. I tug it out and smile. Even in the muted light of the storage area, the colors are gorgeous. After a little more digging, I find another container with mostly fall stuff and load them both into Aunt Paula's ancient sedan, which is so old I'm not even sure what kind of car it is because the emblems have all fallen off.

Although it's technically a peninsula, Sarabella has a secluded island feel because of the way most of its land mass juts out into the Gulf of Mexico. Tourists and natives alike love it here. But to find a mall or large shopping center, you have to drive a good thirty minutes or more, depending upon the time of year.

Like now. My trek to the nearest craft store to buy ceramic paints takes almost an hour each way, but I'm determined to paint the small ceramic pots containing the succulents and cacti that Kade carried in.

Which again shifts my thoughts back to him, dredging up more memories of living under that ridiculous nickname he gave me. I remember him being pretty rough around the edges back in high school, but I always sensed there was more behind those sparkling green eyes.

Seeing Kade yesterday proved me right…I think. He seems different somehow, but I'm not sure. Something has definitely changed. He's reserved but comfortable with himself.

As I park in front of the store, my cell rings and Sasha's smushed face picture shows up. A wave of nostalgia hits me as I remember the day we took these pictures using the window on the fire escape. Sasha got the idea from a social media post. Now, every time we call each other, we look like we're trapped inside each other's phones.

I tap the green button and her actual face appears.

"How's it going?" Sasha never minces words.

I know she chose a video call so she can tell if I'm holding it together or not. "Fine, I guess."

"You guess? That's kind of sad." She pouts, which only accentuates her full lips even more. Sometimes I wonder if my artistic friend should have been a model instead. But her art rocks, so there you go.

I shrug. "Still making peace with this being my life now."

"*For now*. Big dif. In less than a year, you'll put this all behind you."

"I know, I know. But when have you known me to be patient?"

"Never." Her answer is quick because Sasha knows me better than anyone now that Aunt Paula's gone.

"Exactly."

"Where are you now?"

I hesitate. If Sasha finds out I'm about to walk into a craft store, she may start ripping her clothes and throw ashes on her head.

She gives me the side eye. "Amanda, where are you?"

"About to go into a craft store to buy little bottles of acrylic craft paint. Please don't judge me!" My words come out in a rushed jumble.

Sasha leans back from the phone and crosses her arms. "What are you painting? And please don't say a canvas."

"No, nothing like that. Jacob brought me these small cacti and succulents in cute ceramic pots. They're begging to be painted."

She uncrosses her arms and leans forward, looking almost excited as she lists off some suggestions, which include a clear sealant to protect the paint and give a shiny finish. I suspect she may have done something like this in her distant past, but I don't dare ask.

Then she goes off the deep end with ideas. "Oh, and you can paint cute little critter faces on some, too. What animal is Florida known for?"

"Gators. And I don't mean the ones you drive around in."

"I mean cute animals."

"Racoons?"

She gives me a skeptical look. "Depends on who you ask."

I sigh. "Thank you for not judging me."

More than anything, I want to hop in the car with her and take a road trip to upstate New York and see the leaves changing,

"Never. But I gotta run. Call if you need more inspiration."

And then she's gone.

I drop my phone into my purse and get ready to brave the craft store.

Never in a million years could I have imagined the highlight of my day would include painting cute critters on clay pots.

❋❋❋

KADE SAID he'd come by around six. It's now five-thirty and my heart has decided to pick up speed, making my hands shake. Good thing hibiscus flowers have wavy edges because the one

BLOOMED TO BE MESSY

I'm painting is looking rather irregular at the moment. After adding several yellow dots around the matching stamen, I again check the image I pulled up on my laptop for a quick comparison.

"Well, that's as good as it gets." I put the pot down with the others I've been working on. The worktable in the back room is covered with paint bottles, paint splatters, and happy little ceramic pots. Once I seal them, I can put these out with the rest of them. So far, Aunt Paula's runner looks amazing on the display table. And I found these handy clear trays at the craft store that I'll put under the pots so they don't damage the fabric.

I check the time again—5:40. Should I check my hair? I have paint all over my fingers and my cuticles now resemble a bag of Skittles.

Why do I even care? It's been well over ten years since I've had to listen to Kade Maverick's teasing. His graduation day put an end to that irritant. And my graduation two years later marked the beginning of a new life. When I moved to New York, I shed 'Mandy' and became 'Amanda.'

At the time, I figured I might as well make a completely fresh start with no past nipping at my heels. And it's worked, mostly. Aunt Paula still called me Mandy when I came to visit. As did Sally. Only Zane switched to using my full name, but he understood better than anyone why I needed to shake my mother's ties to my nickname.

You've heard of women who have daddy issues? I guess I have mommy issues.

There…I said it.

Being alone in the shop has given me a lot of time to think. Maybe too much.

As I put the finishing touches on another miniature pot, a knock comes from the front of the store.

He's ten minutes early. No time to make sure I don't have something hanging out of my nose or to wash the color spectrum from my hands. Time to face the Maverick Menace.

I chuckle to myself as I walk to the front. Now there's a nickname I can get in line with.

Kade's standing outside, holding an ornate metal display that has me so intrigued I'm walking faster. But then I realize he's not alone…there's a little girl with him. Is he married and has a kid now? For some reason, the thought shoots down my good mood.

Again, why do I care? The guy drove me nuts in high school. I should feel sorry for his wife.

I unlock and open the door. "Hey there."

"Hi." He says nothing else, just stares at me.

I touch my nose to be sure nothing is hanging out of it.

His gaze tracks with my hand. "You've been painting."

I hold my hand up so I can examine how bad the mess is. Yep, I look like a preschooler who broke into the paint stash. Less paint would have wound up on my fingers if those ceramic pots weren't so small.

"Yeah, just my attempt to dress up the plants Jacob brought."

He tips his head at the display he's holding up. "Hopefully, this will help."

Then it dawns on me. He's being subtle in letting me know I need to get out of the way so he can bring it inside.

"Oh, sorry. Come in." As much as I want to take in the gorgeous metalwork of this display, I'm more fascinated by the little girl who's following close at his heels and is the spitting image of him. "And who is this beautiful young lady?"

Kade's smile widens to flash that single dimple/scar on his cheek again. "This is Eliana. Hope you don't mind me bringing a helper."

He raises his brows as if to plead with me to play along, which, of course, I'm happy to do. But I'm guessing there's a deeper story here.

Besides, we ladies need to stick together. "No, not at all. I need all the help I can get."

BLOOMED TO BE MESSY

Sad thing is, I mean it. I do need all the help I can get because I have a to-do list that would stretch the entire length of Mango Lane.

Twice.

Kade positions the new display stand next to the check-out counter where its sad predecessor waits to be retired to the dumpster. Eliana has made a beeline for the table of wee things, much like herself, and is examining my handiwork with an enchanted smile that makes me believe in myself just a little more than I did ten minutes ago.

But it's the display that grabs my attention next. "Wow, it's beautiful! Did you make this?"

"Yes." He kind of laughs as he grabs a stack of greeting cards from the old display and drops them into a slot on the new one. "Should fit all your cards with room to spare."

I'm dumbstruck by the beauty of the vines and leaves that cover most of the framework, but it's the flowers that weave across the top that really grab my attention. Hibiscus with detailed stamens and trumpet flowers cluster the top, and there's even a hummingbird feeding from one of the blooms.

Did I mention I absolutely adore hummingbirds?

"Seriously? You made this." I end with a half question, half statement.

As Kade meets my gaze, something flickers in those green eyes of his, like sunlight peeking out from behind the leaves of a tree. "Yeah, I really made this. Is that so hard to believe?"

I rein in my reaction a bit. "Maybe. Not that I didn't think you capable of such artwork…" Which actually, come to think of it, maybe I did.

Guilty as charged.

"But…" He's waiting for me to finish this thought, so I'm scrambling for what to say that won't make me look like a total idiot.

I shrug. "No buts. It's just amazing. And so perfect for the store."

47

He rewards me with a slow smile that sports the dimple again.

Eliana tugs on the bottom of my shirt. "Uncle Kade did all the flowers today. He worked really hard."

Uncle Kade? Not Daddy…so maybe not married after all? Then I remind myself that I don't care. I'm not interested in anything more than a business relationship here, if even that. Once this transaction is complete, I can get on with business and not think about the way every cell in my body comes to life when he looks at me.

I tear my gaze from his adorable fan to the man who seems intent on playing down his talent. "Just today, huh?"

"I didn't really do that much. Mostly just some clean up." He stares at me again.

Yep, like sunlight activating photosynthesis in plants. My insides are buzzing so loud I wonder how he can't hear it.

Time to redirect before I become a puddle of swoony goo. I touch the hummingbird.

"I can't believe you did that for me." My voice is soft and filled with emotion. As I clear my throat, he drops his gaze and grabs another stack of cards.

"Like I said, it was for another client, but it didn't work out."

Eliana points to the display table. "Did you paint those?"

"Yes, I did. Do you like them?" Maybe I'll get a miniature fan today, too.

She nods. "Can I paint, too?"

Kade looks like he's about to say no, so I jump in. "Yes, of course! Like I said, I can use all the help I can get. That's if Uncle Kade says it's okay."

He studies me as if to make sure I'm not kidding or something.

I give him a small nod to let him know I'm dead serious. Creativity is nothing to be trifled with. That's my motto.

"Sure. But don't get paint on your clothes, okay?"

I hold my hand out to Eliana but keep my eyes on Kade. "No worries. I have an apron she can use."

The apron fits Eliana more like a full-length dress, so I cinch the neckband as tight as possible without choking her and wrap the ties around her twice and tie a bow in the back. "How old are you, Eliana?"

She holds up four fingers. "Four, but I'll be five soon."

I lift her onto the stool in front of the workbench. "What color do you want to start with?"

She scans the bottles lined up at the back of the table. "Pink, purple, and green."

"Okay, three it is." I squirt a dollop of each color onto one of my makeshift palettes. I learned from Sasha that coated paper plates make clean-up easy and are cheaper than disposable paint palettes, which gives me the idea of enticing my best friend to come to Florida for Christmas. What could I do with that brain of hers to spruce up the shop for the holidays?

Eliana goes to work on her first little pot, painting cute little pink flowers with purple centers with green leaves. Not bad for a four-year-old.

I take a step back to glance over my shoulder toward the front of the store. Kade has moved the rest of the cards to the new display and is now heading my way with the old one. I'm tempted to pull out my phone and find Taps to play in honor of this significant moment, but somehow I think Aunt Paula would call it sarcasm.

Kade stops to check out Eliana's work. "Wow, squirt, look at you go. Those are great."

Eliana beams. "Thank you." She grabs the next pot and begins coating every inch of it in purple.

I jump to open the back door. "Here, let me get that."

"Thanks." As he moves past me, I catch a whiff of juniper and metal. His hair isn't black but various shades of dark brown, clipped close on the sides but longer on top. And his beard is starting to show this late in the day, giving him a rugged look.

That's when I realize he stopped walking and is staring at me over his shoulder, one side of his mouth quirked up in a grin. "I can't get this thing out the door with you in the way."

"Oh, sorry. I was distracted."

"I can see that." Dimple flash.

My cheeks feel like I've been in the sun all day as I step back and let him push the door open. He's going to think I'm attracted to him if I don't come up with a reason, but then that could make things worse if I sound like I'm making excuses.

I hear the crash of metal that confirms the final resting place of the old stand. As Kade comes back through the door, I grab my notebook and pretend to study my to-do list, which is legit. I cross off 'get rid of old display' from my list, which I just scribbled on the next line.

"Thank you. One less thing to do." Maybe that will be convincing. Show him how consumed I am with the shop.

"Glad to help."

The smirk he gives me says he's not buying it, but I refuse to give him any ground. Distraction is my best weapon at this point. I grab my key to the cash register from my pocket. I didn't think to grab my checkbook when I ran home earlier. "What do I owe you?"

"Don't worry about it." He waves me off with one hand while he sticks the other into the top of his jeans pocket.

"At least let me cover the cost of your materials."

He points to Eliana, who's covered her fourth pot in all green and wiggled her way over the worktable to nab the bottle of yellow. She squirts enough onto her plate to cover at least two more pots but then proceeds to add yellow polka dots to the green she slathered over her last one. Splotches of pink and purple cover the front of the apron from when she leaned over her palette. And the delight in her concentrated expression is palpable.

"Let's just call it even." As he looks at his niece, his expression softens, revealing a tenderness that melts something in my heart. This just annoys me, because I'm determined not to let Kade Maverick in anywhere near my heart. Some of that may be a lingering annoyance over that ridiculous nickname he gave me, but the bigger issue is I don't plan to stay in Sarabella any longer than I have to.

Romantic entanglements will not serve me well at this point in my life.

I say it to myself again to make sure my heart is hearing my brain.

Romantic entanglements will not serve Amanda Wilde well right now.

Period.

As I'm solidifying this brain-heart agreement, Kade stands next to Eliana and holds a potted cactus so she can paint without getting poked. Then he kisses her head.

There it goes. That agreement is turning into that swoony goo I mentioned earlier.

I've heard women say the sexiest man is a dad in action.

I'm beginning to think it applies to uncles, too.

CHAPTER 6
Amanda

Sally puts a plate of her world-famous—or should I say Sarabella-famous—baked spaghetti in front of me. She only makes this dish when she knows someone is in need of strength. All types—emotional, physical, and I'll throw in spiritual, too, because I need it all.

I'm only a few weeks into getting the shop ready to reopen and I'm exhausted. Who knew owning your own flower shop could be so taxing?

I haven't seen Kade for a couple of days, yet he's become a constant presence in my thoughts. And I can't stop seeing him with Eliana. After she finished that last pot, Kade had to pry her away from the worktable, reminding her she had school the next day. And the way her bottom lip popped out about did me in. Only after I promised I would call upon her when I needed a helper again did she crack a smile.

Kade gave me a hint of a smile through his silent thank you, but I didn't miss the hint of apprehension that brewed behind his green eyes. I still don't know the full story there and asking in front of Eliana didn't seem appropriate. Besides, it's really none of my business. The less I know the better.

Why?

Because the Maverick Menace is drawing my interest more and more. My mind has officially defected from logic and joined the fickle side of my curious heart. Good thing he left when he did because my brain-heart agreement needed some serious solidifying.

It's just a crush. It'll pass. I just need to avoid the man long enough to get over it. Besides, how could I honestly like a guy who came up with 'Root Beer' as a nickname?

"Are you ready for your big day?"

That's the other topic tormenting me at the moment—the shop. Tomorrow is opening day. Or I should say, reopening day. The store still needs so much work, but I can't do more improvements until the place starts earning money.

I drop my head in my hands as the aroma of homemade Italian meatballs, spaghetti sauce, garlic, and Parmesan cheese wafts up my nose. My stomach does a lurch instead of a growl and my nerves are so hyped up over tomorrow that I can't eat. I can count on one hand how many times that's happened in my life, but never, never over Sally's baked spaghetti.

I fiddle with my fork, winding the noodles around the prongs with no intention of eating. "I guess."

Sally slides into a chair with her plate. "What do you have left to do? I can come help after dinner."

I put my fork down and cross my arms, leaning them on the table. Aunt Paula and I spent many a dinner and holiday sitting at Sally's table, talking and laughing. On Christmas Eve, most of the business owners on Mango Lane show up here to celebrate long into the night because they don't have to open their shops in the morning. And Sally, with her legendary cooking and baking skills, makes an art of it. I still think she should have opened a diner instead of a clothing shop.

But then, what do I know? I'm barely figuring out how to run a flower shop. None of my teenage experience in the store prepared me for actually running the business. My respect for Aunt Paula has tripled, if not quadrupled.

"Everything's ready. Those specialty items I ordered for fall and Thanksgiving will come in later this week, which gives me time to figure out how I'm going to display them."

"You should probably start ordering your Christmas inventory, too. People start earlier and earlier these days. Especially tourists, who are already arriving in droves."

I press my hands over my eyes in a useless attempt to pretend that when I remove them, I'll be back home in New York. But then I realize I'm no Dorothy.

"I'm running out of places to display things." I stab a meatball with my fork as if it were some imaginary foe I could take down. And for a fraction of a second, I feel victorious. Short of covering cardboard boxes with scarves like I did in my college dorm, I need to figure out how to display more inventory.

Sally shoots me a rather sly look. "Why don't you ask Kade to help you? He's great at taking old furniture and turning them into display tables and cabinets. And I think Paula had some pieces in her storage unit that he could convert for you."

"That takes money I don't have right now." And more interaction with Kade.

Not happening.

She stabs a chunk of meatball and points her fork at me. "He'd understand and let you pay him when you can, I'm sure." She pops her fork into her mouth and chews as she stares at me.

"I can't afford to be in debt."

"To be in debt or to be indebted to Kade?"

Busted.

"What do you mean?" I focus on my plate, twirling spaghetti on my fork, trying to appear completely oblivious to Sally's accurate assessment.

Sally puts her fork down and sits up in her seat like a mother about to pounce on one of her own, which I pretty much am. "Amanda Wilde, don't you play coy with me. You know exactly what I mean."

"In debt, of course." I keep my eyes diverted because looking Sally in the eye will completely blow my cover.

"Now you're just lying to me. What would your Aunt Paula say right now?"

I drop my fork. "Fine. I don't want to be indebted to Kade."

Sally studies me a moment, then the corners of her mouth wiggle up. "I can think of worse people to be indebted to."

"Sally! That guy tormented me in high school."

"Maybe he liked you." She shrugs.

I push back from the table and cross my arms. "Please tell me you are not justifying a bully."

She holds her hands in surrender. "You're right. I'm just saying that it's possible he had a crush on you then and still might."

"And what makes you think that?" I try to sound casual, but clearly, my thumping heart didn't get the 'no-fly zone' message from my brain.

"Jacob. He said you two could have lit a match with the sparks flying between you."

"Those weren't sparks. That was him using that stupid nickname he gave me in high school and me not letting him have the satisfaction."

"I see." Sally picks up her fork and starts eating again.

I push a meatball around on my plate, imagining I'm rolling a snowball in snow made of noodles. If only yearning could transport me back home. Sasha told me upstate New York had some early and unexpected snowfall already.

Can you hear me whining that I want to go home?

I drop my fork. "I don't need any romantic entanglements. If everything goes to plan, I'll be back in New York in a year."

"Then don't you think asking Kade to do some work for you would help in that plan?"

I hate it when she's right. And she is. As I've said more than once, I need all the help I can get. But I'm resourceful. I'm sure I can figure out some way to make the store more inviting.

Maybe some rugs to cover the patchy floor would cozy up the place and help muffle the squeaks, too. I think I saw some in Aunt Paula's—my storage room.

I shove a chunk of meatball into my mouth and chew. Warm memories flood my mind, which diffuses my anger. Sally's cooking has a way of restoring a person's peace of mind.

And perspective.

Kade *was* rather helpful. He arranged the few cards I had on the new stand so it appeared fuller than it was, and he carted the old stand out to the dumpster. And the way he helped Eliana paint those little pots…maybe time had softened his hard edges after all.

"Eliana's really cute. I didn't know Kade's brother had a child."

Sally puts her fork down. "Neither did he. He died before he found out."

"Oh…" The bite I just swallowed sits like a knot in my throat. "I didn't know."

"I don't know the details, just that Kade's mother was taking care of her until she broke her ankle. So he's helping out for a while."

"What about Eliana's mother?"

"Not sure. Just something about her losing her job and having to find a new place to live, so she left Eliana with Kade's mom until she can figure things out."

Eliana's sweet little face filled with joy as she painted lands front and center in my thoughts. "That poor kid. She must miss her mom terribly."

Sally's studying me, but she doesn't say what I know she's thinking. That, yes, I know what it's like to miss my mother. To cry myself to sleep every night, wondering if my mother would ever take me with her back to LA, especially when she said her career was taking off. As a tween, I searched for her in every movie or TV show I watched but never found her. Yet she insisted she was getting more and more parts. Little did I know what kind.

"So, you'll ask Kade to help you with those displays?"

Oh, she maneuvered me good on that one. "I'll think about it."

She gives me a satisfied smile. "Good."

⁂

ONE CUSTOMER. Just one.

What a pathetic opening day. I'll never be able to sell the business if I don't find more ways to draw people in. I don't know how Aunt Paula managed, but I'm wondering if she ran the place for fun. I haven't sat down to really analyze her books yet, which isn't my strong suit, anyway.

Technically, I'm supposed to stay open until six, but with little to no foot traffic around the shops, I decide to close at five-thirty. Maybe the upcoming Mango Fall Festival will help liven the place up a bit. Sally did say the tourists were arriving in droves. Did they just need a little more time to settle in?

From the shop, I go straight to my storage room (hey, I got it right that time) and find a couple of vintage rugs tucked behind the shelving unit and two pieces of furniture that could be useful at the store. One is an antique breakfront that I can picture the top drawers open with gift items, like fall-themed oven mitts and kitchen towels. Some matching ceramics displayed on top would really be fun, too. Maybe some of those sets that have fun words on them, like 'food is life' or 'kiss the cook.'

But the doors up top are hanging loose, and one of them has no glass. With further inspection, I can tell the wood frame is in terrible shape and needs some serious handyman magic. Maybe I can just remove the doors and use the shelves inside for more display area.

I lift one shelf to see if they're adjustable, but it falls down on one side. Sigh…not the simple solution I'd hoped for.

Sally's suggestion to ask Kade for help floods back. I tug my phone out of my back pocket and pull up the number Sally so conveniently texted to me last night after I got home. The woman is tenacious, which is part of what I love about her so much. Plus, she reminds me of Aunt Paula in so many ways.

The phone only rings once on my end.

"Root Beer…what can I do for you?"

I groan. This just got a whole lot harder. I'm tempted to hang up or make up a story about butt-dialing him. But then one of the doors on the breakfront falls off with a crash.

"Mandy, are you okay?" The Maverick Menace sounds genuinely concerned.

Maybe I could do this.

"Yes and no. I'm fine, but that sound you just heard is the potential new display for my shop. It's large and in need of repair. Any chance you could help me with it?"

"Sure. No problem. I can come right now."

"Oh…" I didn't expect him to rush right over, which makes this so much more real. "I guess that would work. I mean, if it's not too much trouble for you."

"No trouble at all. Sally let me know you'd be calling."

"She did?" Of course she did.

"Yeah. And Eliana's ballet class just started, so now is a good time."

An image of Kade helping Eliana put on a tutu and ballet slippers fills my head and does this weird thing to my heart.

"Mandy? You still there?"

"Yes! That would be great. I really appreciate it."

"Happy to help, but I should warn you, there might be a price."

I should have known his help would come with strings attached. "I wasn't expecting it to be free. Just give me an idea of the cost involved first so I can decide if it's worth it."

"Oh, I didn't mean monetary." He drawls his words out, but

I can't tell if he's trying to be covert or if he's just hesitant to ask for something.

Uh-oh…what new door to the underworld have I opened up now? "Then what do you mean?" I keep my tone firm, as in 'don't toy with me' because I don't like games. And this is business.

Just. Business.

"I, uh, need some help with Eliana."

Oh…well, that doesn't sound so bad. I used to babysit during high school. And Eliana is a pretty cool kid. "Sure, what do you need?"

"How about I explain when I get there?"

"Hmm, sounds serious."

"No, just trying to make good use of our time before I have to pick up Eliana."

"Oh, right. See you in a few."

I'm standing outside my building when Kade arrives in a silver truck that has blue lettering on the doors. As he parks nearby, the blue/teal gradient of the logo becomes clear.

Maverick Metal Works.

The logo is clean and clever, which my experience with graphics and branding can appreciate. Maybe I underestimated Kade's business acumen, which makes me a little more at ease with having a professional relationship with my former tormentor.

"Hey there." He smiles as he climbs out of the truck and shuts the door.

The day is cool, so he rode with the window down, which left his hair in a tousled array that makes my pulse speed up. "Thank you again for helping."

Kade steps onto the sidewalk in front of me, close enough for me to catch that mix of juniper and metal. "No problem."

He just stares at me, and I stare back because I'm intrigued again by that freckle in his eye. Is it brown or is it a darker shade of green? I want to get closer so I can study this enigma, which I Googled and found out is pretty rare.

"Do you want to show me that piece now?"

It's that moment in the movies that sounds like a needle being dragged across a record.

Loud, startling, and oh so embarrassing…

"Yes!" I say this with a little too much exuberance. "Right this way." Calmer this time. Much better, but I am wishing life had an undo button more than ever before.

Kade's heavy boots crunch on the gravel behind me. I noticed when he got out of his truck that the soles had heavy treads that continued over the toe in bands. Heavy-duty stuff, which makes me wonder what he does in that studio of his.

I lead the way to Aunt Paula's—my storage room (rats!), which I'm still struggling to think of as mine, especially since it's still filled with her things. Same with her condo. But that's a project for another day. Every moment of my time and energy is going into the shop right now.

After unlocking the door, I push it all the way open and get out of the way. No need for another awkward door moment, especially when my current embarrassment is still blazing hot on my face and making me want to crawl behind the stack of boxes to the right.

"There are two pieces I'd love to get your help with, if you don't mind." I point at the breakfront. "That one and the stand next to it."

Kade isn't saying anything. He's running his fingers gently over a cabinet door like a concerned lover, which, as you can imagine, heats up the rest of my insides.

"The wood is pretty dried out and the hinges are rusted. I can try to find some antique ones to replace them if you want to match the original hinges, but they'll probably cost an arm, a leg, and some toes." He shoots me a quick glance, I guess to see if I think his silly pun is funny.

I am trying oh so hard not to smile, so I figure talking is my best bet. "I'm not worried about preserving the piece, to be honest. I don't think it's antique-worthy. But it would make an impressive display for the shop."

He gives the piece another look over and nods his head, tugging his bottom lip in as he thinks, which just adds to his attractiveness.

But I don't notice this at all.

At. All.

"In that case, I think I can create something more practical for you."

"Like take the doors off and fix the shelves?"

"Something like that. What if we opened the unit up and put some metal framing around the top corners to create a decorative frame? That would give you space to display some taller items. And I can attach a few small floating shelves to one side for some specialized smaller items."

I can picture everything he's saying, and I'm finding myself…excited. "I love that! And what about the bottom part? Any thoughts on that? Could be used as storage, I guess."

"Do you need storage?"

"I don't know what I need to be honest." I shrug and laugh to make it seem intentional that I just bared a piece of my inner turmoil to this man. The last thing I need is to give him more fuel to use against me.

But instead, he studies me with this concerned look. "That's okay. You'll figure it out, Mandy. You're doing a great job."

I'm dumbfounded and near tears over hearing something I didn't know I needed to hear. Out loud. And the Maverick Menace—I mean, Kade—is the one who said it.

And he didn't use that ridiculous nickname. I'll take my win and save correcting Mandy with Amanda the next time he says it, which didn't sound all that bad for some reason…

Maybe it just reminds me of Aunt Paula. I blink and clear my throat. "Thanks."

He drags his gaze away and crouches as he opens the lower

cabinet doors. "What if I took the center panels out of the doors and replaced them with some matching metalwork? That way you can use it for storing extra display items but would still be visible."

It appears the man is a genius, too. "That's perfect."

He moves on to give me some ideas for the other piece, which is tall and narrow. His idea of adding some metal shelves below will give me even more ways to display seasonal items.

Kade brushes the dust from his hands and dons a sheepish grin. "Now, about that favor."

I'd almost forgotten. "Need a babysitter for a hot date?"

He lets out a soft laugh. "No, nothing like that. Eliana's had some trouble at her preschool, and I think it would be best if another female helped her with it."

"Female? Why?" I can't imagine what feminine advice a four-year-old would need.

"She's dealing with another girl at her preschool who challenges her to…" He rubs the light growth on his chin and pauses to great effect. "To hold things."

"Hold things? Like bugs or worms? Forbidden fruit?"

He chuckles and visibly relaxes some, which is why I said it.

"This kid challenges her to see how long she can go without using the potty."

I about lose it when I hear him say 'potty.' It sounds so *fatherly*.

Seriously…losing my mind here.

"So, this kid is a bully?" I don't know why I'm throwing this out there, only that I see an opportunity to point out that he's the pot calling the kettle black.

"I guess that's one way of putting it."

"Right. Like name calling or using cruel nicknames."

Judging by the way Kade pulls his shoulders back and presses his mouth together, I'm thinking I may have pushed a little too hard. But at this point, I'm like that dog with a bone.

"I apologized for that." If looks could kill, this one might injure me.

"And yet you used it again when you answered my call."

He stays silent for a moment and then nods. "You're right. I'm sorry. *Again*. I didn't realize it bothered you so much. Especially since you seemed to have forgotten who I was that first day and said you preferred Diet Coke."

Now I want to crawl into the breakfront and hide until he leaves. But Kade's grin is growing as I try not to laugh. And fail.

"Point made," I say.

"Point taken," Kade says.

Then he tucks his fingers into the top of his jeans pockets, which brings his shoulders up, giving him this adorable boyish look. "So, can you talk to her and maybe help her understand how that's not good for her…her lady parts?"

Chin tucked, he says the last three words in a fast jumble, and, even in the poor lighting in the storage room, I can tell his cheeks are darkening. I'm beginning to understand how difficult the situation is for him.

"Wouldn't that be better coming from her mother?"

"Probably, but Shannon's not around much at the moment and it's an awkward conversation to have on a phone call."

I can think of several other reasons to deflect this back at him just to make it harder but decide he's suffered enough discomfort. "Sure. I'd be happy to."

"Great. Thank you," he says in a gush of airy relief.

"No problem. We ladies need to stick together against those bullies."

He lifts a brow and hand in protest.

"Just kidding."

And I reward his smile with one of my own.

CHAPTER 7
Kade

Normally, I try not to work on weekends, especially now that I'm responsible for a four going-on fourteen-year-old. But I've spent most of the last two days working on Mandy's pieces, which has put me behind on one of my customer orders. However, the entire process wound up having an unexpected side benefit—ideas to expand my services. So, it's totally worth it.

Besides, Shannon called and wants to take Eliana out for a day of 'mommy-daughter' time, so I'll have the rest of today to play catch up. I've managed to juggle a four-year-old and my business well enough to get by these last few weeks, but the whole experience has given me a new level of respect for single parents.

For Shannon.

No wonder she was overwhelmed. And Eliana can be a handful. Not in a bad way, but even I can see the kid is special. I know I'm biased as her uncle, but she's an unusual kid nonetheless. Just like Devon was.

As I do a final wipe down and polish on the metalwork I created for the cabinet doors, my anticipation of Mandy's reaction to the modifications I've made is growing. And…I admit,

I'm looking forward to seeing her, which may or may not be a good thing. The verdict is still out on that. I have a lot going on in my life right now with my business and taking care of a small human being who needs a lot of my time and attention.

But I am curious. Whenever I'm around her, I experience the same feeling of anticipation I get when I start a new project. And there's nothing more exciting than that.

Not that I consider Mandy a project. At all. More like she's a lit blowtorch and each time I'm around her, my resistance melts more and more.

"Uncle Kade, how long now until Mommy gets here?" This is the fifth time Eliana has asked this.

"Five minutes less than the last time you asked." I could have said 'soon,' but I love watching this kid do calculations. Besides, soon isn't an acceptable answer for the squirt. She wants specifics.

Sitting at the small worktable I made for her, Eliana holds up both her hands, fingers splayed out as her eyes dart back and forth. "So, that's twenty-five minutes less now?"

Like I said, special.

I'm glad Shannon has these outings with Eliana, which helps her feel less disconnected from her mother. But there are still moments that I know she'd rather have her mommy than some gruff and rough uncle who's more comfortable with a blowtorch and has scratchy hands. Eliana has instructed me I need to use lotion more. She even convinced me to keep a bottle by the sink in my studio.

"That's right, kiddo. Did they teach you to use fingers at school?"

"Yes, ten of them twice, which is twenty, but I kept going."

"With toes?"

She bursts out in a giggle that makes me laugh, too. "No, silly. I have shoes on."

The door to my studio opens and Mandy walks in. Like a significant moment in time, I freeze for a fraction of a second before reacting. This is the first time Mandy has been to my studio, and suddenly I feel like an awkward teenager on his first date.

But this isn't a date. So why am I reacting this way?

Eliana races over to Mandy, who puts down the sack she's carrying and crouches to receive Elly's hug. I don't know why that strikes me as significant, but it does.

I wipe my hands with the rag I was using to wipe down the pieces I was working on and hit the lotion pump. No scratchy hands for customers. Has nothing to do with this desire to touch the silky skin of Mandy's cheek and smooth my hand over the waves of her honey-brown hair. I give myself a mental shake. This is just business. Or at the most, an old friend helping another.

If Mandy even thinks of me as a friend...

"Hey, there. Glad you could come by."

She rises back to her full height, which is only a few inches shorter than my six-two, which I really like. And she carries herself with this graceful confidence that easily shifts to playfulness when she's around Eliana.

"Thanks for inviting me. I didn't expect to see your studio."

I shrug. "I just figured it would be easier to do any adjustments here." I point to her bag on the floor. "You brought some of those boxes you wanted to display?"

She grabs the bag and brings it over to the worktable. "Yes, they're all the same size, thankfully."

One by one she pulls out a series of open-faced boxes holding ceramic pumpkins that have metal leaves and curling stems. I pick one up for closer examination. "I like these."

"I thought you might. The metalwork made me think of you." Her eyes widen as she stutters. "And the work you do."

"Right." I try not to grin as I gather the rest of the boxed pumpkins and carry them over to the piece I finished late last night. I slip each box onto the shelf, pleased to see they fit perfectly.

Mandy bends over and swaps out a couple in the order, then straightens. "It's perfect."

I lap up her praise like a thirsty dog. Most of the time I'm the only one in my studio and since I do most of my work for builders, I rarely hear the homeowners' appraisals of what I do, so hearing her approval seems to fill an empty spot I didn't realize I had.

"I'm glad you like it."

She's running her fingers over the metal scrollwork I created for the upper part of the breakfront, and somehow it feels personal. And intimate. I rub the back of my neck and shake off the sensation.

"Like? I love it." She turns to face me. "I love how you matched the other piece you did to bring continuity to the shop."

"You noticed that, huh?"

She gives me this confused frown. "How could I not? It's beautiful."

I think my chest just swelled. "Thanks."

She tilts her head at Eliana, who's coloring her latest masterpiece. "Should I make my payment now?"

"Actually, my terms of service have changed. Eliana's mother is picking her up in a few minutes. I filled her in on the situation, and she wants to handle it herself."

"I totally understand."

The door to my studio opens and Shannon walks in. She looks tired but happy to see Eliana.

"Mommy!" She races over to Shannon, who sweeps her up into a big hug.

"Elly, my sweet girl. I missed you so much."

Once back on the floor, Eliana drags Shannon to where Mandy and I are standing. "Mandy, this is my mommy."

Mandy nods at Shannon. "Nice to meet the mom of this amazing young lady."

BLOOMED TO BE MESSY

The apprehension in Shannon's expression shifts to pride as she smiles. "She's pretty special."

"And she paints so well." Mandy drops her gaze to Eliana. "Be sure to tell your mom about the pots you painted at my store. Most of them have sold already."

Eliana bounces on the balls of her feet. "Really?" She turns to her mother. "Mandy says I'm an artist."

Shannon leans over and kisses her on the top of the head. "I'm so proud of you, Elly. Let's get going so you can tell me all about it, okay?"

Eliana bobs her head before dashing over to her desk to grab her miniature backpack boasting the latest Disney princess, which is the same one on the new dress she's wearing. Another moment of failed resistance on my part.

Shannon clasps her hands in front of her. "Can I speak to Kade for a moment?"

"Oh, sure! I'll just help Eliana clean up her desk."

Shannon draws closer. "I can't thank you enough for watching Elly. I'm almost back on my feet."

I nod. "She's a great kid."

"She's so much like her dad." Despite the nearly five years since Devon's death, sadness still lingers in Shannon's eyes. "I found a new job that pays better but it's less hours. And it's near a great school. Once I have enough money saved, I can get an apartment for Elly and me. Do you mind taking care of her just a little longer? I can do more with her on the weekends, but during the week it's too long of a drive, especially with tourist season starting."

My chest is suddenly tight at the thought of not seeing Elly every day. "Whatever you need, Shannon. I can help you get an apartment, too."

She puts her hand on my arm. "You're already doing enough. Elly practically has a new wardrobe."

I hold my hands up. "I'm a sucker for beautiful women who like to shop."

Shannon sends a glance toward Mandy and dons a teasing smile. "Is she one of them?"

"No, just a customer," says my mouth, but something deep in me wants something way more with Mandy.

"You sure about that? You two seem really into each other."

"Now you're making stuff up."

"No, I saw enough to tell when I walked in. She likes you."

I lift my brows. "More like tolerates."

"Mommy, can we go now?" Eliana is standing by the door, holding Mandy's hand.

Shannon spins around. "Sure, sweetie. Let's go have some fun."

I walk them out to Shannon's car. After moving the car seat and buckling in the squirt, Shannon steps into my arms and hugs me. "Thank you again. I'll bring her by this evening."

An idea hits me. "Why don't you stay at my place on the weekends so you don't have to drive back and forth?"

Shannon studies me for a moment. "Are you sure?"

"Definitely. I can even make myself scarce so you two can have some good one-on-one time."

She dons a sly smile. "Mandy seems really great. You could go out on a date with her."

Then she slips into her car and waves goodbye before driving off.

But her words keep pinging in my head as I walk back into my studio.

Mandy is leaning against my workbench with an unreadable expression on her face. And I realize she had a clear view of what just went down with me and Shannon. Does she think there's something going on between us?

Now it feels too silent in here, too awkward, but then she smiles. "You three make a cute family."

I've never thought of us that way, but she's right. "I suppose we do."

"Are you and Shannon…"

I wait for her to finish but when she doesn't, I decide to finish it for her. "Involved?"

She shrugs and nods.

"No, not like that. If Devon were still alive, they'd be happily married."

Her arms drop, and her expression shifts to concern. Or is it pity? I've seen it all over the years thanks to the scar on my face. But I don't want Mandy to see me that way—flawed, damaged, or whatever she's thinking.

"I'm so sorry, Kade. Sally told me—" She starts to reach out and I know she's only trying to comfort me. But that's not what I want from her. At all.

"You know, I have a few more touch-ups I'd like to do on these pieces. How about I deliver them tomorrow?"

She pulls back, nods. "Sure. I need to go anyway. Almost time to open my shop."

There's confusion, and maybe a little hurt, in her eyes. After she leaves, I smack my hand down on the workbench, feeling like a heel for hurting her like that.

The wound on my face may have healed, but the rest of what went down that day still feels like it's festering sometimes. Maybe I'm just not ready to get involved with anyone.

Especially someone as amazing as Mandy Wilde.

CHAPTER 8
Amanda

No matter how hard I try not to think about Kade Maverick, my heart is not listening, and I think my brain is giving up the battle to remain emotionally unattached.

Why do I suspect this?

Because I can't stop replaying our last conversation over and over again in my head, trying to figure out what went wrong. I thought we were having a simple conversation about Shannon and Eliana—and yes, I was definitely poking around to find out if Kade was involved with Shannon.

See? More proof that my brain-heart agreement has been compromised.

Instead, I seemed to have poked a bear. A really cute and sexy bear, but definitely a bear.

The biggest sigh I've ever made slips out of my mouth as I attempt to rearrange a display of new items I just put out today. An apron that says 'crazy plant lady' with cute little pictures of cacti all over it paired with a matching set of oven gloves. A grow-your-own miniature herb garden designed to sit on a windowsill. And some cute salt and pepper shakers in the shape of watering cans. Normally, things like this would give me extreme delight, but right now, I feel like a big dull dud.

Suddenly, my shop seems stifling, so I grab my wallet, put the 'back in fifteen minutes' sign on the door, and head over to the coffee shop. My predicament calls for a little caffeine and a lot of banana bread.

The odors of coffee, cinnamon, and chocolate fill my nose as I walk into The Last Bean, like a familiar blanket of comfort. I'm instantly transported to the little coffee shop down the street from my apartment in New York. Sasha and I probably spent more of our hard-earned money there than we should have, but the place did coffee and hygge (cozy to the max) better than anywhere else.

I decide to dub The Last Bean as my home away from home coffee shop as I approach the counter.

The owner, Aiden, smiles at me from behind the register. "The usual?"

"Yep, and make the coffee an extra-large and I'll take two pieces of that glorious banana bread."

"Two? Rough day?" He glances at me as he taps my order in.

"You could say that." I hold my phone up to the scanner to pay.

A couple of minutes later, Aiden hands me my coffee and a rather large bag for two pieces of banana bread. I put my coffee down to glance inside. "Um, I think you made a mistake. There's an entire loaf in here."

Aiden grins. "I thought that might help cheer you up."

Feeling lighter than when I walked in, I grin. "Mission accomplished. Thanks."

As I head down the sidewalk toward my shop, I notice someone sitting on the steps, their shape only partly visible through the white wooden railing. I quicken my pace, fumbling with my coffee and the bag of banana bread as I dig my keys out of my pocket.

"Sorry to make you wait."

"No hurry."

BLOOMED TO BE MESSY

I look up and come to a stop.

Kade rises to his feet. "Need some help?"

"Uh…no. I've got it covered." I hold my keys up, then charge up the steps to unlock my shop. "Did you need something?"

I stride to the counter and deposit my coffee and the bag before turning around with a smile I'm not feeling plastered on my face.

Kade swaggers closer, thumbs hooked on his jeans pockets. "Your forgiveness."

I play it cool again like I did the first day I saw him when he called me Root Beer. "Whatever for?" I even add a little bat of my eyelashes, just for fun.

He rubs a hand over his mouth. "For acting like a jerk this morning. I'm sorry."

And now that coolness is turning warm as his sexy green gaze devours me. "Forgiven."

That's all I can say? Forgiven? I spin around and gulp down some coffee. "Oh, hot!"

Kade rushes toward me as I wave my hands at my mouth. "Water?"

I nod vigorously. "Mi-i fri."

Amazingly, he understands I'm saying mini fridge and dashes to the back room. And he's already taken the top off as he hands me the cold bottle. I gulp down a third of the water before I stop and breathe.

"Thank you. Ouch."

"Your tongue?"

I nod as I hold a gulp of cold water on my tongue for a moment before swallowing.

"I can go find you some ice." He raises his brows in question.

I swallow. "No, I think I'm okay now."

Okay…but mortally embarrassed. I want to hide behind the

counter until he leaves. How does one recover from something like this and not look like a total idiot?

Maybe by admitting it? "That was a stupid thing to do."

"I'm sorry if I distracted you." One side of his mouth lifts.

He is so not sorry. I can tell by that dimple trying to make an appearance.

So he's teasing me, but at least that's better than being made fun of. "I can take responsibility for myself, thank you."

He holds his hand up in surrender.

The front door bells jingle as a couple who looks to be in their eighties walks in. The woman lifts a boney finger. "Do you have any palm trees?"

Palm trees? What would this dear older couple do with a palm tree if I had one?

"No, I don't carry anything that large, but I can recommend a nursery to you."

Kade waves at me from the door, then smiles before he leaves. And everything feels right again. The sun is shining, business is improving (even if I don't have a palm tree to sell), and Kade Maverick waited for me so he could apologize.

"Oh, that would be most helpful," says the man.

"Sure." I push aside the bag of banana bread to grab one of Jacob's business cards. "Here you go. Tell Jacob I sent you over. He'll give you a discount."

The couple beams at me, appearing quite grateful for my help, and life as a successful shop owner seems completely doable.

Smiling, I hold up the bag. "Would you care for some banana bread? I have plenty."

CHAPTER 9
Kade

It's Sunday afternoon and I'm buzzing. Shannon took me up on my offer to stay at my place for the weekend, so I took off, looking forward to a day free of schedules and the care and feeding of a four-year-old.

Don't get me wrong. I love Eliana as if she were my own, and I've gotten used to our routine, but I'm stoked to have a day to myself, even if it includes some work.

And I get to see Mandy again today. Maybe I'll take Shannon's advice and ask her out. Despite my screw-up, something seemed to shift between us yesterday. Who knew a run-in with hot coffee could lead to a redemptive moment? I liked rushing to her aid more than I thought possible. Kinda felt like a knight in shining armor to her damsel in distress.

These are things zinging through my head as I drive to my studio.

As I back my truck up to the back sliding door of my shop, I notice Zane leaning against his car. He greets me with a handshake and pulls me into a bro-hug. The thing you need to know about Zane is that he's heroic and humble all at once. That's what makes him a great lifeguard—and a brilliant operations director, too.

Although we went to the same high school, Zane and I reconnected on the beach shortly after I opened my business in Sarabella as a way to reinvent myself after my brother's death. He noticed my motorcycle on his way off the beach from a shift and struck up a conversation that led to an invitation to his parent's house for an unforgettable baked spaghetti dinner. I think he sensed my grief and shifted into hero mode.

Those were difficult days and his friendship helped me a lot.

"Thanks, man, I appreciate you giving up some of your day off to help."

"No problem. I know Amanda appreciates it."

After I unlock and slide the garage-style door up, we head inside to load Mandy's pieces, starting with the biggest one first.

Zane positions himself on one end as I go to the other. "By the way, when I asked you to go with my dad to check out that card display, I didn't mean for you to become Amanda's knight in shining armor."

I stop at Zane's words. If he only knew… "She called and asked for help, which, based on our past history, I'm sure wasn't easy for her."

"History?"

I meet Zane's frowning gaze. "Yeah, I called her Root Beer, remember?"

He gives me a blank stare. "Root Beer?"

"Her initials are A and W."

"Oh, now I get it." He shakes his head. "We ran in different circles back then."

By different circles, Zane means his was the jocks, and mine was the delinquents. Not something I'm proud of. Devon and I weren't the best examples of teenage boys on their way to manhood.

We heft the breakfront into my flatbed and head back inside for the table.

Zane lets out a derisive snort. "That's way less harmful than some of the names slung at her after word got out about who her mother was."

"Yeah, I remember." That was part of the reason I started calling Mandy "Root Beer." I thought it might redirect some of the awful names being slung at her. I may have been a jerk back then, but I recognized pain when I saw it. No way would I add to that.

"That's pretty much why she moved to New York and started going by her full first name."

That's when it clicks in my thick skull that Zane always calls her Amanda. "Duly noted."

Once we tie the pieces down and close the tailgate, we head toward Mandy's—I mean, Amanda's—shop, which is just around the corner.

Zane doesn't say anything else and neither do I, but I can sense he has something on his mind. "For the record, if Amanda had told me you were tormenting her, I would have had to deck you."

He sounds like he's joking on the surface, but I've been around Zane Albright long enough to recognize the steely edge to his voice and his fierce protectiveness over those he loves.

"For the record, I was deflecting. Thought it might create a distraction."

Zane nods. "I wish it had worked. I hated not being there for her after I graduated."

I glance over at Zane before making the turn down the back street that runs behind the shops on Mango Lane. "Have you two always been close?"

"My mom and her aunt were best friends, so we grew up together."

I back the truck in and shift into park.

Zane gets out but then leans down in the open door so I can see his face. "Amanda's like my little sister. I'm kind of protective of her."

There's no missing Zane's subtle point or the look he gives me. "Again, duly noted."

Mandy—I mean, Amanda swings the back door open.

All I can do for a moment is stare at her in my side mirror. She's dressed in these cute jeans that have decorative patches all over the front and a white top that ties to one side. Her hair is pulled up in a ponytail and she has these big silver hoops hanging from her ears. She looks amazing.

That's when I realize Zane is lowering the tailgate and frowning at me in my mirror. I swipe a hand over my face and hop out, then busy myself with untying the ropes.

Amanda holds the door open as we lift the largest piece out of the flatbed first. "I didn't know you two knew each other."

Zane glances at me before landing his attention on her. "Mav and I reconnected a few years ago."

She nods her head but says nothing. Maybe knowing I'm friends with her 'brother' will help earn me some brownie points.

We haul the breakfront to the front of the shop and set it against the wall Amanda directs us to. As I step back, I feel the floor give with a loud creak and nearly tumble into the shelves on the nearby wall.

Amanda runs over. "Oh no…" She bends over and lifts the brittle piece of linoleum that popped up, revealing the original floorboards.

I crouch over the spot and poke my finger at the wood, which crumbles in small puffs of dust. "It's rotted."

That's when I notice the writhing movement below. They built these old places on elevated platforms because of the occasional occurrence of flooding that happens when major storms blow through. But Sarabella hasn't seen a hurricane in about five decades. Just the occasional tropical storm.

Amanda gets down on her knees for a closer look. "They're baby raccoons!" She sits back on her heels. "What do we do?"

Zane leans his hands on his knees to take a better look. "I'll run over to the pet shop and see if Liam can help. I think he helps at one of the animal rescue centers."

He runs out the front door, leaving Amanda and me alone with three little fur balls, two of which are standing on their hind legs looking up at us and the other is lying on its side but not moving.

"I bet they need water." Amanda jumps up and runs to the back room.

Cabinet doors open and slam shut, then water runs. She dashes back with a paper cup and a towel wrapped around her hand. She crouches down again, ready to lower the cup into the hole in her floor.

I grab her hand. "They may be diseased. Do you have string?"

She pauses in thought. "I have some ribbon."

"That'll work."

She shoots up and runs to the back but returns in seconds with a spool of thin, red velvet ribbon.

I raise a brow in question.

"It's all I could find."

I tie the ribbon below the rim of the cup and then lower it down into the hole. The little critters poke their heads into it, lapping at the water. I tug the cup over so some will hopefully slosh over near the one still lying on its side.

Some water lands on its snout, and a pink tongue appears. "That's a good sign."

Minutes later, Zane bursts through the front door, followed by Liam, the owner of Where the Tame Things Are, our local pet store. And he's armed with long gloves and a small animal carrier.

I only met Liam recently, as I've had no reason whatsoever to go into a pet shop until Eliana entered my life. That place is now on the squirt's list as her favorite place to go on weekends. And Liam is great about it. He lets her hold the bunnies and pet his resident feline, who goes by the name of Badger because of the black stripes of fur that run over her eyes.

The three of us stand back as he lifts the raccoons into the carrier that's lined with an old towel.

"I'll run them over to the shelter now." He lifts the sick one in last. "Not sure about that one. I'm guessing they belong to the raccoon I saw on the side of the road a few days ago. Probably the mother. Hit by a car."

Zane offers to help Liam and leaves with a wave once I reassure him I can finish bringing the last piece in myself.

Silence fills the place after the door shuts, but then I hear Amanda sniffle.

I turn to her. "They'll be okay."

Nodding, she wraps her arms around herself and stares at the hole. "I'm an awful person."

"Why do you say that?"

The look she gives me is so vulnerable that I have to ball my fists at my sides to resist the urge to hold her.

"Because I'm more concerned about what this is going to cost me and how long I will have to close the shop than about those poor raccoons."

I rest my hand on her shoulder, which seems to draw her a step closer. Maybe I'm not off base to feel this need to comfort her. "That doesn't make you a bad person, Ma—Amanda. This is your business now. Of course, it means a lot."

She wipes her tears away with a step back and turns to face me. "Do you know someone who can repair this quickly without breaking my bank? This really messes with my plan to sell the place."

She mumbles those last words as if speaking more to herself.

My thoughts about whether she'd notice that I used her full first name fly down the hole in the floor. "Sell?"

"Yeah, thanks to my crazy aunt, I have to run this place successfully for a year before I can sell it and go back to New York."

Her words knock the air out of me, like a while back when my dirt bike flipped. I landed so hard it took me a good ten seconds to breathe again—seconds that felt like forever. I remember wondering if that was how it felt to drown, knowing you couldn't get air into your lungs because they filled with water.

I suck in air with a sudden gasp that's noticeable enough to make Amanda blink. I don't know why this is affecting me so deeply, just that it is.

"I did construction work for several years before starting my business. I can do the labor if you can cover the materials. And I know some places that have discontinued lots of flooring."

At first, her eyes widen, but then she shakes her head. "No, you've already done enough, Kade. I can't ask you to do that."

"You're not. I'm offering."

We stare at each for a long moment. I'm not sure what's passing between us, but it feels deep.

And dangerous.

Especially if she has no plans to stick around.

I tear my gaze away. "I'm sure I can rope Zane into helping, too." I head toward the back door. "I'll go get that last piece in for you. The sooner we get that floor fixed, the sooner you can reopen."

Guess I will spend my free day ripping up old flooring and loading wood beams from the hardware store.

I hear her footsteps scurrying to keep up behind me. "I don't know how to thank you, Kade. Really. You're a lifesaver."

Or a knight in shining armor? I let an ironic laugh slip out. "I think that's Zane's title."

Definitely not mine. I couldn't save my brother. I'm just a former troublemaker keeping his head down to make the best out of this life.

I feel her hand tug at my elbow. "Seriously…you're what my aunt would call a godsend."

That's a name I never would have associated with a Maverick.

But I'll take it.

CHAPTER 10
Amanda

I have a hole in my floor.
A hole!

And raccoons. They may not be monster raccoons—according to Liam, they're called kits and are actually adorable. But not in my shop!

This can't be happening. I'm already a month into this venture, open barely a week, and now I have to close again.

After Kade pulled away the rest of the rotted wood, which filled 'The Can' nearly to the top, he headed off to the hardware store for supplies to repair the hole, which is now four times as big.

I called Mr. Tate to find out if I could still operate business as usual if I roped off the damaged area, but he advised strongly against it, saying a lawsuit would cost me much more than any lost revenues. After locking the front door and taping a sign I hand-lettered stating I'm 'Closed for renovations,' I shuffle to the back room and drop onto the stool.

At least I brought my laptop with me today. I still need to find more ideas for the shop to draw in more business. I don't know how Aunt Paula kept the place running with just flowers and floral arrangements. Maybe she had plans to add more with that renovation Sally mentioned. Based on the reports I pulled from the register, business had been on a steady decline.

But nothing I've found fits my growing vision for Bloomed to Be Wilde. I've even played with some designs for mugs or home items, but nothing feels…original. Just another reinvention of the same old stuff out there.

A knock comes from behind me. I spin around on my stool, mustering everything I have left strength-wise to open the back door and help Kade haul in the materials he purchased. I'm dreading that receipt. I may have to go back to eating Ramen for a few weeks.

But it's not Kade standing at my door. It's Sally.

"I heard you had a little excitement this morning."

I step back so she can walk in and see the disaster for herself. "Who was it this time? Mr. Tate? Zane? Kade?"

She gives me a hug. "Does it matter? You keep forgetting you're not in this alone, Mandy. People are looking out for you."

She's right, just like Aunt Paula always was. I guess I've gotten used to making it on my own. The only person who looked out for me in New York was Sasha. And I looked out for her. The folks on Mango Lane may 'talk' a lot, but they put action to their words, too.

Sally bleats out a sighing whistle combo as she studies the hole with her hands on her hips. "Yeah, that's quite a hole."

"You think?"

She raises a brow at my sarcasm. "Don't jeer when you can cheer."

Another one of her pithy sayings. But I don't think a pair of pompoms would help this situation. "Then what exactly do you suggest I do here?"

"Make a plan."

"I did. And now that plan is on hold until I can open my doors again."

"Then let's make a new plan."

I cover my face with my hands. "Like what?"

"One, the festival is next weekend. Did you sign up for a booth?"

I drop my hands. "No. I didn't see the point. Flowers aren't really something people come to buy at things like that. Besides, I don't really have time. The shop needs every bit of my focus."

"But the festival draws a large crowd. All the shops will be closed so they can manage their booths. If there are no more booths, you can have mine. That would give you great exposure and let the regular tourists know the shop is under new management."

As much as I love her enthusiasm, I'm still only seeing the negative side of this whole fiasco. Or should I say *hole fiasco*? Because that's what this has become—another *pitfall* in my plan to get back to New York.

And yes, I intended every pun there.

"But only half of the items I've ordered will arrive before then. I don't see how I could be ready in time."

Sally drops her hands to her sides. "Then let's go find something."

"I've looked everywhere online. Even on Etsy. Nothing seems to fit the shop, and now it's too late to get anything custom-made."

"I wasn't talking online. I mean local. Grab your purse and let's go. I have an idea."

"Another one?"

When Sally shifts into mother mode, her chin goes up and her shoulders pull back, making her look at least four inches taller. Downright intimidating. "Amanda Wilde, do you want to find unique inventory for your shop or not?"

She's right to ask that question, I know. And as much as it stings, I also know I have only one appropriate answer. "Yes, ma'am."

Sally settles back to her usual height. "All right then. Let's go."

"Shouldn't we wait for Kade to get back?"

"Send him a text and let him know the back door is open. We'd just be in his way anyhow." She grabs my wrist and leads me to the back room.

I feel like a teenager again, being dragged along for some outing I have no interest in. But what choice do I have? If I want my old life back, I have to do the work.

"What if he needs help?" No, I'm not making excuses again. It's just that Kade is being so generous with his time, and I don't want to appear ungrateful. Nor do I want to take advantage of his generosity.

After a brief pause, she grabs my purse and hangs it over my shoulder before heading out the back door. Sally tosses her last word on the subject over her shoulder as she sprints around the back of my shop to Mango Lane.

"I already texted Zane to come help."

Of course she did.

BY THE TIME I catch up with Sally, she's already on the phone with someone, talking about something to do with seashells. She ends the conversation with a time affirmation, which—I glance at my watch—is an hour from now.

Sally is like a soldier with marching orders. Facial expression determined and a look in her eyes that tells me if I don't keep up, if I don't fully commit to this new plan, I will regret it for the rest of my life.

"Where to first?" I adopt what I hope is a more bubbly tone so she'll think I'm all in. My goal is to reach that point by the time this day is over. Because Sally has that same determined spark my Aunt Paula had, and I witnessed these two women not only become successful businesswomen—for the most part—but forces to be reckoned with in the Sarabella business community.

"First, we're going to visit a friend of mine. She's a glassblower."

"Glassblower?"

"Exactly." She says this as if she thinks I know exactly what she means, but I don't and I figure if I just keep playing along, this will all make sense at some point. At the very least, I'll have a little adventure to help me forget about the misadventure the flower shop is becoming.

The next street over, Lime Avenue, is a short walk and very close to Kade's studio. I've noticed the area has adopted the label of an artist's district. Perhaps Sally is really on to something.

The front of the studio looks more like a small gallery with stark white walls and floating shelves displaying gorgeous glass vases, bowls, plates, and statues. Sunlight streaming in through the glass door highlights swirls of color that fascinate the senses. I barely have time to study the pieces though, because Sally is dragging me through another door to what I assume is probably the work area where these stunning pieces are created.

The shift is startling, from bright white and clean to bare cement flooring and lots of clutter. Metal shelves line one side of the large work area like a library but, instead of books, glass shapes in a wide range of shapes, sizes, and colors fill them. An open area on the left houses a furnace and various other contraptions, which I assume are integral to the glassblowing process.

A woman somewhere in age between Sally and me walks toward us, wearing a heavy leather apron and her hair pulled back in a bun. Wisps of blonde hair streaked with pink hover around her face.

She smiles, revealing a perfect set of white teeth, one of which boasts a pink diamond. "Sally, what brings you my way?"

"Marnie, this is Paula's niece, Amanda. She's a product designer." She tugs me to stand next to her.

Feeling super exposed to be introduced by my profession when I'm feeling like the biggest failure on earth, I shake her hand, noticing the pink polish on her nails matches her hair.

"Nice to meet you, Marnie."

Sally takes over the conversation. "At our last think tank, you mentioned something about those glass mangos you were playing with."

"Oh, right. They're over here."

Marnie leads us around the row of shelves to a back shelf I hadn't even noticed. She points to these cute, mango-shaped pieces in shades of greens shifting into oranges and reds, like true-to-life mangos when ripening. Metallic specs in gold and bronze speckle the glass as well.

I reach toward the shelf but pause. "May I?"

"Of course." Marnie's exuberance to share her art shows as she jumps forward to pick one of the pieces and deposits it into my hands.

As I hold up the mango, light filters through and makes the metallic pieces sparkle. "It's gorgeous. What are you going to do with them?"

"That's what I was telling Sally. I had fun making them, but I really don't know what to do with them."

I turn the piece, studying the colors and imagining potential uses for them. Just stacked in a bowl like fruit seems a waste of their beauty and a bit cliché. These babies need to be hanging. That's when the idea strikes me they'd look amazing with some kind of metalwork wrapped around them, like the vines in the shelf accents Kade created that would culminate in a leaf or two with a stem to hang it. They'd be great for windows.

Or even Christmas tree ornaments! What better souvenir to take home from Sarabella, the mango capital of the US, than a hand-blown mango ornament that people can enjoy year-round.

I'm so excited, I'm bouncing on the front of my feet.

"Marnie, I'd like to purchase every one of these for my shop. I have an idea that will turn them into something truly unique. If they sell well, would you be willing to make more?"

Marnie's eyes lift, tugging up the corners of her mouth. "Sure. I'm game."

Sally beams with pride as she turns from me to face Marnie. "I knew she'd think of something."

CHAPTER 11
Kade

Amanda's text pops up on my phone just as I arrive at my studio to gather additional tools.

Back door is open. Sally is dragging me off on a mission.

Probably a good thing she won't be around while I do the repair work. I don't need someone hovering, asking how they could help. During my years of construction and handyman repair—I call those years 'Kade just getting paid'—I learned I worked best alone or with a partner when the work required four hands.

I wasn't doing what I loved then like I am now. Straight out of high school, I knew I wanted to build things, so construction seemed the logical choice.

But it never satisfied my need to create.

However, I had bills to pay and a mother who was getting older and needed to slow down. She'd worked two, even three jobs sometimes when Devon and I were young just to pay the bills and put mostly decent food on the table.

And I did my duty as the oldest son by doing my part, helping out. Until one horrible day sent everything crashing to the ground.

I don't enjoy dwelling on the past. It is what it is.

But I'm at the point now that I can look back and see the good that came out of it. Now I have a life I can be proud of, doing—creating beautiful things that people like. And they pay me for it.

Even with the 'munchkin interruption,' I have a great life. A better life, if I'm totally honest. Having the squirt around reminded me of the importance of being connected to the people you love. Which I guess is why hearing Amanda say she wanted to go back to New York kind of threw me.

Okay, more than kind of.

Maybe a lot.

I let myself think there could be more between us. At least I found out before I became too invested. Time to stay squarely in the friend zone.

After filling my tool bag with the items I'd need, I head back to Amanda's shop. Zane is sitting on the back doorstep waiting for me again. He walks over to my truck as I get out. That's when I notice a nasty scratch on one of his cheeks.

"Did one of the raccoons do that?" It didn't look serious, but we're talking about a wild animal known to carry rabies.

He shakes his head as he touches his cheek. "Thank goodness, no. While Liam helped the kits get settled, I wandered over to see the domesticated ones. Guess I got a little too friendly with an old orange tabby with an attitude problem."

I can't help but chuckle at the image his description conjures. "I didn't know you liked cats."

"Not sure I do anymore." He follows this with a sarcastic laugh. "But I do like dogs and one rescue really caught my eye."

"Are you going to adopt it?" I lift my tool bag from the back of the truck.

"As much as I'd like to, no. I'm not home enough."

Then I realize that Zane is back here instead of going home. Or off to do something more fun on his day off than dealing with baby raccoons and grumpy cats.

I pause at the back door. "Why are you hanging around here?"

"Mom texted and said you needed help with the hole repair, so here I am."

I know I said I enjoy working alone, but Zane is my best friend and this is most likely a job best done with four hands. Nevertheless, I have to offer. "I can manage if you want to go."

He pats me on the back with a wide grin and a fresh load of sarcasm. "And miss more of the fun?"

After dropping off my tools inside the back door, we head back to the truck to unload the wood. That's when I see Amanda and Sally walking toward us.

Amanda is holding something and has the biggest smile on her face. She's practically glowing as she breaks into a jog, heading my way. I'm so struck by her beauty and her energy for life that I can only stare.

Despite knowing she has no plans to stay in Sarabella, I feel myself drawn to her. In a powerful way. Drawn to her goodness, her beauty…sucked into an abyss of hope every time she looks at me.

Zane pats me on the chest. "Breathe, man. You're turning blue."

I take a deep breath and shove all that into my mental locker, spin the dial, and walk away. Friend zone, friend zone…

She stops in front of me, cheeks flushed and eyes sparkling as she holds out her hands. "Look at this."

What feels like a minute slides by before I can drag my gaze from her face and imagine welding that locker closed for good. This will not be easy.

But then I'm sucked into the beauty of the glass piece she's handing me. I lift it up to the sun and marvel at how the sunlight reflects off the metallic pieces and illuminates the green, red, and orange glass and how the colors mingle to create deeper shades.

"Looks like a mango."

"Exactly." She says this as her eyes widen; as if she thinks I know where she's going with this.

"It's beautiful. What's it for?" I hold the piece out to her to hand it back.

I remain silent, waiting for the punch line. And for Amanda to take the glass mango back, but instead, she's cups the back of my hand with one of hers as if to help me hold it and traces the glass with a finger as she speaks.

"Can you finish it with your metal work, like you did on that card rack? A delicate framework that would hold it and look like part of the design. With leaves at the top and a stem."

As I digest what she's describing (and try to ignore what her touch is doing to my pulse), Zane leans over and studies the glass. "Did Marnie make these?"

Sally nods. "Yeah, but she didn't know what to do with them."

Then I catch Amanda's vision. "A stem that would allow you to hang it in front of a window to catch the light."

"Yes!" She gives me a light smack on my arm. "You can picture it, can't you?"

I nod. "Totally."

"Can you do twenty of them in a week?"

My gaze shoots up, taking in her sober expression. She's dead serious.

"Twenty?"

"Twenty," she says, without blinking.

Sally rests her hand on my arm. "I can help with Elly, so you have more time. I told Mandy she could have my booth at the festival if there weren't any left. This could really help get the word out about the changes she's making at the shop."

I will say I'm intrigued by the idea. Just not sure I can do what she's asking. I glance at the floor, which Sally notices right away.

"If you and Zane can repair the hole today, Jacob and I will call in some favors to get the rest of the flooring done."

I want to do this for Amanda. More than I probably should in light of the reality that we can't be more than friends. Staying away from her would make my life so much easier.

But it's the silent pleading I see in her eyes that sinks my resolve to keep my distance. Besides, friends help friends, right?

"Sure. Sounds like a plan."

Amanda bounces on the balls of her feet before throwing her arms around me in a hug.

The musky scent of her hair fills my nose, and it's all I can do not to bury my face in those silky strands.

She takes the mango and chats excitedly with Sally as they go inside the shop. Zane gives me a look that confirms what I'm already thinking.

Keeping that locker shut may take a bigger blowtorch.

CHAPTER 12
Amanda

They say fake it until you make it, but my motto seems to be fake it until you break it.

I turn off the torch and push up the front of Kade's spare face shield, which makes me feel like a bobblehead.

Since I can't open my shop yet, I'm spending the day at his studio, helping him save my business. How? By learning how to weld metal bits together. Today I've learned what flux and solder are, and how to use a blowtorch.

Well…kind of. The piece I've tried to solder (apparently it's a noun and a verb) falls apart yet again. "Okay, I give up. This is too hard."

Dropping the front of his face shield and mine, he takes the torch from me. "No, you're doing great. It just takes practice to get the hang of it."

His voice sounds clear and professional, and he does in mere seconds what I've been trying to do for at least ten minutes. After turning off the torch, he pushes his shield up as do I.

"There. Once it cools, a good sand and polish will finish it."

He puts the torch down and tugs off his face shield, which leaves his hair mussed and kind of sexy. "Want to give it another go?"

"No, maybe I should work on the leaves." I struggle to take off mine, so Kade helps me.

He stalls when our eyes meet, then brushes back the strands of hair that fell into my face when he tugged the gangly thing off of me.

It's all I can do not to close my eyes and lean into his hand. If I wasn't still wearing his spare gloves that fit me more like oven mitts, I'm afraid to think of what I might do. Because the image slamming my thoughts of holding his hand against my cheek is feeling almost real right about now.

He clears his throat and turns toward the table behind us to remove his gloves. "Or I can do them."

I give his arm a light shove. "Hey now! You said you could use some help, so here I am. I can think of a bunch of other things I could be doing right now."

He chuckles but shoots me a serious glance. "Am I keeping you from a hot date?"

I don't miss his reference to my same inquiry when he asked me for help with Eliana. I wonder if he's forgotten to call in that favor…

"Um, not likely. I own a flower shop. Every guy who walks in is buying something for a girlfriend, fiancée, or wife."

"We buy stuff for our mothers, too."

"In case you missed it, that holiday already passed, buster."

Kade takes one of the leaf shapes he cut from a piece of brass and secures it halfway in a vice. Then he hammers the free side down. Once he finishes, he releases the vice and holds the leaf out to show me.

"That creates the center. Then we just take it over to this block and, using this shaping hammer, we give it texture. Like this."

He seems to instinctively know where to hit the metal to create subtle curves and textures. Then he rotates the leaf to gently curl the edges and the tip. Using a cloth he grabbed from the workbench, he gives the leaf a quick brush. "I'll polish them more thoroughly once we attach them to the mangos."

"We?"

"Okay, me." He turns the leaf back and forth, smiling at it as if lost in the detail of what he created.

And I find myself entranced, sharing in that delight, much like he did that day when Eliana painted the pots. I understand what he's silently feeling. That satisfaction that comes with creating something beautiful. Or witnessing it. It's a deep kind of peace that pushes away all your cares and worries and connects you with something bigger than yourself.

Aunt Paula always said that was God. That he created us to create. Part of that whole 'made in his image' spiel. I never paid much attention to it until now. And I think I understand somewhat better what she meant.

And why I've felt a little…empty the last few years, implementing my boss' designs instead of creating my own.

"It's perfect."

He blinks at me as if he forgot I was there. "Thanks."

Silence returns and hangs heavily between us. My mantra flies back to me.

Romantic entanglements are not allowed.

I clap my hands to break the current buzzing between us. "Okay, I think I will figure out how to wrap the mangos with the wire so you can attach the leaves."

"Great idea." He pulls out a sketchbook from a drawer in his workbench and begins sketching the shape of the mango in quick, bold lines. "I was thinking we could follow the upper part of the groove Marnie left near the top, so the stem will stay more stable."

I hold my hand out to the pencil he's holding. "May I?"

He shoots the pencil up with his thumb and forefinger. "Go for it."

I build upon his line to create a winding flow of lines that will wrap the shape in a spiral and add a small, curling tendril that will complement the leaves. "I know mangos don't grow on vines, but I think the effect suits the design."

"I agree." One side of his mouth quirks up as he studies me. "I keep forgetting you're an artist."

I snort. "Why? Because I bunch flowers together? I'll have you know that's an art form in and of itself."

"Oh, no doubt, but the work you did in New York…you must miss it." Suddenly he seems awkward as he asks me this.

Is he asking out of curiosity or is he fishing for something? "Yes and no. I miss the potential of what my work could be."

His expression shifts to a studious frown, which deepens the scar on his cheek. "Not what it was?"

First, I shrug and then shake my head as I fiddle with the sketchbook. "Not that part. I was still more of an assistant to my creative director. He's been training me for the last two years to do more with product and communications. Mostly implementing his designs."

"You don't sound very excited about it." He's studying me so intently that a band of heat forms around my neck and travels up to my cheeks.

Hopefully, he'll think it's from the heat the blowtorch generated. "Not yet. Once I get my own accounts, it'll be great."

"And when will that be?" He drops his gaze, studying the picture we just created together.

"Soon I hope. That's my plan. To get my shop running well so I can sell it and go back to my actual career."

"In New York." He glances up and captures my gaze.

I want to compare that freckle and the shade of green in his eyes to the green in the glass mangos because both reflect the light in a way that takes my breath away. But I have a feeling that if I do, whatever this is between us will level up to a kiss.

Not that I don't want that…I do…but I can't.

I drop my line of sight to the sketchbook. "Yeah…New York. Daniel said he'd have a job for me when I was ready to come back."

"Daniel?"

"My creative director. I call him Bossman." I let out a soft laugh, hoping to break the tension that's zinging between us. Maybe he thinks Daniel is more than just my boss?

Kade takes a deep breath that swells his chest before he lets out a noisy breath. "Then we better get back to work. I think I'll make a few more leaves while you take care of wrapping the glass."

Kade turns back to the counter behind us and picks up a small sheet of brass.

I'm drawn to the sketch again and notice the page is near the back of the book. I flip to the front and discover page after page of drawings. Of ornate designs and ornamentations. Mixed between are sketches of his motorcycle, flowers, and seashells. I stop at a sketch of Eliana.

The lines are simple and easy but catch her likeness perfectly. I flip to the next page—what I think at first is a self-portrait but realize the face seems younger.

And no scar.

"Is this Devon?"

He looks over my shoulder before reaching over to close the sketchbook. "Yeah...I was trying to draw him from memory."

I lean my back against the heavy workbench, facing him. "Can I ask what happened to him?"

He shrugs and gives me this half-smile that looks more pained than happy. Usually, the scar on his face almost disappears when he smiles, except for the dimple it creates, but right now, it's vivid all the way to his hairline, as if highlighted by his thoughts. "You can, but I wish you wouldn't. Let's just say...it was...tragic."

I want to hold him, comfort him, but I know that would mean crossing over into something that could lead to more. Crawling into someone's grief is like a silent promise that you're committed to walking through it with them. Mix that with the way I feel drawn to him, and you have what I fear might be a cocktail to heartbreak.

"I'm sorry." For him. For me…might have been nice to talk to someone who understands the loss of a loved one. Losing Aunt Paula hasn't been easy—getting the shop up and running has been a great distraction. But at night, alone in her condo with all her memories there…that's been rough.

His features tighten, but he pretends to smile. "You know, it's late. Why don't I drive you home?"

He needs me to leave, and…I understand. We stepped into a 'no ventures allowed' zone. But I'd be lying if I said it didn't sting a little.

"I can drive myself. How about I take the mangos and work on them at home? I'll bring them by in the next day or so."

"Sounds great."

The distance between us is two feet max, but it feels more like a mile now. And cool to the touch. He helps me rewrap the glass mangos and put them back in the box along with a spool of thin brass wire.

"Here's a pair of snippers to cut the wire. Be careful not to poke your fingers. The edges can be sharp." He adds the snippers to the box and then, as an afterthought, throws in the gloves I was using earlier.

"Got it."

And I do. The box and the understanding that Devon is off limits.

As I leave his studio, the coolness of the night air folds gently around me as if to say, "Pay attention. The season is changing."

And it's right. Perhaps faster than I want it to.

※❀※

After flipping the camera on my phone, I dangle the glass mango near the sliding door leading to my balcony so that Sasha can see how the metal flecks reflect the light. I'm pleased with how the brass wire complements the metal flecks in the glass, and the delicate coil I created to mimic a tendril on a vine turned out even better than I'd imagined.

"Amanda, it's gorgeous!"

"I know, right?" I gently lay the mango on the counter and flip the camera again. "And they'll look even better once they have leaves."

Somehow, having Sasha's seal of approval helps put most of my fears to rest. At least the ones to do with the festival, which is only three days away. I wound up texting Kade the next day that I didn't have the mangos quite where I wanted, and he replied he didn't have the leaves finished yet either.

But in truth, I think we're avoiding each other.

Like I've said before and will say again, I wish life had an undo button. I'd be smacking it all the way back to New York right now.

"Those are going to sell out within minutes. What else are you going to sell?"

"I plan to have some 'grab-and-go' mini bouquets, the line of fall decor items I managed to get shipped in time, and a bunch of those small plants in the pots like I painted with Kade's niece."

I notice how my voice trailed off when I mentioned Kade's name and suddenly I can't seem to look at my best friend in the phone-face.

"Amanda, why do you look like you just imagined your worst nightmare?"

I'm careful to school my face to innocence with just a touch of outrage as I gape at her. "That's a bit dramatic, don't you think?"

Sasha turns her head ever so slightly and gives me her penetrating side-eye. "Did something happen between you and Kade?"

"No. I'm just nervous about the festival and a nervous wreck about the shop. The entire floor wound up having to be redone, which will most likely empty my bank account."

"Are you sure that's all this is?" She leans back and crosses her arms. I see our apartment in the background, which makes me long to be back there, sitting on our couch as we gripe about our jobs. Or laughing at the neighbor below us, who set up a table umbrella on the fire escape to protect him from any more of Sasha's paint clean-ups—something we apologized for profusely and promised never to do again.

"And missing my Aunt Paula." Might as well play every card I have.

Her expression softens a little. "Fine. I'll give you that one, but I still think there's something going on with Kade. You usually light up like a Roman candle when you talk about him. Not look like you lost your best friend."

I growl and then let out a loud sigh. "It's nothing, but it's complicated."

She bounces back with a wicked grin. "I knew it! Now fess up."

"Seriously, it's nothing. I found a sketch of his brother and asked him about it. And he closed down tighter than a clam."

"Maybe he's just not ready to talk about it."

"Well, that's obvious. All he said was it was *tragic*. But it's been five years."

"People deal with grief in different ways, and based on what you told me about that scar on his face, he probably was part of the accident."

"Could be. I haven't mustered up the courage to ask and now I won't. He may keep his leaves and leave my mangos bare."

Sasha giggles at my double entendre. "Listen, I have to go, but I'm FedEx-ing you a box of some items I collected from my gals in the artists' co-op. I told them my best friend needed a Hail Mary, and they were happy to help. Should get to you tomorrow."

"Sasha! That's great. Thank you!"

I throw her a kiss and a wave before ending the video call. The silence of the condo surrounds me again as the excitement of talking to Sasha fades away.

I've spent a fair bit of time the last couple of days packing Aunt Paula's clothes for donation and gathering other items that I don't want to keep. I even took myself out on a date one evening for sushi and a run to Target for a new bed cover.

A few years after I moved to New York, Aunt Paula sold the house I grew up in to downsize to this condo, which suited her better since she didn't have my help with the upkeep of both inside and out. Her time was better spent at the shop, she said.

The place still feels like hers, but now a little of me is showing up in small touches. Except for her special chair with the side table by the window that looks out toward the ocean. I know that's where she started every day with her herbal tea, her Bible, and a fancy journal. She loved the ones with flowers and an inspirational quote on them.

Maybe it's because when I look at it, I can picture her there so clearly, which makes me feel less alone.

I rewrap the mango I showed Sasha and return it to the box with the others.

Time to put on my big girl pants and face the Maverick Menace.

CHAPTER 13
Kade

I guess I blew it again. Amanda must think I'm a fickle grump.

After she left, I played what went down in my head again, and realized I pretty much told her to leave with my attitude. When it comes to Devon, I still have a hard time talking about him.

About what happened.

Doesn't help that my mother never wanted to talk about it either, other than to make it clear that I should have done more. Only recently has Shannon started talking more about Devon because Eliana has started showing interest in the man in the pictures with Mommy.

I blame myself for his death, even though I technically didn't cause it. But I wasn't able to save him, so isn't that the same thing?

Amanda's on her way over with the mangos and I'm scrambling, trying to figure out how to apologize (again) and make it up to her. She deserves better than my grumpy mood.

Eliana is sitting at her miniature worktable, coloring her latest masterpiece. With the push to get Amanda's pieces done as well as some client projects, I haven't spent enough time with the squirt this week, so today I told Sally I'd pick her up from preschool myself and brought her back to my studio.

The squirt runs up to my workbench and holds up her picture. "I made leaves, too!"

I take the page and pretend to study the detail. She likes it when I do this because she's seen me do it with my work. "This is top-notch, squirt. You nailed the detail perfectly."

Her smile grows big enough to push her nose up and almost blinds me. Warmth spreads through my chest. Life before the squirt consisted of my shop, occasional runs to the grocery store, and my apartment. Unless I had a delivery, I could go an entire day with no human interaction. I didn't realize how alone I felt most of the time until I had to add Eliana to the mix, and now I look forward to taking her places and taking care of her.

"Thank you, Uncle Kade. Now I'm going to draw the mangos." She pauses at her table, then spins around. "When is Mandy coming?"

"A-manda, remember?" I'm trying to retrain Eliana to use Amanda's full name, which she says doesn't *sound* like Mandy at all. I know what she means, but I still want her to try now that I know it's important to Amanda.

I check my phone to see how long ago Amanda texted she was on her way. "Any minute now."

And as I say the words, Amanda walks in. Like Eliana's smile, I'm dazzled by her brightness, and that buzzing in my body returns; like every cell is alert to her presence.

"Mandy!" Eliana races over to hug Amanda.

"Hi there!" She sets the box on the edge of my workbench. "They're ready for leaves."

"Eliana?" I raise my brow as a reminder.

She makes a sour face at me, then looks up at Amanda. "Sorry. A-mand-a."

She emphasizes every syllable as she rolls her eyes, which makes me roll mine, too. So much for subtlety.

Amanda looks confused now. "What am I missing?"

I run a hand over my face. "Zane mentioned that since you moved to New York, you preferred to go by your full name."

She makes a small circle with her rosy lips. "I see. Well, Eliana has my permission to call me Mandy." She smiles at the squirt. "Only my special friends are allowed to call me that."

Eliana gives me a smug smile. "See?"

And I'm jealous—jealous of my four-year-old niece, who seems to have found her way into Amanda's heart with little effort.

Has to be a kid thing. I'm so tempted to ask if I can be one of her special friends, too, but then I remember her plans to go back to New York and slam the locker shut again on those growing feelings. I may have to upgrade the size of my mental storage space.

When Amanda returns her gaze to me, her smile appears somewhat forced—not her usual affable grin that makes me want to grab her hand and tug her closer so I can get a better look. Like I do when I'm creating a piece and want to lose myself in the detail.

I put down the leaf I was finishing. "Listen, about the other day...I'm sorry I shut down. I still have a hard time—"

She holds her hand up to stop me as compassion shifts her expression. "No apology needed. I get it." She holds that same hand to her chest and, again, the temptation to grab it almost pushes me over the edge. "I'm struggling to deal with losing Aunt Paula. Grief is...messy."

She shifts her hand to my arm, and before I can even think about it, I grab and hold it to my chest, right over my heart.

I don't know why I did that. I'm at a loss for words and as shocked as Amanda is, judging by how big her eyes are right now.

I let go of her hand and tug the box closer. "Let's see those mangos."

"I want to see, too!" Eliana bounces up and down with her excitement.

I shoot a quick glance at Amanda to see if she's moved on from that awkward moment. Kind of like doing damage control. There's not a lot I can do or say with Eliana here. As my mother says, small pitchers. Damage control will have to wait until another time.

She drops her gaze to the box as soon as she sees me looking at her and grabs a small bag out of the box. "I almost forgot. Eliana, these are for you. Do you mind painting more pots for the festival? The paint bottles are in the bag, along with a couple of paint brushes."

The squirt jumps up and down with pure glee on her round face. "Yes! I'd be delighted."

Then she grabs the bag and takes it to her worktable to spread out the contents.

Amanda meets my surprised gaze with her own. "Smart kid, that one."

"You have no idea."

I hold up one of the mangos by the stem, studying how she worked the wire around the glass in such a way to complement the shape of the glass and culminate into a delicate coil at the base of the stem.

"You have a knack for this, Root Beer."

"Hey! I thought we agreed." She sounds offended, but the smile on her face is cute and teasing.

Maybe I didn't screw things up as badly as I thought. "Sorry. My bad."

"Root Beer?" Eliana shoots a frown at me and crossed her arms. "Are you being mean to Mandy?"

Amanda turns her head just so and lifts one brow as if to say, "See?"

I drop my chin at first and then grin apologetically. "I'm sorry, Amanda. I guess my excitement got the better of me."

Amanda drops her gaze to Eliana, who gives her nod of approval, and then she brings those deep, golden brown eyes back to mine. "Forgiven. And you can call me Mandy, too."

There's an unspoken message of acceptance and understanding in that statement. I got my wish, and I didn't even have to ask. And I can only describe what I'm feeling as…connection.

Like one of those small cacti she has in her shop that's about to bloom, I get the sense something between us is about to grow into something more.

I don't know what to make of it yet, only that I know it feels right.

CHAPTER 14
Amanda

The big day has arrived—Festival Day—and I...
I am a bundle of nerves.

The last time I came to one of these was during my last year of high school. Back then, it was just a smattering of booths (more like tables) by local businesses, a table of baked goods hosted by a local church, and an arts and crafts cabana set up for kids to get their faces painted.

But this...this is a full-scale FESTIVAL.

There are vendors here from all over the state of Florida and several other states as well. At least fifty booths fill the center pavilion and park in downtown Sarabella, which is only about a half mile away from the beach. There are food trucks, a farmer's market, and several bouncy houses for kids.

And Mr. Green, who owns the Sarabella Golf Club and Course (yes, seriously), loaned several of his golf carts to transport back and forth those who park on the outlying streets.

Aunt Paula told me the event had grown quite a lot, but college classes were either in session or I was working full time, so I never had an opportunity to come and see for myself.

So this...this I didn't expect. At all.

I'm still moving things around my booth to make sure everything is arranged just so and will give a 'filled' appearance. Thanks in part to the box Sasha sent, my booth has more to offer than I'd expected. I'm afraid to ask her what the shipping cost was because I fully intend to reimburse her for that. But, wow, what a treasure trove—small, matted, limited edition prints; custom buttons with crazy designs and inspirational words; hand-crafted jewelry; and a quirky set of coastal-themed coasters I'm positive Sasha threw together just for me.

Because they have seashell designs on them, and Sasha hates the beach. To this day she won't tell me why, but she does. I think my chances of getting her to come for a visit are slim, but I'm determined nonetheless.

I created a special sign for the items she sent to promote them as *Crafted by New York Artists*. And I put a sign by the small pots that says *Hand Painted by Eliana*. I've already gotten a few 'ohs' and 'ahs' over these from the tourists and the locals.

The good news is, the floor in my shop is now finished—and gorgeous!—thanks to Sally and Jacob, who enlisted the aid of a friend in the flooring business to get the job done fast. And cheaper than I expected. I was even able to open up shop yesterday and make a few sales.

Since the replacement of the floor wound up costing less than I expected, I invested in a decent printer to create my own fancy labels for the mangos, which I can't wait to show Marnie and Kade. Because these babies are a joint venture in my mind, I credited Marnie and Kade's businesses for their parts of the design.

Two of the glass mangos sold already and the festival only opened twenty minutes ago, so needless to say, my hopes are soaring even higher than the seagulls over at the beach at the moment.

Yep, things are definitely looking up for Amanda Wilde. I may just conquer this small business owner thing yet.

The tantalizing smell of giant pretzels, popcorn, and fish

tacos makes my stomach growl, and I remember I never ate breakfast.

"Mandy!" Eliana's sweet voice filters through the hubbub. I search the growing crowd for her little face and see a wave coming from the direction of the bouncy houses. Kade's standing near the opening, holding her hand as she climbs out.

After helping her slip on a cute pair of bright pink flip-flops, Eliana leads Kade over to my booth like a dog pulling on a leash. And Kade is holding one of those giant pretzels I've been drooling over for the last half hour.

"Hey there, guys! How are you?"

Eliana frowns at me. "I'm not a guy."

"Oh, it's just an expression, but you are right. You're a gal." I tweak her nose and am rewarded with a smile.

From Kade, too. A smile that says he's glad to see me. At least I think so. But I can't help but look longingly at that pretzel he's holding.

And what's worse, he notices and looks down at that beautiful twist of brown bread and salt. "Are you happy to see me or just my pretzel?"

My stomach growls so loud I can only imagine how red my face is based on the heat spreading through my cheeks. I'm scrambling for some kind of witty answer but drawing a total blank.

And then Kade does the most adorable and unexpected thing. He hands me his pretzel.

"I think you need this more than I do."

The delicious smell of pretzel dough wafts up my nose and fills my mouth with saliva so quickly, I'm afraid to say anything for fear of spraying instead of saying, as Sally says.

He gives his hand a little lift as if to say, "Go ahead and take it."

I take his sweet and salty gift, tear off a piece of warm bread, and pop it into my mouth. Honestly, I don't know if I'm just that hungry or this is THE BEST pretzel I've ever had in my life.

And I think my eyes rolled back in my head as I groan. Reality slams back as I cover my mouth. "Sorry."

Kade has this silly grin on his face, and his eyes are smoldering.

All from a pretzel?

Thankfully, I'm saved from the rest of this embarrassing moment when a cute couple walks up behind Kade. I recognize Aiden right away from his shop, The Last Bean, home of the best banana bread I've ever had the pleasure of consuming. I think the cute redhead on his arm is his girlfriend.

Aiden pats Kade on the back. "Hey, man. How's the metal biz?"

They shake hands and begin to talk. Eliana has discovered the items Sasha sent and is studying each one in great detail, just like her Uncle Kade.

Meanwhile, I'm staring at that cute redhead, trying to figure out how I know her. Because I'm pretty sure I do. She gives me this little wave, which tells me she knows who I am.

Now I want to lean down to Eliana and ask her if my face is as red as this woman's hair.

And then the memories flood back. "Emily?"

She runs over and gives me a quick hug. "Mandy, it's so good to see you!"

Emily and I were inseparable in middle school. Then her parents moved to northern Florida because of her dad's job, and we lost touch.

"When did you move back to Sarabella?"

"Last year. I lost my job and came to stay with my grandmother for a while. And then I met Aiden." She looks at Aiden with a love glow to rival Romeo and Juliet (without the family war I hope) and holds up her left hand to display a beautiful round but modest diamond surrounded by small red rubies.

"We just got engaged. The rubies are his way of reminding me he loves redheads."

That has to be one of the most romantic things I've ever heard. I look up from the ring. "That's so precious!"

And it is. Because I remember how much Emily hated her red hair in school, which was a constant source of ridicule and teasing by the same group of kids that made my life so miserable in high school when they found out about my mother's true profession.

"I wanted to come see you sooner, but the bakery has been overwhelmed with orders for the festival. I'm the pastry chef at Bake My Day."

I can't help the little gasp that slips out. "All those hours with your Easy Bake Oven paid off!"

She laughs. "I can't believe you remember that."

"How could I forget? I was your best customer, remember?" I'll never forget *that* either. That's the summer I discovered that chocolate could cause acne. I was devastated.

She leans toward me with a conspiratorial expression. "From what Aiden tells me, you still are. The banana bread is my recipe."

I gasp. "No way!"

She smiles and nods with pride. "He pointed you out as we walked over, and that's when I recognized you."

Warmth floods my chest. To be reconnected with Emily is an unexpected surprise and a gift. "I'm so glad he did."

"Me, too."

I feel a tug on my right side.

Eliana stares up at me, holding one of the sun-shaped pins Sasha sent. The hand-scripted words 'Be the Sunshine' arc over a sunburst in shades of pale yellow, mustard, and orange. "Can I buy this one?"

I squat down and pin it to her pink and white polka dot dress just above the image of Ariel on the front. "Consider it payment for all your hard work painting those pots for me."

Eliana's eyes widen to match the cute little circle of her plump lips.

I think I've made a friend for life.

As I rise I notice Kade watching us, and he has this look in his eyes that sets my heart on overdrive and, at the risk of sounding a wee bit cliché, weak in the knees.

I drag my attention back to Emily, who's become the object of Eliana's awe because of her red hair that's just like Ariel's.

"Are you a mermaid?"

Emily giggles. "No, but I always wanted to be one."

Kade is still staring at me. That is, until Aiden elbows him in the side.

Aiden saunters over and wraps an arm around Emily's waist, but I can tell he's up to something. "I just had the best idea. How about the four of us go on a double date?"

Emily is bouncing her gaze between Kade and me, and her delight is as palpable as my mortification. "That's a great idea!"

Kade looks as if he just got sucker punched, which he did. Yet he's looking at me with this question in his eyes. Like he's letting me decide.

What do I do? Even Eliana is looking at me with hopeful expectation. She is one profoundly astute four-year-old, whom I do not wish to disappoint.

At least, that's what I'm telling myself.

"Sure. Why not?"

The festival yesterday couldn't have gone better. By the end of the day, I sold out of all but one of the mangos, which I held back as a sample to take preorders after I sent a quick text to Marnie to make sure she could make more. I also told her I wanted her to create a line of bud vases for my store, which garnered a dozen happy face emojis and a GIF of a chick doing a happy dance. And by chick, I mean the feathered kind.

Then, while Sally and Kade managed my booth, I went and explored the others and connected with close to a dozen other vendors—some local and some from out of town—to add unique inventory to my shop.

Even Kade is going to create some additional items he has in mind. Along with the leaves for the glass mangos.

Which reminds me again that we have a date.

A date.

An honest-and-for-true date.

Tonight.

Emily somehow got my number and texted me the details for dinner at a new seafood place later that evening. Good thing I noticed Kade was included on the same text before I asked something embarrassing.

Like, *Do you think Kade really likes me?*

Because I had it typed in and ready to send.

My stomach does a flip-flop just thinking about it.

How did I wind up in this position? It all happened in a matter of seconds yesterday, and then a rush of customers came into my booth, giving me no chance to talk to Kade, let alone figure out how I feel about it.

And I do…feel about it…a lot.

I can't stop smiling as I imagine what it will be like to go on a date with him, along with all those romantic expectations we've managed to avoid until now. And then the butterflies swarm in and I want to puke.

Oy…

Is this *really* a good idea, considering I have no intentions of staying in Sarabella? I've never been a casual dater, and I get the feeling Kade isn't either. I don't think so anyway. I've yet to see him out with anyone. Although, lately, he has spent a fair bit of time at my shop, bailing me out of some mess, or I've been at his studio, *helping him* bail me out.

Oy again…

Maybe I should call Sasha and see what she thinks. Or

better yet, maybe I should cancel or come down with a nasty stomach bug that magically goes away in twenty-four hours.

But as much as I'd like to figure this out, my shop is about to reopen in a few minutes, and I am like one of those Roomba vacuums, scurrying all over the place, getting ready.

Any leftover stock from the festival has joined the rest throughout the store, and Sally dropped off two platters of cookies from the bakery last night to help welcome new customers. I even lit a sugar cookie candle to add to the ambiance.

After I place one of those cookie trays down on the checkout counter and tug off the cellophane, the front door bells jingle.

An older woman dressed in white jeans and a floral top breezes in with her friend, who also is wearing capris and the cutest little pink sandals that match her pink toenail polish and pink tank top.

I know, weird that I notice these things, but I'm a designer and colors are my jam.

"Welcome to Bloomed to Be Wilde, ladies. Is there anything I can help you find?" I stand with my hands behind my back and a massive smile on my face as I stand on my brand-new wood floor that gives the place a light, airy feel. I just know these two ladies are browsers and will probably be here for a while.

"Oh, we're just looking around," the first woman says.

"Trying to get a jump start on some Christmas shopping," says her friend.

I called that one. Tourists love to find gifts in Sarabella to take home with them. The more original, the better.

"Where are you ladies from?"

They both say Vermont at the same time, then giggle.

"I used to live in New York myself," I say as I grab the cookie platter from the counter and take it over to them. "Can I interest you in a cookie? They're from our bakery just a few doors down."

The first woman studies the array of maple leaf shaped

cookies decorated in fall colors, either undecided about which one she wants or if she even should. But her friend swoops in with a delighted squeal and scoops one up.

And that's when I see it.

And they do too, judging by their screams.

A giant cockroach about the size of my thumb scrambles out of the cookies and up the second woman's arm. She tosses the cookie across the room and jerks her arm over her head, trying to fling the black monster off.

Which she does—right into the other woman's hair.

Now they're both screaming and stomping around on my new floor. I drop the tray back onto the counter, intending to help, but three more cockroaches come crawling out of the cookies.

I jump back and bounce into the first woman who has now turned her perfectly coifed do into a rat's nest in her mad attempt to expel the cockroach.

"I am so sorry! Here, let me help you."

Before I can get anywhere near her, the other woman has grabbed the rat nest lady's hand and is dragging her out of the store. "Let's get out of here. Now!"

Out they go, running down the front steps and onto the sidewalk, still writhing and squealing as they run away from my shop.

I rush to the back area because, if that tray has roaches, the other most likely does, too.

And it does...a few under the plastic wrap, several crawling on the worktable, and a few scurrying away from my feet.

There are many things I can tolerate, but cockroaches are not one of them. This way surpassed my encounter with 'The Can,' and makes those raccoons under my floor a pure delight.

After a visual check that the back door is still locked, I grab my purse from the chair, head back to the front, flip the sign to closed, and lock the door.

As I collapse on the second front step, my phone rings. Sasha's phone-smushed face shows up, and I hit accept.

Her real face smiles at me. "How's it going?"

I burst into tears. The full-on sobbing, can't talk for the first few seconds, body-racking kind that only come out with an impending apocalypse. And that's what this might as well be—the end of my world as I know it.

I suck in enough air so I can form the only words that best describe my situation.

"My shop is possessed!"

CHAPTER 15
Amanda

After Sasha talks me down from setting my shop on fire (just kidding...well, mostly), I walk over to the Pink Hibiscus, looking for Sally, but she's not there today. Nor is she at home, because I forgot that she and Jacob always take a vacation after the festival, and I refuse to call and disrupt her wonderful getaway from the chaos of running a business.

Especially when the chaos has reached the 'you've-got-to-be-kidding-me, blow-your-brains-up' level. You know the emoji I'm talking about.

I'm sure I'm being overly dramatic, but there are real, rather large cockroaches all over my shop, and Bloomed to Be Wilde is shut down.

Again.

At this rate, I'll never get the place running smoothly in time to sell it. And, yes, I know a year is the minimum requirement, but the longer I'm gone, the more I fear I'll lose that job my former boss promised would still be there.

Zane is most likely on duty or overseeing training for a new class of lifeguards, so I can't bother him.

And...I'm right around the block from Kade's studio.

I'm standing on the corner, frozen in my indecision of what to do.

So not good.

I recognize the signs.

The Overwhelm.

In my last year of art school, I wound up with appendicitis right before final portfolios were due. Talk about feeling overwhelmed as I dealt with recovery, falling behind, and hoping to still graduate. I produced my final projects in a mania Sasha still calls my Van Gogh period.

Thankfully, I survived with both my ears intact.

But I did nothing but sleep for two weeks straight afterward. Sasha even called Aunt Paula because she was so worried about me. Fortunately, I pulled out of it and landed my almost-dream-job a few weeks later.

I cannot go there again. I have a business to run. I need help.

That propels me toward Kade's studio. He must know someone in this town who knows how to eradicate cockroaches. And I do mean ERADICATE. As in, do whatever is necessary to get rid of every single one of them. FOREVER.

Yeah, and it snows regularly in Florida.

I've lived here long enough to know that's impossible, but I need a drastic miracle NOW.

As I approach the door to his studio, he sees me through the glass and saunters toward the door with a smile, which shifts to concern as he draws closer. So much so his brows are nearly touching in the center as he pushes the door open.

What must I look like to cause that reaction?

"What's wrong? What happened?"

I don't know what possesses me other than the need for a hug. Aunt Paula always gave the best hugs right when you needed them. That's the hug I want right now. So much so, I step into Kade's studio and don't stop until I'm against him in the hopes he'll do just that.

Wrap his arms around me and hold me.

That logical voice telling me this could lead to more can take a flying leap.

Because right now I don't need logic. I need a hug.

And he does exactly what I'd hoped. His arms wrap around me as I bury my face against his shirt. I can smell his soap and a mix of ozone and smoke fumes. He's been working this morning and I've interrupted him.

I lean my head back. "I'm sorry I interrupted your work."

"Don't be. I didn't expect to see you until tonight. I'm not complaining." His smile finishes the implication of his words and that logical warning voice is getting louder again.

"I can't even think about tonight right now. Not when my shop is infested with cockroaches."

His eyes bug out.

Yes, pun intended. Maybe that's a good sign that I'm not completely losing it?

"Seriously?"

I nod. "And it gets worse."

I relay the entire debacle that played out with those two poor women from Vermont, who will tell everyone they know about the horror that is living inside of Bloomed to Be Wilde with their final warning of 'stay away from that place.'

My business is probably ruined and my reputation tanked.

As I finish, the chuckle Kade has worked so hard to hide behind his hand breaks loose into a full-on guffaw. And there are actual tears streaming down his face.

He's laughing so hard he has to lean against his workbench as he tries to apologize between breaths.

I stare at him, at first offended that he could laugh so hard at my horror. But then this giggle wells up from my gut, and before I know it, I'm laughing just as hard as he is and whatever tears I had left from my earlier heart-rending sob are now making their way down my cheeks.

Once we regain composure and I find a paper towel to sop up the remains of my mascara, Kade picks up his cell phone.

"I know just the guy to handle this quickly for you."

"Oh, bless you. You are a good man, Kade Maverick."

Kade then stares at me with this shocked expression on his face, and I haven't any idea why.

KADE'S FRIEND, Buck—an older gentleman who wears a full-on jumpsuit with the logo 'Buck the Bugs' on the left side—is down on his hands and knees with a flashlight in one hand and his head poked in the crawl space under my shop.

"Yep, you have an infestation. Probably because of those raccoons you had. Once they were gone, the roaches moved in to consume the leftover garbage."

I physically shudder. "What do I do?"

"Nothing. I'll take care of it."

"How long will it take?" I must sound as desperate as I feel, because he shoots a concerned glance at Kade as he maneuvers to his feet again.

His studious expression tells me he's trying to answer me as delicately as possible. He scratches his head, too. "Well, fumigating the shop won't take too long. It's the crawl space that presents a bit more of a challenge. Kind of hard to seal that, so I'll have to lay down bait. That's what might take a little longer. The suckers have to eat it and die."

"Then when do you think I can reopen?"

He scratches his head. "Two or three days."

That's when I notice Kade's hand on my shoulder—he gives me a light squeeze of comfort.

I turn around and plant my face against his chest. This seems to be my favorite place today. And I seem to have no shame or reservations about going there.

The rumble of Kade's voice in his chest comforts me as he tells Buck to get started as quickly as possible.

And I'm so grateful. I don't think I can deal with one more mess, one more piece of drama, one more heart-wrenching disappointment today.

Kade shifts me so I'm under his arm as he leads me down the walk, away from my shop and into a sweet little patch of shade near a palm tree. Then he turns me to face him, but I'm staring at my feet and wishing I could go back to the day I bought these cute blue-gray sandals with Aunt Paula on one of my visits from college. That was a blissful day full of laughter and good food as we explored shops along the coast further north of Sarabella.

He stops, pulls his phone from his pocket, and starts typing.

"What are you doing?"

His thumbs fly over the small keyboard on his screen. "I'm letting Aiden and Emily know we need to reschedule…" He trails off.

Or is he hesitating because he's struggling with the whole date thing, too? Could this disastrous day be a blessing in disguise?

If so, then why does that make me feel worse?

"Reschedule?" I need to know I'm not just a piece of drama in his life that he's tolerating. But what's the alternative to that? A relationship? There go those warning bells again.

"Yeah. We'll do it tomorrow." He looks up. "Right now, you need to see fuzzy critters."

"Excuse me?" That sounds like the last thing I need.

"I'm picking up Eliana early so I can take her to the animal rescue and see those raccoons Liam rescued from under your shop. That'll be way more relaxing for you, which is what you need right now."

"Are you asking me to go with you?"

He tilts his head and does this confused smile thing that rolls out the dimple again. "Unless you'd rather not go."

I hold my hand up. "No, it's not that. I mean, I do want to go. I just wasn't sure…"

"Yes?"

I take a deep breath, close my eyes, and blurt it out. "I didn't think you'd be interested in being around a nut job who seems to have the worst luck possible right now."

Dead silence. I peek one eye open.

Kade is staring at me with what I can only describe as deep compassion with a touch of something more that makes my heart go *kathump* and makes it very hard to breathe.

A soft breeze tugs several strands of hair into my face.

Like that time at his studio, Kade brushes those errant tendrils back, and I'm once again captivated by those green eyes as he leans toward me. No one—and I mean no one—has ever looked at me like this. As if he sees every part of me.

His lips part like he's going to say something, but then he stops and leans back.

My heart is screaming for him to finish what I think he just started.

"You could never be a nut job."

Not exactly what I'd hoped for but still sweet. "Do you not know me?"

One side of his mouth tugs up in a smile—the side with the scar dimple. "Not as well as I'd like."

CHAPTER 16
Kade

Mandy thinks I'm a good man. That's all I can think about as we drive to the animal sanctuary. Mandy's turned around in her seat so she can talk to Eliana, who is chattering away about her day at preschool.

I wonder if she'd still think that if she knew about my past. She hasn't asked any more questions since the last time I shut things down—shut her down—with her questions about Devon. Maybe one day I'll be able to talk about him and what happened. I almost feel like I could with her. That she'd listen and not judge.

Of course, she'd just experienced a cockroach invasion, described in epic proportions, and probably would have thought any person who helped her at the moment was 'good.' I'm not a fan of those little creatures myself, and I use the word 'little' subjectively here.

But the thought still scares me—not the larger-than-life cockroaches she described, but the idea of her thinking I'm a good person. What if I tell her more about myself and she decides I'm the horrible man my mother seems to think I am?

Then again, why am I having this argument with myself

when I know a future with her is off-limits for so many reasons besides the fact that she has no desire to stay in Sarabella?

I'm talking myself in circles like this a lot lately. An earlier version of myself would have just gone for the ride as long as it lasted, but Mandy deserves way better than that.

Better than me.

I pull into the gravel parking area at the animal rescue and park my truck as I shove this inner war into a locker next to the one that's supposed to be holding my feelings and longings for Mandy and bring out that imaginary torch gun to redo the seals. I think I need some kind of magical flux because these welds don't seem to last very long.

But the imagination tends to have a mind of its own, right?

As Mandy gets out, I reach back and unlatch the buckle on Eliana's car seat. The squirt must have fallen asleep right before we arrived and has her face snuggled against the side of her seat. I slide my hands under her arms and lift her up onto my shoulder. She snuggles her face into my neck and wraps her small arms around me with a squeeze of complete trust.

This is one of those times I'm struck with how small and delicate she really is, and that fierce sense or need to protect her from everything bad in this world overwhelms me so strongly that I either can't breathe or I want to punch the hood of my truck to make a statement—if anything or anyone comes near her, I will protect her with my life.

That's when I notice Mandy is watching me with this intent expression that's unreadable to me. I know some women aren't keen on men with children. And before Eliana, I was one of those guys who would have steered clear of any woman with a kid. Eliana may not be mine, but she's pretty close to it. She not only changed my life, but she also changed me. Helped me realize how alone I'd been living my life.

And Mandy seems really fond of Eliana and the squirt adores her.

"Hey, squirt, you ready to see those raccoons?"

She nods her head as she rubs her eyes.

Mandy grins at her. "I hope they have some kittens, too."

Now Eliana is on full alert as she wiggles to let me know she's awake and wants to take off.

"Kittens?" Her voice almost squeaks with her excitement, and she runs toward the entrance.

Once inside, I explain we're there at Liam's invitation. The receptionist makes a call to the back and shortly after, the door behind her swings open. Liam comes through with a grin on his face. "Hi, guys!"

Eliana tugs on Mandy's hand.

Mandy leans down. "What's up, sweetie?"

"He called me a guy," Eliana whispers loud enough to be heard.

Liam puts his hand to his chest and leans back as if struck. "My sweet Eliana, forgive me. How could I ever mistake your radiant beauty for a guy?" He draws 'guy' out for emphasis and turns guttural at the end, which has Eliana giggling and her frown has shifted to a smile that competes with the sunlight streaming through the front windows.

Liam drops his hand and grins at Mandy. "Ladies it is, from now on."

Did he just flirt with Mandy?

I check Mandy's reaction to see if I'm right.

Her blush is barely visible, but I notice it.

Those feelings I locked away are rattling that locker door—hard. I want to put my arm around Mandy and give Liam a clear message to back off, but I have no right to do such a thing. Nor would I. Mandy's not a possession. She's this beautiful embodiment of everything good, pure, and kind.

"You coming?" Liam's slamming me with visual question marks, and I realize I'm staring at Mandy as she follows Eliana through the doorway.

I blink and force a grin. "Yeah, let's go see those raccoons."

Liam pats me on the back as I pass him and whispers, "You sure that's all you're here to see?"

I give him a look I hope gets the message of 'off limits' across. Today is about a little girl, raccoon babies, and kittens, as long as none come home with us. My attraction to Mandy and anything to do with my love life is not part of the day's agenda.

Liam leads us to a decent-sized enclosure outside that has several dog houses, some toys, and several shallow bowls that are either empty or hold water. There's a jungle gym-type structure in the middle that's actually an old tree with several small platforms attached.

Eliana squeals next to me and bounces like a spring as she points to three little faces poking out of one of the dog houses. "There they are!"

Liam takes her hand and guides her into the enclosure. "Let's give them some food, okay?"

He looks at me and must see the concern I didn't realize I was showing. "They've been checked and they're healthy. No diseases."

"Can I come in, too?" Mandy holds her hands together under her chin and has a hopeful smile that competes with Eliana's earlier outburst.

"Sure." Liam waves her in, then focuses on me. "You, too."

Liam secures the enclosure once we're inside. "Normally we don't let this many people come at once, but since it's just the three kits right now, it's okay."

The smallest one is clinging to my boot now. "Is this the one we didn't think was going to make it?"

Liam nods. "She's a tough little guy."

Eliana lets out a noisy sigh. "Not a guy, a girl."

"You're right again, Elly." Liam helps her dump out the small bucket of food into the bowl. "How would you like to see some squirrels?"

"Squirrels?" The squirt is bouncing again and clapping her hands.

After Liam secures the raccoon habitat, we follow him to a smaller enclosure on the other side of the grounds. He points to a squirrel near the top of a cage that's taller than me. Two other squirrels are climbing the lower parts of a jungle gym that resembles a small tree.

"Those two down there will be released soon, but that guy—and yes, Elly, he is a boy—has become one of our permanent residents."

Eliana looks up at Liam with a confused expression. "Does that mean he can't be free?"

Liam shakes his head. "He'd die if we let him loose. Charley can't take care of himself out in the wild anymore. He was too badly injured."

"Oh." She seems lost in her thoughts, but I'm wondering if she's overthinking things. The kid has an amazing way of applying things like this to her own circumstances.

I tousle her bangs. "It's okay, squirt. He has friends he can play with and people to love him."

"That's right." Liam opens the enclosure. "And Charley likes to be held, too. Would you like to hold him?"

Eliana nods her head with a vigor only a four-year-old can handle.

Liam reaches toward Charley, who then leaps onto his arm and scurries up to his head. Liam then cradles the fur ball and hands him to Eliana.

"He's so soft." Eliana stares down at the little guy with complete adoration. Then she giggles as Charley climbs up to her shoulder. "He tickles."

Sudden movement alerts me to the fact that Charley is now airborne and heading toward me. A flurry of movement blinds me for a moment and I hear Mandy's yelp mingling with Eliana's. Then everything goes quiet.

And a very fuzzy tail is hanging down the front of my face. I don't move for fear of scaring the little guy, but I can't help but chuckle at my situation. "I don't think this is how you're supposed to wear a coon hat."

Liam reaches up and extricates the squirrel from my hair one paw at a time. Eliana is giggling, and so is Mandy.

Now that my hair is hanging in my eyes, I attempt to brush it back, but Charley did quite a tease job to my head.

"Here, let me help." Mandy runs her hands through my hair, combing it back with her fingers. And I'm lost. Lost in the feel of fingers brushing over my ears and across my scalp. It's taking every fiber in my being not to lean in and pull her closer. Her mouth is too close for comfort, so I close my eyes.

"I don't know how you managed to stay so calm."

I snap my eyes open as her words jerk me back to reality. "I didn't want to scare the little guy any more than he already was."

She's still so close as she continues to fiddle with my hair. I can smell her floral scent mixed with a hint of something spicy, like clove or cinnamon. Since she's not looking directly at me, I have time to really study her brown eyes, which appear to be more hazel when the sun hits them like it is now. A dark brown ring surrounds her irises, too. My gaze falls to her lips again, and I want so much to find out if they're as soft as they appear.

"There. That's better." She lowers her hands as I bounce my gaze back up to hers.

It's like slow motion after that as she moves back without breaking eye contact, then blinks and drops her chin as she runs her hands down the front of her jeans.

I reach up and run a hand over my hair that's now surprisingly smooth. "Thanks."

Thankfully, Charley has distracted Eliana and Liam.

Once Liam puts the rogue squirrel back in the enclosure, he rubs his hands together with a mischievous grin. "Okay, let's go check out those kittens."

Eliana grabs my hand. "Let's go, Uncle Kade."

"Lead the way, squirt." I glance over my shoulder to check on Mandy, who seems to be intentionally lagging behind.

After a few steps, Eliana stops, turns sideways, and holds her hand out to Mandy. "Come on, Mandy."

She hesitates a moment as our eyes meet again, but then she smiles at Eliana and rushes forward to hold her hand.

The path is wide enough for the three of us to walk side-by-side. I turn my head just enough to see Mandy in my peripheral vision.

Eliana is talking about how much she loves kittens and Mandy is asking her why.

And I'm the guy listening to the two most important 'girls' in his life chatter about fuzz balls. It's a peaceful moment—comfortable and almost familiar. As if I'm catching a glimpse of what my life could be like with a family.

I rub a hand over my mouth. When did my life become so simple and so complicated all at once?

And how and when did I fall so hard for Amanda Wilde?

CHAPTER 17
Amanda

I'm going out with friends.
 I'm going out with friends, and Kade happens to be one of them.
 I'm *just* having dinner with some friends.
 And Kade.
 I groan and drop my head in my hands as I plop down on the sea of discarded outfits covering my bed.
 Doesn't matter how I frame it, it's still the same.
 I'm going on a date with Kade Maverick, former high school nemesis, turned sexy distraction who's not only the dominating thought in my head these days but also rapidly taking up more space in my heart.
 Oh, so much more, which has me in a near panic.
 Why?
 Because yesterday, being with him and Eliana like that… well, let's just say that as the three of us walked together to see the kittens, the idea of what life could look like if I stayed in Sarabella formed into a definitive image and left an indelible impression.
 Me holding Eliana's right hand. Kade holding her left. Almost felt like we were holding hands by proxy.

And I haven't been able to think of anything else since.

I have to face facts here—not impressions, wistful thinking, or anything of that ilk—if I want to survive the next ten months in Sarabella and stick to my plan to get back to New York as fast as possible.

With a grunt that's more like a growl, I shove off the bed and turn around, facing my imaginary self sitting on the bed.

"You can't fall for him. That totally wrecks your life plan, Amanda. This is serious, so I hope you're listening closely. You cannot fall for Kade Maverick…or his adorable niece." I run my hands over my face only to realize too late that I probably rubbed my eye shadow down my cheeks, and drop onto the bed again.

"Who am I kidding?"

My cell phone starts to vibrate and ring. Is it bad that I'm hoping it's Kade calling to cancel? Or Emily calling to say she and Aiden can't make it because of a family emergency?

No, I don't wish that on anyone.

I release the breath I was holding and answer Sasha's video call.

"Why is your eyeliner all over your cheeks?" Typical Sasha. Right to the point.

I wave my hand and roll my eyes. "I decided to try a new look."

Sasha leans away from the phone and gives me her side eye again as she holds up her index finger. "I can honestly say *that* is not working for you."

"I knoooooow." I jump off the bed and grab a tissue in the bathroom, then prop the phone on the counter as I attack the smears on my face. "I'm getting ready to go out with friends and can't figure out what to wear."

"You mean the date with Kade?"

"It's not a date!" Again, who am I kidding?

"I thought the whole point of this was a double date."

"I'm choosing to look at it as going out with a group of friends."

"Then why are you having so much trouble figuring out what to wear?"

"Because…because the weather has started to change, and you know how that throws me for a loop. It's not so hot, but it's not that cold. Can I wear a light sweater, or will I wind up too hot?"

"You realize you're just making excuses, right?" She's leaning in now, overfilling the phone screen so that I can only see her eyes and nose, but that's more than enough to put me on the hot seat.

"Okay, fine. It's a date." I whine my words as I plop down on the vanity seat and start fixing my eyeliner.

"Why is that so hard for you to admit?"

I pause mid-stroke of reapplying liner on my right eye. "Because falling for Kade Maverick isn't part of my plan."

"Who said anything about falling for him? It's just a date, Amanda. Go out and have some fun. You need a break after dealing with monster cockroaches."

I shrug and mumble, "And kits and kittens."

"What?"

"Nothing." Back to fixing my makeup.

"Unless you're already having feelings for this guy." She leans in again. "Are you?"

My eyes sting with the threat of tears as I face the truth. "Maybe."

Sasha covers her mouth as she laughs softly.

"What's so funny? I'm falling apart here, and you're laughing at me?"

"I just never thought I'd see you in this place and yet, here you are." She holds her hand out for emphasis.

"What place is that?" I toss my eyeliner back into the cup holding the rest of my color spectrum. That's the thing about artists. We don't limit our color to canvases and computer screens. A face is just another kind of canvas.

"Falling for a guy."

"What do you mean? I kind of had a crush on Daniel for a while."

"Your boss? No, no, no." She has that finger up again. "That doesn't count. That lasted all of what, two weeks? And then you found out he got engaged."

"Still counts."

"Okay, so you go out and have a little fun with friends. Maybe you and Kade see each other more. What's the worst that can happen?"

"I fall for him completely. Him and his adorable niece."

She nods. "All right, let's say that happens. Then what?"

"We'll both get our hearts broken when I move back to New York."

Sasha stays silent for a moment. Blinks and then clears her throat. "As much as it pains me to ask this, but as your best friend, I'm required to. Have you thought about staying in Sarabella?"

"Sarabella?" My voice squeaks as I say it, but I don't get upset because she's asking what I've already thought about way more than I'd like to admit.

She rolls her eyes. "Yes, Sarabella."

"I'm only doing all this so I can sell the shop and get back to New York." Even I don't miss how I stumbled over the word 'sell,' so I know Sasha heard it, too.

"Right, to be a production assistant to a boss who promised to mentor you to be a full-fledged product designer three years ago."

"And told me I'd have a job waiting for me when I come back."

Sasha shakes her head. "What I'm obviously doing a terrible job saying is, are you sure that's still what you want? You not only light up when you mention Kade. You're like a Roman candle when you talk about your shop."

"Which is becoming more and more like a shack in serious need of repair."

"Which can be fixed." She lifts one finely drawn brow. "Just think about it."

I lean closer to the phone. "That would be quite the change of plan, Sash."

She looks up as she holds her chin. "Didn't you once tell me an unchangeable plan is just a box that limits you?"

I hunch my shoulders and manage a sheepish grin. "Maybe."

Sasha nods and points at me. "Yeah, ya did."

"No, you did not!" Emily giggles and gives Aiden a light punch on his arm.

Our table is by a window at the back of the restaurant, giving us a beautiful view of the bay.

Aiden's grinning ear to ear at me and Kade after confessing he didn't like Emily's banana bread the first time he tried it. "No, I'm serious. I've never liked walnuts." He turns to her, holding up his hand. "Which I didn't know she used until I took a bite."

"I told you it was banana bread, and banana bread usually has walnuts."

"No, you simply called it banana *bread*. Bread doesn't normally have nuts."

"Some do. But I watched you eat it more than once. Why?"

He takes her hand and kisses it. "For you, I'd eat anything."

Emily turns a wide-eyed grin our way before leaning closer to Aiden. "And I'm only finding this out now."

"That's because you already agreed to marry me. No take backs."

"Banana bread? That's what brought you two together?" Kade chuckles through his words.

Aiden holds a hand up. "That's our story, and we're sticking to it."

Emily giggles. "Believe it or not. He came in everyday for a piece of my banana bread and then, after three weeks, he finally asked me out."

Aiden nods, then shakes his head. "Longest three weeks of my life."

"But if you didn't like it, what did you do with it?" I'm on the edge of my seat, waiting to hear if Aiden will totally fess up.

"I gave it to Zane. He loves her banana bread." He leans forward on the table. "I think he gained five pounds by the end. He was so glad when I finally asked Emily out, but don't tell him I told you."

I barely swallow my sip of iced tea before I burst out laughing at the thought of Aiden giving his banana bread to Zane on the sly. Bananas always were Zane's favorite fruit. Now I have something to poke my brother bear with or future blackmail material. "What a story you two will have for your grandkids."

Kade, who's sitting next to me, has that goofy grin on his face that brings his scar dimple out to play and makes it hard for me to look away. He insisted on picking me up at my condo, which made our 'date' feel even more like a *date*. And to make matters worse, he shed his jeans for a sleek pair of black slacks and his boots for some soft black lace-ups. And don't get me started on the long sleeve green button-down that makes his eyes pop even more.

Did I tell you I'm all about the walk and the legs when it comes to guys? The way a guy carries himself says way more than words.

And I can say, Kade carries himself *very* well.

Did I mention that his green shirt makes his eyes even more fascinating?

Snort.

Emily's voice breaks into my meandering thoughts. "Don't you think so, Amanda?"

That's when I realize I had rested my chin on my hand and was staring at Kade. I pop up and straighten in my seat. "Um, sure. I think so?"

"You think so?" Emily is staring at me with this mix of confusion and borderline offense.

I'm scrambling, trying to figure out how to fix this, when I feel Kade's arm go across the back of my chair. He then gives my shoulder a quick squeeze of reassurance. "I think what Amanda means is that she loves the idea of doing the flowers for your wedding, but with the latest challenges with her shop, she's feeling a bit off-kilter."

I hope he sees the extreme gratitude I'm sending him before I turn to face Emily. "Exactly, but let's talk about what you want. I've never done arrangements for a wedding before, but I'm getting pretty good at figuring things out."

Emily crosses her arms in front of her on the table. "Actually, I'm glad you're not familiar with what's the norm." She makes air quotes with her last word. "I want to do something more creative and different."

I can't help but grin. She just stepped into my wheelhouse.

"Then count me in. I think it would be totally cool to do a mix of mediums. Not just flowers, but incorporate things that express who you and Aiden are as individuals and a couple."

Aiden and Emily both look stunned.

Are those tears welling in Emily's eyes?

I'm in a panic again. Did I screw up again? Miss something that was said while I was in Kade La-La Land?

Emily reaches out and puts her hand on my arm. "You just spoke what's been on our hearts, and yet, not one single florist we've talked to has grasped that."

Relief floods me in a giant *whoosh;* like a wave hitting the beach. "Make your wedding what you want."

"Amanda, you're a godsend!" Emily gives my hand a quick squeeze.

"Oh, I don't know about that."

Kade's studying me again like he does when he's working, but there's something more. Is that pride I see in his eyes? Is he proud of me?

Heat crawls up my cheeks so intensely I can only imagine what I look like at the moment. Will this evening of embarrassing moments never end?

Thankfully, our food arrives, saving me the mad dash to the bathroom.

Once our server leaves, I ask the only logical question that comes next when faced with helping with someone's wedding.

"Have you two set a date?"

Emily nods vigorously. "Yes! The first Saturday in November."

The bite of food I had in motion never makes it to my mouth as my fork drops on my plate.

Math was always one of my better subjects, as I could do most calculations in my head. But let me tell you, the calculation sitting in my brain right now is giving my heart a workout.

"That's three weeks from this Saturday."

Aiden pulls out his phone, I assume to look at his calendar. "Yes, you are correct."

"How, um, how big is the wedding?"

"Oh, not too big. About a hundred and fifty people or so. We're doing a sit-down dinner, so we'll need centerpieces and maybe some additional arrangements for the ceremony. And my bouquet, of course, but I'm not sure I really want flowers for that."

Aiden agrees with Emily. "Right, and how great would it be to add some of those extra touches you mentioned around the venue? We can take you there and show you where the wedding will be staged and the reception room."

"Oh, yeah, that would probably be a good idea." I take a sip of my iced tea and then gulp down half the glass to stave off a wave of heated panic that reminds me of those intense hot flashes Aunt Paula would get during menopause.

Emily gives me a cautious stare. "So…do you still think that's doable?"

She has that cringe about her now. You know, that look that tells you they don't want to be disappointed but are in the deepest fear of their lives that they will be. It's a mix of hope and dread that makes you want to do whatever is necessary to make it better. This leaves me only one possible reply because I don't think I could live with myself if I were the reason Emily didn't have the wedding of her dreams.

Like I told Eliana, we ladies have to stick together.

I hold my hands up with a shrug. "My Aunt Paula used to always say, 'where there's a will, there's a way.'"

Emily bounces up and down in her seat, then grabs Aiden's head with both hands and kisses him with a loud smack on the lips.

Kade leans over and his lips brush my hair as he speaks, sending chills down my neck and back. "You're an amazing woman, Amanda Wilde."

I attempt to control the grin I give him and fail miserably, so I look away and pick up my fork.

Aiden and Emily look as if they just had the world handed to them. And I get it. This is a big deal for them, and I will do all I can to help them have that beautiful wedding.

I may regret this in the biggest way possible, but somehow, in this very significant moment that has everything to do with entangled hearts, expectations, and dreams, I refuse to see it any other way than hopeful.

Not to mention that my heart is so tangled up in feeling Kade so close to me, to feel his lips brush my ear, and the effect his words are still having on me…on *my* heart…

How did I end up exactly where I tried so diligently not to be?

Falling hard for one Kade Maverick.

CHAPTER 18
Amanda

Once I unlock the back door to my shop, I peek my head in first. Buck said the fumigation worked, and that there were quite a few dead cockroaches around the place to be swept up, which he did as part of his services. I don't know if that's his normal MO, or if he did it as a favor to Kade, *or* if he took pity on me.

I really was a mess that day. And Kade was so kind and caring. I can't stop thinking about how much he's done to help me without even being asked. I've grown so accustomed to taking care of myself since I moved to New York. And even before that, I learned early on I was the only one who was going to look out for me. And Aunt Paula, but now that she's gone…

In a pinch, I know I can count on Sally and Jacob and even Zane. They proved that by the way they stepped in to help solve my floor issue. But I've already imposed on them enough, so that makes getting this shop running well on my own even more important. I can't deal with—let alone afford—any more setbacks, so from now on, it's all or nothing.

And I certainly can't keep running to Kade for help.

After pushing the door open and scanning the floor and counters, I breathe a sigh of relief at seeing no more evidence of the nasty critters. Although I have this mad urge to disinfect the place. My hint of OCD demands I at least wipe down the worktable and counters in the back room. Buck must have disposed of the cookies, too, because not even a crumb remains of the plate I dropped on the floor. I may have to add Buck to my Christmas list.

I have several boxes of new inventory that need to be priced and displayed, thanks to those agreements I made with several of the vendors at the festival, and Marnie is bringing over the blown glass bud vases she created just for my shop, as well as my order of glass mangos. Which means Kade will come by later to pick them up after I finish wrapping them with the brass wire.

My stomach flutters—actually flutters—at the thought of seeing him again. After our 'date' (it's getting easier to think of it…of him that way), he drove me home and walked me to the door of my building. The memory of how he lagged back as I stepped onto the landing of the building entrance floods my mind again.

We stood there staring at each other for what seemed like minutes, but I'm sure was only seconds, under a full moon that drizzled silver streaks in his dark hair—hair that had felt thick yet soft between my fingers as I smoothed the unruly mess left by that nutty squirrel.

Then before I could brave a word, he said good night and left me standing there wishing he'd come back and, well, kiss me, for crying out loud.

But…maybe it's for the best. If Aunt Paula were still here, I'd be on the phone asking her for advice and a few prayers, too.

As I grab my keys off the front counter to unload my car, sunlight glints off the key I've yet to discover what it opens. Aunt Paula's condo and storage area accounted for two of the keys, and the shop door and cash register for two others. And with all the chaos of getting the shop back open, I hadn't even thought about it. Maybe Sally might know what that last key is for, but that's low on my to-do list.

I'm expecting another inventory delivery later today—I found this amazing artist on Etsy that makes the most adorable Christmas ornaments out of seashells and driftwood and another makes these adorable amigurumi animals that remind me of the crocheted doll that Aunt Paula made for me when I was a child.

And there's a small unused room not much bigger than a walk-in closet that I plan to set up with things like this for both human and fur babies. In just the short and very limited time I've run the shop, I've noticed tourists and locals are shopping for Christmas gifts much earlier than usual. Setting up that room is one task on the list.

Just as I reach the back door, I hear a knock.

Zane's smiling face greets me as I swing the door open. And he's holding a bag from The Last Bean that has the distinct aroma of banana bread in one hand and two coffees in his other. "I brought breakfast."

My nose and mouth are doing a happy dance. "Wow. What a nice surprise, but what brings you my way?"

He puts the coffees on the worktable and then unloads the bag. "Can't I just come by and say hello? Maybe offer a little moral support?"

I nab a slice of banana bread and pop a chunk into my mouth. "I don't know. The moral support part has me concerned. Have I been immoral somehow?"

Zane drops his chin as he laughs. "No, nothing like that. It's just an expression, although I'm sure my mother would love to see you at church on Sunday."

I grunt. I admit, when I moved to New York, going to church kind of fell by the wayside. With classes, work, and then, yes, surviving the grind of the marketing world that never rests and a city that never sleeps, well, I just didn't have time.

He sits on the stool, takes a bite of banana bread that equates to half of the slice, and sips his coffee. "I have the day off and thought you could use some more help."

I lean my hip against the counter. "And?"

"What?" He mutters this over a mouth full of bread and coffee.

"You know what your mother says about that." I point at him.

He swallows. "Yeah, yeah, don't spray, just say."

I pick up the bag from The Last Bean. "Are you sure this isn't about the rumor mill talking about Kade and me going out with Emily and Aiden a couple of nights ago?"

"You mean your date?" His perfectly chiseled jaw twitches with the laugh I know is killing him to hold back.

"It wasn't really a date." I swat his arm.

"That's not what Aiden said." He lifts his brows and shakes his head.

"And what did Aiden say?"

"That you kept staring at Kade. A lot. He said Emily noticed it, too. They think you two are a perfect match."

"Yeah, well, they can think whatever they want. It's not happening."

Zane leans back, elbows on the counter behind him, and studies me. "Care to unpack that for me?"

"Nothing to unpack. Nothing can happen between Kade and me." Now that I've said it out loud, even I'm having a hard time accepting it.

"Does this have anything to do with that goofy nickname he had for you, because you really should just let that go—"

"No, it has nothing to do with that, you goof. It's just common sense. I have no plans to stay in Sarabella, so romance is off the table."

His expression turns serious. "Have you explained that to Kade?"

"I've made it very clear that I need to get this place running well so I can sell it and go back to New York. He knows."

He nods but remains silent, as if lost in thought for a moment. "Too bad."

"Why?"

"Because you're good for him. And I think he'd be good for you."

Zane thinks we're a good fit? My 'brother,' who wouldn't let any of his friends near me when I started high school, actually thinks a guy is good for me?

I study the top of my coffee cup. "I guess it's just not in the cards."

He gives me a pointed look. "Maybe you should try a different deck."

MARNIE'S BUD vases sit in the front window, capturing the afternoon flood of sunlight that hits around this time of day, warming the front of the shop significantly, too. I pull myself away from admiring how amazing they look to lower the thermostat. It may technically be fall, but this part of Florida hasn't gotten the memo yet.

Zane cleared the extra room, moving the few things stored in there into the back, which now looks like a disaster zone, but at least now I can begin planning the displays for that room. He told me about a woman on his team, who also creates adult coloring books. I told him to tell her to come see me. I can already picture a display of tropical-themed and inspirational coloring books with packets of markers and colored pencils for sale as well.

Even though they're not finished, I arranged some of the glass mangos without leaves in the front window to complement the vases, and of course, included some succulents and cacti Jacob brought in my latest delivery. I hope Zane remembers to bring the pots Eliana painted.

A few customers have come in throughout the day. Even the two ladies from the cockroach invasion ventured in carefully at first, but then charged in full blazes once they found out I had the place fumigated. I gave them each a pumpkin-scented candle to apologize and to thank them for coming back. They seemed to really appreciate that.

I custom-ordered several wall letterings that I hope will capture the tone I'm trying to create for the shop, too. I'm on a ladder right now, applying a Ralph Waldo Emerson quote, 'The earth laughs in flowers.'

The letters are about six inches high in a flourished font I am loving more and more. But smoothing it onto these older walls is proving more challenging than I expected.

Zane walks up to the ladder and looks up at me. "Need some help?"

"No, I think I got it." I resorted to using a plastic spatula I found in the back to reach all the swooshes on the top of the letters. There's one left to go, but it's somewhat of a reach, and I refuse to move the ladder again.

So I do the logical thing—reach over and give it a firm rub. But then the ladder starts to tip and before I can straighten back up, continues its descent. The next thing I know, I'm flung in an arc by a strong vice around my waist that turns out to be Zane's arm.

I slam against him as the ladder smacks the floor, toppling a small glass table with several small plants. Dirt and glass now cover the area where I would have landed.

"That was close." Zane somehow swung my legs up in the scenario so that now he's holding me against him with his other arm under my back.

I link my hands behind his neck, holding on for dear life as my heart pounds like a hammer in my ears. "Good thing you were there."

He lets my legs slide down, but they're still like rubber from the scare of nearly tanking onto the floor. I hold on to his shoulders and lean against him.

Zane rubs my back as a chuckle rumbles through his chest. "Yeah, no kidding."

BLOOMED TO BE MESSY

The front door bells jingle.

I crane my head around to see who walked in, only to meet a set of very serious green eyes. "Kade!"

I don't know why I feel the need to jump away from Zane. It's not like I'm in a relationship with the man. And besides, for all intents and purposes, Zane *is* my brother.

Kade takes a step closer, observing the mess all over the floor. "Having a little too much fun perhaps?"

"Only if you call hauling dusty boxes around fun." Zane lifts the ladder back to an upright position. "I'll go find a dustpan."

Kade tucks his hands into his jeans pockets. "If you needed help, you could have called me."

"Zane showed up this morning with banana bread and coffee."

"Ah, the infamous banana bread." Kade gives a tight smile that doesn't reach his eyes.

"Then he wound up hanging around to help. And I didn't plan to fall off the ladder."

Why do I feel the need to explain why Zane is here? Besides, there's nothing official between Kade and me, therefore he shouldn't be jealous.

Even though I kind of hope he is.

Don't judge me.

He drops his hands and looks around. "Your shop is really looking great." He points to the letters that stayed on the wall. "Nice touch."

"Thanks."

Zane comes back in and begins sweeping the dirt and glass into the dustpan.

Kade runs a hand over his mouth. "Listen, I don't have a lot of time. Sally picked up Eliana for me, so I'm on my way to pick her up there. Just wanted to come by and get the mangos."

"Oh, right!" I rush to the back room to grab the box Marnie brought them in and hurry to the front window to load the mangos.

Kade grabs a piece of the packing paper and wraps one as I do the same. Neither one of us says anything. We're just standing there, wrapping glass mangos, while Zane dumps a load of glass and dirt into the can in the back room.

Once loaded, Kade hefts the box under his arm and gives me a mock salute. "I'll get these finished and back to you as fast as I can."

And then he leaves. No chit-chat, small talk, how do you dos, or what's up.

Zane returns to the front of the store. "Where's Kade?"

"He left."

"That was fast."

"He said he had to pick up Eliana from your mom's."

Zane frowns and checks his watch. "That's weird. Mom just texted me to let me know she's still at the beach with Eliana. She was going to make spaghetti tonight."

"Oh, well, maybe Kade didn't know they were delayed."

"Yeah, maybe." Zane has this funny expression on his face that borders on mirth and mischief.

"What?"

He chuckles and shakes his head. "You may think there's nothing happening between you two, but I think Kade does."

"What does that mean?"

Zane holds his hands out. "I could be wrong, but I don't think he appreciated seeing you in another man's arms."

Okay, yes, I'd be lying if this didn't make me just the tiniest bit happy, but I won't tell Zane that.

"But he knows you're like my brother."

"Yes, but you see it in movies all the time. Two friends who wind up as more." He waggles his brows as he says this. To me. The girl he buried in the sand, except for my toes, because he wanted to see if the crab he found would eat them.

"Ew, and just…ew. He knows we're just friends."

Zane belly laughs. "But we don't share blood."

I punch him in the arm. "Now you're just being gross."

CHAPTER 19
Amanda

I pick up my phone for what has to be the hundredth time to see if anyone has texted me.

And by anyone, I mean Kade.

But it's been dead silence since yesterday evening.

After I closed the shop last night, I sent a text, asking if he had an idea of when the mangos would be ready. In actuality, I was trying to see if he was upset over seeing me in Zane's arms, which, for the record, I still don't see why that would upset him.

For crying out loud, I fell off a ladder and Zane—thank goodness—was there to catch me. Or I'd most likely be freaking out in a hospital at the moment instead of standing in the back room of my shop, obsessing over a text I still haven't received and a man who is taking way too much space in my thoughts.

Zane gave me the scoop on the guy reasoning behind that thinking, but I still think it's Neanderthal malarky.

How could Kade actually think Zane and I…? Granted, Zane is blond, muscled, and tan.

But, *eww*.

I check my phone again. Still nothing. And it's almost noon. Maybe he's just busy with Eliana. Maybe he had a meeting with a client and hasn't had a chance to reply.

Or maybe he's intentionally avoiding answering me because he doesn't want to talk to me anymore. What am I saying? Of course, he *has* to talk to me. He has two dozen of my glass mangos held hostage, which means there will have to be negotiations.

This. Is. Ridiculous.

I should just call him. As I reach for my phone, the front bells jingle. The place has been quieter than a tomb most of the day and now someone comes in, just when I've worked up enough courage to call Kade?

"Hellooo?" A woman's voice calls out, reminding me I have more important things to concern myself with than the Maverick Menace.

I deposit my phone face down on the worktable and slap a smile on my face as I rush to the front.

"Hi there! So sorry. Is there anything I can help you find?" I should focus on how wonderful it is to have someone walk in the door finally and see all the hard work Zane and I put into this place yesterday. He took off the door to that walk-in closet and helped me paint and set up the room for the pet and children's items. And every piece of inventory is displayed, along with several new orchids Jacob brought by this morning. The shop has never looked so good. The only thing missing is the mangos.

Which brings me right back to, yes…Kade. I'm dying to check my phone at the moment.

"Actually, I'm looking for Amanda Wilde."

Caution and curiosity are doing this weird little jig in my head. No one has ever come into the shop asking for me by name. "That's me. You found her."

She holds her hand out. "I'm Bettina Stringer, the mayor's wife. I was hoping you could help me with an upcoming event."

Ah, okay. That's right. This is a flower shop and people need flowers. Duh…

"Oh, of course." I turn around to grab my notepad from the

counter. "When's the date of the event and how many arrangements do you need?"

"I'm not interested in flowers, actually. Though I will keep that in mind." She does a quick, circular scan of the shop. "I was actually looking for glass mangos. One of my friends showed me the one she purchased at the festival and gave me the most brilliant idea. But I don't see any. Are you out of stock?"

She's facing me now with an expectant look on her face; as if I hold the key to her brilliant idea.

"No, not at all. They're in production even as we speak and should arrive this week. How many did you want?" My hand pauses over the paper, ready to take down details.

"Fifty."

My pen jerks across the page, leaving a trail of black ink. "Fifty?"

"Yes, and I'd need them in four weeks. I'm throwing a private dinner for fifty of Mayor Stringer's supporters, and we want them to have a special gift as a thank you. Is that possible?"

My brain is doing math calisthenics as I try to figure out how I'm going to convince Marnie and Kade to help me create fifty more mangos. All while I'm creating those 'unique' arrangements for Emily's wedding, which turns out she'll need at least a dozen for tables and three or four more for the ceremony. And her bouquet and special items for attendees to take home as a memento of the wedding.

"Absolutely! That's no problem at all. I can put the order in today with a deposit."

"Wonderful." She claps her hands back and forth, but they don't actually touch. "When I saw Hillary's, I just knew they'd be the perfect gift and so perfect, because we're the mango capital, of course."

"Of course."

She pauses and holds a French manicured finger over her mouth for a moment, like a dramatic pause. "I knew your mother, by the way."

"You did?" I'm not surprised, really. More surprised the topic of my mother hasn't come up sooner. Sarabella has grown, but it's still a small town.

"Yes, same high school. I lost track of her after she moved to Los Angeles. How is she?"

I can tell Mrs. Stringer is fishing to find out if my mother is still there in pursuit of her dream to be a movie star, which she is, but not the kind Mrs. Stringer would appreciate, I'm sure.

"I honestly don't know. I haven't seen her in years."

"Oh, I'm so sorry. I thought she kept in touch."

I shake my head as I keep my smile in place.

When word got out about my mother's acting profession during my sophomore year of high school, I tried denying it at first, saying it was just a coincidence that this person had almost the same name as I did—Wild without the e—and resembled my mother, but no one believed me, of course.

Then I tried to act as if my mother was about to break into major motion pictures and would soon whisk me away to LA to live with her, but even I didn't believe that one.

Aunt Paula used to tell me I was only responsible for my own behavior, not others'. I knew she was right in theory, but it did little to dull the jabs at school. So, I learned to ignore the teasing or pretend I didn't hear it.

Mrs. Stringer pats my arm. "Well, dear, I'm so glad you had your Aunt Paula to raise you properly."

"Yes, ma'am." I'm not ashamed to say I add a little of my aunt's Savannah accent to my reply. I can appear the good southern girl for effect, too.

Mrs. Stringer continues a running dialogue as she checks out the rest of the shop. By the time she's made a full circuit, which normally doesn't take that long unless your superpower *isn't* talking and shopping at the same time, two hours have passed. She's made four trips to the counter to add more things to her purchases, pausing to tell me whatever story the item she's found brings to mind. Then she adds several pet items to her growing stack (*ka-ching*) and concludes with the longest tale—or should I say *tail?*—of her cat, Mr. Pickles, who has an unusually long—

Yes, you guessed it. Tail.

After doing one more cursory pass through the shop to see if there is anything else she can scoop up for whoever's left on her shopping list, Mrs. Stringer leaves with several full bags and a receipt for fifty glass mangos.

If that's the worst confrontation I face having to do with my mother, I can survive the rest of my tenure in Sarabella.

I dash to the back room to retrieve my phone, ready to text Kade and Marnie with the news. Why a text and not a phone call? Because I'm a big chicken who's afraid to see their expressions when they hear that I've committed them to fifty more mangos.

I start with Marnie, who answers almost immediately, first with a shocked emoji, then a smiling emoji, and then several clapping hands. Now that I know she's on board, that leaves Kade.

My finger is paused over the little text bar on the screen with his name.

I could text or I could put on my big girl pants and confront the grumpy menace face-to-face.

What better reason to go see him and find out what exactly is going on than under the guise of this great news? More orders for me, more work for him and Marnie.

It's a triple win. The best kind.

So, of course, it makes sense to stop by and present the news in person. And make sure he's still willing to work with me. Otherwise, I'll have to figure something else out. I'm betting Amazon probably has brass leaves of some sort. Or the craft store.

But they'd never look as good as Kade's…

Okay. Fine. I can do this. I'm a grown, you-know-what woman, and I am not about to kowtow to some guy's misconception of a friend saving another friend from a mishap.

I'll close the store a little early and head over there now.

Because ladies and gents, I just put on my big girl pants.

CHAPTER 20
Kade

Nearly a full day has passed, and I'm still unsettled—Okay, fine. I'm angry.

I'm mad about what I saw at Mandy's shop yesterday. Why am I upset? I don't know, to be honest. It's not like she and I are dating or anything more than friends.

I just know seeing Zane holding her like that did something to me. I know he's like her brother, but how many stories have you heard about the best friend becoming more? Mandy's been living in New York for a long time and now she's back. Who knows what that could stir up between them?

With a growl, I grab the box of glass mangos and drop it onto my workbench before I remember the delicate cargo it holds. Fortunately, a cursory examination confirms nothing broke.

I should have paid attention to the yellow flags popping up since the first day I ran into her. The last thing I need is a messy relationship with a woman who has no plans to stay in Sarabella. Especially now with Eliana in my life. And having Shannon there on the weekends has turned out to be nice.

Comfortable even.

And I'm glad I'm here to help. It's the least I can do since

I'm kind of the one to blame for the situation they're in. If Devon were still alive, Shannon and Eliana would have a much better life. A happier life. At least, that's what I believe.

I unwrap the glass mangos one by one and lay them out on my workbench. This shouldn't take but a few hours at the most, because I made the leaves ahead of time between job orders and installations.

Plus, this will be a welcome distraction from the anticipation eating at me about a large project a regional builder contacted me about. A brand new subdivision is being planned for an old golf course. The style will be the usual stucco that's common in Florida, but the homes will have a Tuscan influence, which means they want metalwork to complement the stonework they're incorporating not only on the exterior designs but the interior as well.

That means I would have guaranteed work for at least one to two years because they have a plan for a second phase if the homes sell well. Which they will. I've seen the plans and the location. I've no doubt it will succeed simply because of how the area has grown in just the last year alone.

I submitted a proposal as requested, and now I'm waiting to hear back if it's been accepted or not. If my numbers seem too high, they could wind up hiring someone out of the area to keep costs down, but I did a hard sell on my guarantee to personally install every piece and make sure the work is done right.

Another reason I should stay away from Amanda Wilde. I have too much riding on this contract to get distracted by a romantic entanglement that will ultimately wind up hurting us both.

My future is here in Sarabella. And it's a good one. Maybe even one my mother would approve of and finally admit I cleaned up my act and did something good with my life.

So why do I keep imagining all the places Mandy's fingers have touched as she wrapped the mangos with the brass wire? I'm touching those same spots as I attach the leaves, which makes the entire creative process almost spiritual as I feel more connected to her.

We're both artists, so there's a strong connection there, but I'm finding myself more and more drawn to her. Especially since she referred to me as a 'good man.'

She's the only person who's ever told me that.

I'm so engrossed in all this that I don't realize Shannon and Eliana came in until the squirt has her arms wrapped around my legs. I switch off the small torch and slide off my safety shield so I can heft her up into my arms.

"Hey, squirt. Did you have fun with your mom today?"

She bobs her head with more excitement than the norm. The pink remains of strawberry ice cream around her lips explain the sugar rush. "We went to the playground and then got ice cream. And then," her voice gets even louder, "we went shopping!"

"Let me guess. More tights?"

She wiggles down and runs over to Shannon, who's holding a rather large bag. After yanking down the bag and rustling through the contents, she pulls out a mass of purple fabric with an overabundance of lavender gauze.

Eliana holds the dress against herself and spins around. "I'm going as a princess for Halloween!"

"Wow, it's gorgeous." I glance at Shannon, who looks like she could use a nap at this point. "Busy day, huh?"

Shannon nods and yawns, proving my observation correct. "Yes. I wanted to go back to your place, but she insisted on showing Uncle Kade her dress now."

"I'm glad you did."

As I mentioned, having Elly around has made me rethink what I want out of my future, and having Shannon around on the weekends gave me legs for that vision. But I admit, they still feel pretty wobbly.

My cell phone buzzes in my pocket. I slip it out and recognize the name of the builder I've been negotiating with.

"I need to take this."

Shannon nods and helps Eliana put her dress back in the bag.

"Hey Steve, great to hear from you."

"Kade! I've got great news. The team looked over your proposal, and they're good with the numbers."

My head is buzzing so loudly that I'm sure Steve can hear it over the phone. "That's great. I've already started some preliminary sketches using the architectural renderings you gave me. When would you like to meet next?"

"Glad to hear you're already on the job. The team is excited to see your ideas. I'll text you some dates and times and you can let me know what works for you."

"Perfect. See you soon." Keeping my cool, I end the call. Then I let loose with a downward thrust of my fist. "Yes!"

My shout startles both Eliana and Shannon.

The squirt giggles. "I think Uncle Kade needs ice cream."

Shannon walks over to me, her expression growing in excitement. She looked over my proposal before I hit send, just to make sure I didn't have any typos or miss anything. "You got the job?"

"I did. And this is a big one, Shannon. This will more than pay the bills for at least a year."

She covers her mouth with a hand as tears well in her eyes. "I knew you'd get it."

I shake my head. "I wasn't that sure."

With almost a jerk, she drops her hand and frowns at me. "Why? Kade, you're an amazing artist, and you run your shop with integrity. What's not to like?"

I'm speechless. Really not sure what to say. I guess compliments aren't easy for me to accept. Or believe.

Shannon hugs me. "I'm so proud of you. And Devon would be, too."

Hearing her words and hearing Devon's name associated with that brings up a surge of emotions I'm not prepared to handle at the moment. I hug Shannon back and hope those feelings will go back to wherever they came from before I make a fool of myself.

"Mandy!" Eliana's excited voice interrupts our exchange.

Shannon lets go and greets Mandy, seeming unfazed by her sudden appearance, whereas I feel like the proverbial kid who just got caught with his hand in the cookie jar.

"Hi, Mandy." I give her a weak wave. Correction, seriously lame wave.

After hugging Eliana, Mandy straightens and sends a hesitant glance my way. "Just thought I'd stop in and check on those mangos."

"I'm almost done." I can't bring myself to face her, and I don't know what to say. I'm that awkward high school guy again, who knows he screwed up and doesn't know what to do about it.

"I can come back." She turns toward the door, but Eliana runs in front of her.

"We're going to get ice cream to celebrate. You can come with us?"

Mandy shifts her gaze from the squirt and bounces it between Shannon and me. "What are we celebrating?"

Shannon brings her hands together in front of her. "Kade got a big contract with a builder. They want him to create some ornate metal designs for a new subdivision and install them."

Eyes round, Mandy smiles at me. "Wow! That's so great!"

"And…" Shannon glances at me, "I was about to tell Kade that I found a place and put down a deposit."

I feel the gut punch at the same time the rush of excitement for Shannon hits me. It's a double whammy for sure.

"That's really great, Shannon." The emotion of it makes my voice sound rough. I clear my throat of the knot threatening to choke me. "Lots of great news today."

Shannon's eyes stay on me for a moment. I know she heard it. She knows me well enough. "We move in next week."

I nod and shove my hands into my apron pockets. "That's really great."

Can't think of any other word than great at the moment. It is…great…but hard.

Mandy is studying me, too. She sends a curious glance at Shannon before settling back on me. "Well, I guess I can add some exciting news to the mix as well."

I'm afraid to ask. What if she found a way to go back to New York ahead of schedule? What if she's here to tell me she realized she has feelings for Zane, after all?

But I'll ask anyway because she deserves it. "Oh yeah, what?"

"My shop looks absolutely amazing now with all the new items, and…I have more orders for mangos." She cringes at me with that last statement. "Which I hope you're still able to help me with now that you're mister big shot designer."

The tension I've been holding for a day breaks, and I chuckle. "I will always have time for your mangos."

Mandy rewards me with a smile so warm, I feel the heat through my entire body. "Thanks."

"How many?"

"Fifty. And it's for the mayor."

"Fifty?" Shannon bursts out what I want to say but can't suck in enough air to say it.

"The mayor?" My voice sounds more like one of Eliana's friends.

Mandy nods and stares at me as if she's waiting for me to either dash her hopes or help make her dream to sell her shop and go back to New York come true.

I'm not a selfish man at heart. I never have been. Being the man of the house from a young age taught me to put others first. My mother and Devon needed something on a regular basis.

Right now, every bone in my body wants to be selfish and say I can't do it.

But I won't, because I would make a hundred of the things if it made Mandy happy.

I toss my hands out from my sides. "Like your Aunt Paula used to say, where there's a will there's a way."

Mandy and Shannon chat with excitement.

Eliana is jumping around like a pogo stick on steroids. Or sugar, in her case. "Let's get ice cream!"

And me? Let's just say, jumping for joy isn't the emotion I'm feeling at the moment.

CHAPTER 21
Amanda

Somehow I got roped into ice cream. Technically, no rope was involved, nor did any cowboys enter the story. Nor were any animals harmed during the course of these events, but I can't say the same about my waistline.

And it only took the sweet, imploring green eyes of a four-year-old. My resistance to Eliana is practically nonexistent now. I fully understand how the squirt, as Kade calls her, is the best-dressed four-year-old in Sarabella.

Then ice cream wound up transitioning to a walk on the beach. A different set of green eyes compelled me into that one. I seem to have no boundaries when it comes to the green eyes of this family. I'm guessing Kade's brother also shared them and that Shannon fell to their charms as well.

Based upon that drawing Kade did of Devon, they could have almost passed for twins. I've heard many a story of widows marrying the brother of their deceased husband. I wouldn't fault Shannon for falling for Kade, too, even though it makes me want to hate her.

But I can't because she's so nice and such a great mom to Eliana. They really seem like a ready-made family.

Perhaps that's another reason there can be nothing between Kade and me. And I need all the reasons I can get to fight off this growing attraction to him.

"You're dripping."

"What?" I track his gaze to my hand holding a waffle cone filled with strawberry ice cream (Elly's favorite, too, by the way) and note the pink ooze making its way toward my hand. I lean over and run my tongue around the top edge of the cone.

When I turn to thank Kade, he's studying me again and the green of his eyes has darkened to match the deep green of the ocean to our right.

I shoot my attention straight ahead. "Wow, that's quite a sunset."

The sun's descent has streaked in reds and oranges that make the sky look like it's on fire. Just like my face. I'm grateful for the cool breeze calming my errant blush.

Note to self. Do not eat ice cream in a cone when one could be embarrassed by drippy messes.

He chuckles with a deep resonance enhanced by the gentle sound of a gentle tide. "Yeah, it's a good one tonight."

Shannon and Eliana are about fifteen feet in front of us, walking onto a sandbar that shoots off at an angle from the shore. Seagulls surround them, pecking at a slew of scallops the afternoon storm brought in.

Eliana picks one up and dances excitedly to the next one.

"She's an amazing little girl." I don't know why I say this. Maybe I'm making small talk, or maybe my subconscious has its own agenda tonight.

"Yes, she is."

I dare a glance at Kade. He's staring at Shannon and Eliana as we slow our steps.

"Is it going to be hard for you?"

He crouches over the water lapping at our ankles to wash off the ice cream that dripped on his hand. Now why didn't I think of doing that instead of embarrassing myself by licking my cone?

"Is what going to be hard?" His words mock innocence, but his tone is full of the heaviness I saw settle in on him when Shannon shared her good news.

I'll play his game. For now. "To not have Eliana around every day."

He rises to his full height, shaking the water from his hands. For a moment, I wonder if he's going to answer me at all until he takes a deep breath and finally locks eyes with me. And then I see the battle in him, to open up or remain stoic, which I'm noticing he's really good at.

"Uncle Kade!" Eliana is jumping up and down and waving at him to come see the object she found in the sand.

He heads her way, walking through a deeper band of water that gets the bottom edges of his jeans wet.

"Saved by the kid," I mumble under my breath.

As Kade crouches down with Eliana, I have this mad urge to take a picture so I do. I noticed Shannon heading toward me on the edge of my view screen. And I take a few more shots as she stops next to me.

"That's a great shot."

I lower my phone and scroll through the pictures I took. "Reminds me of an assignment I did in a photography class in college. I took a bunch of pictures at a park one day, what I thought were just random shots. When I looked at them later, this adorable little girl was in most of them."

Shannon smiles and points to the one where both Kade and Eliana are looking down and their heads are touching. "I love that one. Will you send it to me?"

"Of course."

I give my phone to Shannon so she can fill in the phone number for the text. "Is it hard for you?"

Shannon gives me a confused look. I must be the queen of

short, vague, and redundant sentences tonight. "I saw a sketch Kade did of Devon, and they looked so much alike. Does it make it difficult for you to be around him?"

Shannon tilts her head as she studies me and a small smile ticks up the corners of her mouth. "Are you asking me if I'm into Kade?"

"No! No, I mean, well, I was just wondering. Forget I asked." I wish the sand under my feet would turn into quicksand and swallow me whole.

"I was at first." She swivels her head to watch Kade and Eliana. "When I found out I was pregnant with Eliana, I was scared out of my mind. Didn't know how I was going to take care of myself, let alone a baby." She shifts her attention back to me. "But I realized he could never replace Devon, and I didn't want him to."

"That must have been awful."

"It was. Especially for Kade. He was there when it happened."

I touch my cheek. "Is that what caused his scar?"

"Yeah." Shannon takes a deep breath. "He and Devon loved to ride motorcycles together. One evening they went for a ride. The driver didn't even see them. Just pulled out and hit Devon, knocking him into Kade. Devon died at the scene."

My eyes are burning, and before I can stop it, a tear slips down my left cheek. "Kade never told me what happened."

"I'm not surprised. He won't even talk about what happened with me. And I won't even bring up his mother in that scenario."

"I think you just did." I raise a brow to signal my attempt at lightening the mood.

Shannon lets out a soft laugh but says nothing more because Kade is heading toward us with Eliana on his shoulders.

After plopping her down on the sand, he pauses, staring at me. The sun has dipped below the horizon now, exchanging its fiery reds for more pinks and purples. The effect is dazzling, as it highlights Kade's form from behind.

I lift my phone again, wanting to capture the moment.

And the man whose story keeps pulling me deeper into a tide of emotions that just may drown me.

CHAPTER 22
Kade

I haven't seen Mandy in three days, and I think I'm having withdrawals.

Our evening on the beach seemed to shift something. I didn't miss how she kept taking pictures of Eliana and me on the beach. Really cute, you know?

But then she took that last picture of just me.

I stood there, letting her snap the shot and aching to ask her why—why did she want a picture of me?

After she lowered her phone, we stared at each other, and I had this weird sense she was recording a memory; like someone would do on a vacation.

Or saying goodbye to someone.

Then we left the beach, and I never had a moment to ask that didn't include two extra sets of ears. Now it's three days later, and I still can't bring myself to call Mandy, because if my gut is right, she drew a line in the sand that evening.

So I've kept my distance, and it's killing me.

On top of that, I have to help Shannon and Eliana move into their new place today. Don't get me wrong. I'm excited for her and the squirt, but suddenly I feel like my life is becoming empty again.

Shannon walks out of Eliana's room with yet another box. "How can one little girl have so many pairs of tights?" She lifts the box. "That's all that's in here."

I chuckle. "She's your daughter."

She adds the box to the growing stack by the door. "And your niece, who you've clearly spoiled."

"She's easy to spoil." A knot to match the tangle of tights I'm imagining in that box fills my chest.

Shannon walks over to where I'm standing. "You've changed. I like this new side of you."

What is she talking about? I'm the same guy I was before Eliana moved in with me. "What side?"

She gives my arm a soft punch and turns around. "The soft, teddy bear side."

I follow her into Eliana's room. The squirt is at school for another few hours, so we're taking advantage of the uninterrupted time to pack. "There's no teddy bear here except for that purple one on the squirt's bed."

Shannon is loading another box with stuffed animals, including the purple bear I pointed at. "Mandy sees it, too."

Her words stop me in my tracks and twist that knot I mentioned earlier so tight, my chest physically hurts. "Doesn't matter."

I turn around and leave the room, but Shannon's soft footfall is close behind.

"What do you mean, it doesn't matter?"

As I open the fridge to get some orange juice, she pushes it shut.

"It doesn't matter. Nothing can happen between us."

"Why not?" Shannon doesn't get mad often, but something is definitely brewing in her tonight.

"Because she's not staying in Sarabella. You know that."

She picks up her phone off the counter, swipes at the screen, and then holds it out to me. "Look at the pictures she sent me from the beach the other night. You're in every one of them."

"So is Eliana."

Shannon snaps her phone back, moving her finger across the screen before turning it toward me again. "She's not in this one."

Yep, it's that last shot Mandy took of just me. I'm almost fully silhouetted by the setting sun, but you can still see my face enough to see my expression, which says more than I realized.

"It's just a picture." I tug open the fridge and grab the OJ.

Shannon makes this noisy clicking sound with her mouth. She does this when she's frustrated and wants to make sure you know she is. "It's not just a picture. It's you looking at her as if she's the center of your world. Trust me, I know that look."

I pause my juice pour and stare at her, recognizing the grief that passes more infrequently over her face these days, but I can't find any words that will refute her keen observation.

"Don't you want to know if there can be something great between you two?" She's pleading with me now.

Everything in me wants to scream yes, but for my sake—and Mandy's—I can't go down that path. "Shannon, trust me. What you and Devon had was one in a million. Besides, I told you, she's not planning to stay in Sarabella."

Shannon makes that sound again and throws her arms to her sides. "Then move to New York!"

"I can't. My business is here." I gesture to her. "You and Eliana are here. I need to be around for the squirt."

"Then make Mandy fall for you so hard, she's willing to move her life here."

"I can't mess with her dream, Shannon." Now I'm the one sounding exasperated.

"Are you sure it's just that, or are you afraid?"

"Afraid of what?" I yank the fridge door open, shove the juice carton in, and then slam it shut.

"That she'll still pick New York over you and leave." Shannon's aim is dead on.

Takes me a few seconds to untangle my voice from the emotions holding it captive. "I admit, it's a risk."

"Maybe one you should take." Shannon puts her hand on my chest. "Kade, Devon died. He didn't leave you—us. Life is messy. Love even more so, but you'll never know unless you take the risk."

Tonight I've discovered that roundabouts aren't just great for traffic flow, they're outstanding for indecisive idiots.

Like me.

There are two roundabouts between my place and Mandy's condo, and I've turned around twice. I'm basically driving a big loop between the two as I make up my mind.

Work up my courage.

After dinner, I left Shannon and Eliana to finish packing while I left to go see Mandy. Shannon didn't even ask where I was going and judging by the look she gave me, she knew.

Yeah, Shannon is right.

I'm afraid.

I lost my best friend as well as my brother five years ago. And I'm still recovering from Devon's loss. If Mandy and I wind up pursuing something, I don't know if I could get over losing her. I'm an all-in kind of guy.

But I won't know unless I try, right? So, here's me, whipping around the circle again, but instead of making a full loop, I go straight.

Don't think. Just do.

That's my motto tonight. I keep saying it over and over again until I'm at her condo door.

Last hurdle? The knock.

Don't think. Just do.

I knock on the door but hear nothing. Wait for a few seconds longer, then knock again.

The scurry of feet bleeds through the door just before it launches open. Mandy stands in the doorway, her cheeks flushed with most of her hair in a messy bun and the rest in a wild disarray around her face.

I don't know if she was sleeping or working out. And I don't care.

Don't think. Just do.

I step forward as I reach for her, pulling her against me and claiming her lips like a man parched from a walk through a desert. That's what my life has felt like until she walked into it.

And she meets me with the same ardency, quenching my thirst for her until the kiss slows to a tender exchange.

As the kiss ends, she slides her hands from behind my neck to my chest and stares at me. A mix of unspoken questions flies through her brown eyes, from curiosity to wonder to confusion.

But mostly surprise.

I push a hand through my hair. "Hope you don't mind me stopping by."

She touches her lips, then smiles. "It's a delightful surprise."

"Can we talk?"

She steps to the side and swings out her hand. "Come in."

As she follows me into her living room, I perch on the edge of the couch with my elbows on my knees. I can see her bedroom from where I'm sitting and notice a pile of stuff strewn all over the bed and the floor.

"Did I catch you in the middle of something?" I gesture to the bedroom first, then to the closet that looks like it barfed its contents into the hallway.

Mandy flops onto the other end of the couch and picks up a set of keys lying on the coffee table. "I'm trying to figure out what this key goes to. My aunt's lawyer doesn't know, and so far I haven't been able to figure it out."

I take the keys from her for closer observation and almost grab her hand to pull her next to me. But we need to talk first and maybe the mysterious key is a good segue.

"Doesn't look like a house key."

"I didn't think so either."

I try to read the engraving to see if it holds any clues, but nothing stands out. "It's small, though, like a key for a locker or a lockbox."

She takes the key ring from my hand, lingering with her fingers as if she wants to explore the feel of my hand. "That's what I was thinking, so I started emptying the closets to see if my crazy aunt had one hidden somewhere."

"Did you try under the bed?"

"That's where I started." She scoots closer. "Are we starting something here, Kade? Or should I call you Mav? I haven't figured that one out yet, and I—"

Taking Shannon's advice to convince Mandy, I stop her nervous chatter with another kiss. As she leans closer, I cup her cheek, memorizing the feel of her skin and the way she smells. Her floral scent reminds me of the roses that bloom near my shop in the spring.

I lean my head back enough to speak. "Does that answer your question?"

She blinks and nods.

"And Kade is fine."

"Noted." Her eyes dart back and forth as she stares back at me.

I want to kiss her again, but I need to know how she feels about this.

Us.

"Now I have a question."

"Shoot." She leans back, widening the distance enough to make me feel the loss of her warmth.

"Do you want to start something? Between us, I mean."

"Isn't it a little late to be asking me that? I think you already initiated things." She laughs softly.

I chuckle as I tuck my chin for a moment. "I know, and I'm

sorry. I should have asked first, but when you opened the door—"

She jumps forward and brings her lips to mine with the same hungry demand I had at the door. And I meet her request with everything I have.

Again, the kiss softens just before she pulls away to speak. "Does that answer your question?"

"Yes. I just wanted to be sure—"

She kisses me again. "And that?"

"Yes, but if you keep doing that, I won't be able to finish this conversation." I lift my brows, hopefully making my point.

She drops her head back onto the couch. "I'm sorry, but I know what you're trying to ask."

"You do?"

Mandy nods. "You want to know if I'm still going back to New York."

I clench my jaw and nod my head.

She leans forward again and puts her hand against my cheek. "Can that be the one question I don't answer right now?"

I drink her in, memorize her face, and inhale her scent again. Maybe that's enough for now.

"Sure." I drop my gaze. Then, with a sigh, I stand. "I should probably go."

"Kade?" She entwines her fingers into mine as she looks up at me.

"Yeah?"

"Would you like to spend the day together tomorrow? My shop will be closed since it's Monday."

"I'm helping Shannon and Eliana move into their new place tomorrow."

She grins. "I'll come help."

"Are you sure you want to spend your day off—"

She jumps up and kisses me again, soft and tender this time, then pulls away.

I chuckle. "Is this how we're going to communicate from now on?"

"Works for me." She gives me an impish grin that's making it really difficult to leave.

Mandy follows me to the door. "See you in the morning."

With a soft growl, I steal one more quick kiss. "Be at my place at ten."

CHAPTER 23
Amanda

Riding in the front seat of Kade's truck is giving me the opportunity to relax and enjoy the passing scenery as we follow Shannon and Eliana to their new place.

Except relaxed is the last word I would use to explain what I'm feeling.

Kade has held my hand for most of the trip, running his thumb in light circles over the back of my hand. Not constantly to make a sore spot, but enough to keep my heart beating in this weird staccato and my mind in an endless loop of remembering our kiss last night.

Correction. Kisses.

Needless to say (but I'm saying it anyway), I didn't sleep much last night. Euphoria has a crazy way of doing that to you. I kept replaying that first unexpected kiss in my head, allowing myself to dream a little before reality came crashing back in with the dawn.

I'd planned to call Sasha this morning, but I woke up with barely enough time to get dressed and gulp down a cup of coffee. So I sent her a brief text.

The kiss happened. More soon…

That's our agreed upon code for letting each other know

when we have experienced a kiss so incredible that the earth shook, the sun and moon froze in their trajectories, fireworks ignited, and the term 'swoon-worthy' doesn't do it justice.

Oh, and let's not forget, blew my socks off.

Except I wasn't wearing socks. Florida is too hot for them.

And…that was the first time I've ever used our code. Sasha still hasn't. And her wide-eyed emoji reply confirmed she's as shocked as I am.

We're on a country road now, which reminds me of my trips with Sasha to see the northern countryside explode into glorious shades of burnt orange, gold, and red. Colors so vibrant and astonishing that we couldn't say a word because they literally brought us to tears.

Funny thing is, I almost feel that way when I sneak a glance at Kade and take in the wave of his dark brown hair and the way the sunlight streaming into his side of the truck is making the green of his eyes lighter and highlights the set of his jaw, neck, and shoulders.

I could depend on those shoulders. I could hold on to those shoulders. I could…love…those shoulders.

All of that terrifies me.

How is this possibly going to work? You know the funny thing about euphoria? It doesn't last long. And in slides worry like a beast.

Kade turns my way for a moment and then does a double-take. "A copper for your thoughts?"

I can't help but grin at his turn of phrase. "Spoken like a true coppersmith."

Eyes on the road, he grins. I can't see the left side of his face, but I can imagine his dimple deeper than ever because that is one of the best smiles I've seen him flash to date. I don't think I've seen him smile that easily, come to think of it.

"So?"

Did I mention I haven't stopped smiling either? I keep my face forward. "A copper won't cut it."

"Oh?" He chuckles. "I see. Maybe I need to switch to silver."

"Why not gold?"

He doesn't answer me until he reaches the four-way stop we're nearing and turns to stare at me with a look so loaded I can barely breathe.

"I was thinking the same." His voice sounds husky.

I catch his meaning because he explained to me the difference between a silversmith and a goldsmith while we worked on the mangos at his shop. A silversmith creates large and small things, whereas a goldsmith works on smaller items like jewelry or rings…

Generally speaking, that is.

Technically, he's more of a brownsmith, but most don't know what that is so metalsmith is his go-to.

There goes my brain, running down bunny trails because the big sign at the end of this road we're on says L-O-V-E. And that rant I created about no romantic entanglements is hunting me down.

We remain comfortably silent in his truck as we leave the stretch of country road and pass houses first, then businesses and strip malls. Shannon's left blinker turns on just before she turns down a narrow street. The neighborhood is older, with your typical Florida flat-roofed, stucco houses, but the trees and palms are tall and the lawns are green and manicured. She pulls into the carport of a pale green stucco house with white trim. A line of hibiscus bushes runs along the left side and a large oak dominates the small front lawn.

Eliana races out of the car straight to the oak tree. She scrambles onto a low branch that's grown parallel to the ground before making an upward descent.

"This place is great." I climb out of Kade's truck.

Shannon walks down the drive toward us, smiling. "Isn't it?"

Fists on his hips, Kade studies every part of the exterior and the roof. "You found a sweet deal."

"I know. The owner's a friend of a friend. He bought and refurbed the place for his mother, but she got sick and had to go into full-time care. He didn't have the heart to sell it, so he decided to rent it. I was in the right place at the right time."

I point to where Eliana is hanging from the tree like a monkey. "Eliana already loves it."

Shannon smiles at her daughter. "Wait until you see her room. That bed Kade bought her will fit perfectly."

Kade lowers the tailgate, and we haul in boxes and the few pieces of furniture for Eliana's room.

Inside, the house smells of fresh paint. The walls are a sandy color with a soft white trim, and a terracotta style floor runs throughout the entire house, which is small. Two bedrooms, a bathroom, a cute kitchenette, and a cozy living room.

As I look around I can picture art on the walls. A beige sofa and matching chair already fill the living room, and a cute parlor-style table and chairs create a picturesque scene by a window in the kitchen. "It's perfect."

"I found most of what we need used. Kade insisted I let him buy me a new bed. That gets delivered later today." Shannon finishes with an eye roll. "When he makes up his mind about something, you can't change it."

"Oh?"

She holds her hand out toward me. "Don't get me wrong. I love that he wants to help. He's a generous person. But he never does anything partway. It's all or nothing."

That's when I notice Kade is like a soldier on a mission, unloading the truck and setting up Eliana's bedroom. I glance at Shannon and raise my brows in question.

She shakes her head and waves me into the kitchen. "Like I said... And he's gotten really attached to Eliana."

"What's not to love? She's a great kid."

Shannon smiles and gets this warm, fuzzy expression on her face that makes my ovaries stand up and salute. "She is."

I glance over my shoulder out the front window as Kade

unloads the mattress for Eliana's bed. Now's my chance to get the deets.

"You mentioned Kade's mother. Does he have any other family besides you and Eliana?"

Shannon hands me a bottle of water from the fridge. "No. Devon and Kade's father walked out on them when Kade was around Elly's age."

"That had to be rough."

Shannon's voice grows softer. "Devon didn't really remember him, but Kade had to be the man of the house from an early age. His mother is kind of…difficult."

The sound of a motor comes from outside. Shannon leans to one side to look past me out the front windows. "Speaking of whom. Looks like you'll get to meet her for yourself."

I follow Shannon out the front door. Kade is by the sedan, opening the driver's side door. A woman about Sally's age, maybe a little older, gets out. She has the same dark hair as Kade but not the green eyes.

"Gramma!" Eliana races from the tree and wraps herself around Kade's mother, who leans over to kiss Eliana on the head.

As I walk over with Shannon, Kade takes my hand. He's smiling, but his jaw looks like a vice and there's deep apprehension in his eyes. "Mom, this is Amanda." He glances at me next. "This is my mother, Jackie."

I feel like a bug under a microscope as I hold my hand out. "Pleased to meet you, Jackie."

She shakes my hand as she stares at the one Kade is still holding. "Kade didn't mention he had a girlfriend."

I tug my hand free. Or Kade—who now resembles a bug under her microscope, too—releases it. I'm honestly not sure which. Maybe both?

This day is feeling like a sandcastle at high tide. "Oh, I don't think we've made anything official."

Kade takes his mother's elbow. "Come see Shannon's new place."

I lag back as he keeps pace with Jackie, who has a slight limp. Eliana skips ahead of them, chattering about her special room and the new bed Uncle Kade bought her.

"See what I mean?" Shannon stays in step with me, and I'm wondering what her definition of 'difficult' is because that was more like torturous.

"Maybe I should wait in the truck."

Shannon giggles. "And miss all the fun?" She heads inside, and I push myself to follow. Somehow, those raccoons and cockroaches don't seem so bad.

But I can't help but wonder what else may lie in wait for me.

"I'm sorry about my mother." Kade stares out the front windshield as he drives us back to Sarabella.

"It's okay. She just doesn't know me. Maybe me coming was a bad idea."

Shannon strategically kept Kade's mother busy organizing her kitchen, while I helped Kade set up Eliana's room. Then he ordered pizzas for a late lunch and Jackie drilled me on what I did, where I used to live, and why I returned to Sarabella.

Again, bug under a microscope.

"I think it was a great idea. A perfect idea." He reaches over and takes my hand, entwining our fingers together.

"Why?"

"Because she had someone else besides me to focus on."

He's joking, of course, but I still give him a playful smack on the arm.

"That's so messed up."

Silence settles in for a few moments, giving me time to gather my thoughts. And my questions.

"Did you know she was coming?"

"No. Or else I would have definitely told you not to come." He lets out a derisive laugh.

"Kade, she's not that bad."

"On a good day. And you caught her on a good day. She got her cast off yesterday."

I nod and settle into silence again as I work up the courage to ask the other question that's been eating at me all day.

"She thought I was your girlfriend."

"Yes, she did."

"What did you think when she said that?"

He glances at me. "Are you asking me if I think you're my girlfriend?"

The lid is now officially off the can of worms. This is so not how I wanted this convo to go. "No, of course not. It's too soon. That would be silly."

He glances at me as his mouth forms into a wicked grin. "Why don't you just admit it? You want to be my girlfriend."

I take my hand back. "That's not true. You're the one who showed up on my doorstep last night and started all the," I wave my hands around, "all the kissing. If anything, it's you who wants to be my boyfriend."

He tugs his bottom lip under his front teeth in that shy, kind of sexy way he does. "And what if I did?"

The counter-argument I was preparing in my head goes out in a fizzle as I let his words soak in. And I'm at a loss for words because that warning bell that's supposed to remind me there can be no romantic relationships with Kade is not going off.

At all.

"Don't leave a guy hanging here." He gives me this part petulant, part seductive expression as he stops at a traffic light.

I swallow my urge to kiss him silly. "I'm still thinking about it."

Kade turns his head to the side so all I can really see is the back of his head. And it's a fantastic view—the back of his head, I mean. One of the best back of the heads I've ever seen.

But it's not his face. And I so want to see that face right now, so I can try to figure out what's going through that complicated head of his.

When he faces forward again, his expression is blank. Well, mostly. I can clearly see his jaw is tensed and that little muscle just below the ear pulses every so often. I know it's crazy, but right now, I want to touch that muscle and smooth the tension from his face, because I'm pretty sure I'm the one who caused it.

He pulls into his apartment complex and parks next to my car. We're back where the day started, and I so want to restart it again. Actually, I'd like to restart it from last night.

Would the Amanda I am now, who's had more time than she probably should to think about it, let Kade into a place in her heart she thought safely barricaded?

As I open my door, Kade hops out of the truck and jogs over to my side to hold the door open. The side of his mouth that supports that dimple quirks up as he shuts the door.

I stand there, trying to figure out what to do with my hands as my brain scrambles for something to say.

Kade leans against the truck and crosses his arms. "Thanks for your help today."

"Thanks for letting me help." Letting me help? What am I, a parrot or something?

He chuckles softly as he drops his chin. "Just to set the record straight, Root Beer, you're not my girlfriend."

I know he's saying what my fight-or-flight reflex wants to hear, what my brain is demanding to establish, and what my logical, career-driven paranoia is relieved to know. However, my heart just took the leap of sacrifice and is groveling on the tarmac beneath our feet.

And he called me 'Root Beer' again. I lift my chin to meet his taunt. "Good. I'm glad we cleared that up."

"I figured that would help."

Why is he being so obliging? "Help what?"

"Help relieve that concern that's had you tangled up all day."

"What are you talking about? I haven't been concerned about it. I just didn't want to hurt your feelings."

"My feelings?" He pushes away from the truck and drops his arms as he straightens himself to his six-foot-something. But then his dimple deepens slightly, and I can tell he's trying not to smile.

"Yeah…" The fun of our banter slides into more serious territory. "And mine." I release the breath I was holding.

The smile's gone. He nods and opens my car door. "You have nothing to worry about."

As I get behind the wheel, I want to ask him what that means in the grand scheme of things. Or in the measly one…

But I'm too afraid of his answer. So I do the only thing I can.

I drive away.

CHAPTER 24
Amanda

What do you get when you cross the mayor's wife with fifty glass mangos?

More business!

It's no wonder the mayor was re-elected. The woman is a powerhouse. I haven't even delivered her order yet, but she has told everyone she knows that Bloomed to Be Wilde is the place to shop for the upcoming holiday seasons. Good thing I ordered a lot of fall and Christmas-themed items to accommodate.

Turns out, she has a lot of friends and supporters not just here in Sarabella but in New York, too. The steady flow of customers in the last three days alone has doubled my sales for the month so far, which is great. The downside is, I can only work on inventory and orders after the shop closes, so I've been working late every evening at the shop.

The upside of that? I haven't had a lot of time to think about Kade and the fact that we haven't seen each other in a week. I could be mad at him for not even texting, but the minute I start to feel that way, I remind myself that I haven't texted him either.

Plus, I don't even have time to do anything about it because

I'm seriously freaking out. Emily's wedding is this coming weekend. I designed an arrangement I can do ahead of time except for the addition of the fresh flowers. After assembling the prototype, I did five more, which means I have twelve more to do. Plus the arrangements for the ceremony, which are essentially the same design, just taller, and a special arrangement for the wedding party table.

And let's not forget the bridal bouquet. I'm still working out sketches for that one.

Marnie brought over the first half of my order for the glass mangos with a promise to bring the rest by the end of the week. So those need to be wire wrapped so Kade can work his magic to finish them. Just in time for Mrs. Stringer to pick them up next Monday.

So, you see, this is what kept me up most of the night and brought me to my shop at dawn to use the one day the shop is closed as a workday to catch up.

And why I've called in the big guns.

Sally's on her way over. So is Emily, who insists on helping and is bringing her bridesmaid, who flew in from California for the wedding.

My phone buzzes on the worktable and shows me Sasha's face. "How's it going? Are you freaking out?"

No greeting, just right to the point. Of course, it doesn't help that I sent a long text to Sasha before dawn, which was more of a panicked rant. "No, help is on the way."

"Good. I wish I could be there to help you."

"Me, too."

"Any more interchanges with Mr. Lucious?" Sasha makes air quotes as she says 'interchanges,' which is her code for kissing.

I roll my eyes. "I told you, I think that ship has sailed."

"Then call it back."

"Not a good idea."

"Why not?"

In the world of Sasha, only one form of logic can exist—hers. But I will attempt to sway her to mine. "All the same reasons I went over before. Kade is established here in Sarabella—"

"He can move his business."

I stare at the ceiling of my shop as I list *my logical* reasons. "He wants to be nearby for his adorable niece—"

"That's what airplanes are for."

"And around, in case Shannon or his mother needs help."

Sasha crosses her arms and pouts. "You're seriously bursting my vicarious balloon here."

"Sorry."

She leans in closer. "Are you? Are you really?"

I know she's mocking me in her playful, sometimes dark way, but I can't ignore the shriveled balloon my own heart now resembles. Because it's been one long, emotionally frustrating week. Emily's wedding, wire-wrapping mangos, and running my shop are the only things that kept me from storming into his studio.

"More than you know."

For some reason, this catches Sasha by surprise. "Oh… wow."

"What?" I wag my finger at her image on my phone screen. "What's all that about?"

Sasha drops her arms, tilts her head, and looks at me as if I'm the saddest case of pathetic on this earth. "You already fell."

"What? Noooo. *Phtt!* What are you talking about?"

"Okay, moving on, since you clearly don't want to talk about it. How's your shop?"

"Great!" I flip the camera and take Sasha on a tour to see all the changes I've made, all the unique items I'm carrying now, including new items from local artists, and the centerpieces I'm working on for Emily.

Sasha is grinning from one multi-pierced ear to the other. "You did it, Amanda. You've made your shop a success."

"Yes, despite rotted floorboards, raccoons, cockroaches, and over committing myself." I laugh.

Sasha looks thoughtful for a moment. "You realize you're essentially operating as a product designer, right? And not only that, you *own* the business."

I mentally jerk from the electric shock going from my figurative toes up to the obligatory light bulb floating over my head.

Bling! And there was light!

She's right.

As I digest what my best friend said, something shifts in me. It's like someone opened a set of beautiful floral curtains mimicking the outside to reveal a real live enchanted garden outside just waiting to be explored.

And it's amazing. It *is* kind of like being a product designer/communicator only the products are in my hands, and, instead of creating graphics under the direction of a creative director to promote them, I have this wonderful shop that's all mine to run as I please.

My eyes burn and then fill with tears. Is it possible that I've found what I've wanted all along right here in Sarabella? And if that's true, could that mean Amanda Wilde is allowed to have a romantic relationship with, say, one Kade Maverick?

"Amanda? Are you okay?"

I swallow and shake my head with a vigorous nod. "Yeah, crazy as it sounds, the best I've been in a long time."

As I say goodbye to Sasha, I hear a knock coming from the front door. Emily is standing there with another woman I assume is her friend, and she's holding what looks like a tray.

The aroma of banana bread fills my nose as I open the door. I can barely greet them over the deluge of saliva filling my mouth.

Emily holds up the tray. "I brought sustenance. Straight out of the oven fifteen minutes ago."

I stand back as they file in. "You're my hero."

Emily giggles and gestures to her friend, who could give Sandra Bullock a run for her money. "This is Callie. She used to live in Sarabella, too, but fled the coop like you did. I'm trying to convince her to come back." She lifts her brows with a silent hint that I could move back, too.

I'm not saying a word until I get to take these new thoughts out for a one-to-one discussion with myself after the dust of this chaotic week settles. "Emily told me you flew in from California. What part?"

"Los Angeles."

"Not to be an actress, I hope." I crack the joke before I can stop myself. Like I said, I have mommy issues.

"No, definitely not." Callie seems a little on the shy side, despite her killer looks.

Emily puts her hand on Callie's shoulder. "No, she's a head lifeguard, like Zane."

Callie gives Emily a somewhat pained expression, which seems to send Emily's proud grin into a grimace of regret.

Best to leave bestie secrets between besties is my motto, so I don't ask. I take Emily and Callie to the back room where I have all the elements for the wedding centerpieces spread out on the worktable and counters. Once I show them how to wrap the glass jars with fairy lights and hide the battery pack in the eucalyptus woven grapevine wreath that sits on the mouth of the jar, they take over like pros.

On the day of the wedding, I'll fill the jars halfway with water to sustain a small bouquet of three white hydrangea blooms interspersed with purple pea flowers and a sprig of eucalyptus. Emily flipped over the design.

"Amanda, these are even better than your sketches!" Emily's cheeks are bright pink with her excitement as she takes pictures with her phone. "I'm totally going to add some hydrangea flowers made of fondant down one side of my wedding cake. I just love how this is all coming together. Can we do a similar design for my bouquet?"

"I actually had the same thought." I grab my sketchbook from the counter to show her my latest designs, when the bells on the front door jingle, reminding me I didn't lock the door again.

I rush to the front prepared to tell whoever I'm closed today but breathe a sigh of relief that it's Sally, and she's holding two carriers filled with cups of what smells like coffee and chai tea. Although, I don't think coffee will rival the buzz I'm already experiencing over the paradigm shift about my life as a business owner, thanks to Sasha's observations.

But I am dying to talk to Sally about it. She's one of those people who can put aside her own preferences to give an objective opinion.

I take one of the drink carriers from her and notice the bag from Bake My Day. The aroma of baked goods alerts my mouth and stomach that some yummy goodness is coming their way, even though I've already consumed two pieces of Emily's banana bread.

Unable to resist, I peek into the bag. Donuts, muffins, and, yes, more banana bread. One can never have too much banana bread. "Did you leave anything for the other customers?"

Sally does a laugh, snicker combo. "Some. However, Aiden got this concerned look on his face when I came in with the bag to grab some coffee for us. When he found out it was for those of us *slaving* over his wedding, he had everyone in the place making a full array of caffeinated drinks, free of charge, and with the instructions to call if we need him to bring more."

"Wow, I'm impressed." I nab a coffee and take a sip. My eyes close as the warmth of the potent brew mingles with the banana bread I've consumed. Now I can face whatever comes next.

I head toward the back room with the bag of goodies as Sally follows me with the second drink carrier.

After greeting Emily and Callie, she leans against the counter. "Zane said he'd stop by later and give us an update."

"Update? On what?"

"The hurricane." As I set the cups down for Emily and Callie to choose from, I notice Callie has turned a pale shade of green. "Callie, are you okay?"

She glances at Emily, who puts a hand on Callie's arm. "Oh, I'm fine."

Something is definitely up with her, but I'll keep my nose to its normal size. Maybe she prefers earthquakes to hurricanes.

Sally smiles and waves her hand in dismissal. "I'm sure the hurricane will miss us. They usually do."

In the last twenty years, most of the bigger storms and hurricanes have missed Sarabella. It's almost a superstition now that our little peninsula is magical or protected somehow. I don't recall any major hurricanes coming through, even when I was a kid.

Sally and I return to the front counter, where I've set up a portable table to work on the mangos.

"So, this hurricane…do I need to be worried?" I give Sally a wary look, ready to gauge by her reply if this is a major threat to worry about or just a gnat to swat away.

"Possibly. It's still south of the state, below the Keys."

Which means it would have to swing up into the Gulf and angle our way. Seems unlikely. But if Zane is concerned, then I'm concerned. "Why is Zane stopping by?"

Sally shrugs and tilts her head as she studies the wire we'll be using. "It's already a category two, and he wants to take a look at your shop."

"My shop?" My voice squeaks out. I take a deep breath and push down my surge of panic. "Seriously, do I need to be worried?"

Sally pats my hand, sits down at the worktable, and picks up a glass mango. "No, everything's going to be fine. He always did that for your aunt, too."

I start to breathe again.

She smiles up at me. "These are so pretty!"

CHAPTER 25
Kade

Reminders of Mandy cover my workbench. Specifically, the leaves for the glass mangos, which need to be finished before the weekend. She texted me this morning to say she's bringing half of the order over later to attach the leaves, and the thought of seeing her is making me antsy.

But not seeing her for an entire week has been worse, but I'm determined to protect her feelings. I told her she had nothing to worry about, and I intend to keep that promise.

And it's not like I'm avoiding her, not really. Shannon has needed help with things at her new place, so every evening after I closed the shop, I've made the trip to help and spend time with Eliana. A couple of times, I bunked on the couch and came back in the morning.

So I'm not twiddling my thumbs—or driving circles in roundabouts—trying to figure out where I stand with Mandy. I'm safely back in the friend zone and will stay there.

For her sake.

As I finish attaching a stem to another leaf, I turn off my torch and shove my shield back. The anticipation of knowing I'll see her later is almost too much to take. Maybe I'll just walk over to her shop and put myself out of my misery sooner than later.

After shedding my gear, I grab my keys just as Zane walks in, looking sterner than I've ever seen. "Hey man, what's up?"

"Not the barometric pressure."

"Come again?" I drop my keys on the workbench.

He's studying my ceiling now and checking my windows. "These aren't storm rated, so you'll need to board up."

"I thought the hurricane was still below the keys."

"Yeah, but it's looking more and more like we're going to get a direct hit. I'm going around to the downtown businesses and making sure folks are aware of what's coming."

I point to a stack of plywood in the corner. "I think that's left over from the previous tenant. Will that work?"

Zane flips through the panels and nods. "Those are fine." He walks over and lays a map on the empty end of my workbench. "Doesn't your mother live in this area?"

I study the maze of streets and point to where her trailer park is located. "Yeah, right there."

"That's a flood zone, so you probably want to move her somewhere safer."

"But she's more inland."

"Right, but if the squalls are as high as they're predicting, that's going to flood the inlets which run right by her."

"Okay, I'll take her over to Shannon's place. She's a good five miles more inland."

"Good." He folds up his map. "I'm headed over to Amanda's shop next."

"Mind if I tag along?"

Zane studies me. "Something I need to know about?"

"Nope." I say it fast and firm.

"That good, huh?"

I don't say a thing. Just focus on keeping my face as blank as possible, because I've had more than enough input from

Shannon over the last week and one more opinion might send me over the edge.

He frowns at first, then relaxes his expression. "Yeah, sure. I may need some help boarding her place up. If you're available."

"Sure. No problem. Glad to help."

As we walk over to Mandy's shop, my heart is thumping hard in my chest, and it's not from the brusque pace we're keeping.

Despite the closed sign on the door, Zane walks in and I follow.

Zane is taller than I am and fills the doorway, so I know Mandy probably doesn't see me at first when she greets him.

When he moves to the side, our eyes lock.

"Kade, it's good to see you." She's smiling as if she's genuinely pleased to see me.

And I feel myself smile in response. Zane walks over to where his mother is sitting and now it's just Mandy and me in this microcosm that has room for no one else.

Just her and me.

I know it's only been a week, but she's even more beautiful than I remember and I am falling fast and hard again. Clearly, the friend zone doesn't have strong enough boundaries for what I'm feeling for her.

"Zane said you may need help boarding your place up."

Her eyes go round with fresh panic. "He did?"

Zane walks back over to the near disaster about to happen in front of me. "It's just precautionary, Amanda. Don't worry."

"But I am worried. I just got this place running well and now a hurricane is coming? When are they predicting it will make landfall?"

"Possibly Friday night or Saturday morning."

A shriek comes from the back room. "What? No! That's my wedding day. Tell that thing to wait a day."

Zane is visibly trying not to laugh, and so am I, because the hysteria in the place has reached epic proportions. Why do weddings do weird things to people's logic?

Mandy rushes over to Emily, who's now standing in the doorway to the back room and matches the off-white color of the walls. "Zane said not to worry, so…so let's not worry. It's still early in the week, right?"

Still looking like a possum caught at night, Emily nods. Another woman I don't know comes up behind Emily, takes one look at Zane, and freezes.

Zane's mirthful expression shifts to surprise before becoming guarded. "Callie?"

Callie attempts a wan smile. "Zane, I didn't expect to see you."

Mandy bounces her gaze between the two of them. "You two know each other?"

Zane turns to face me. "Mav, I'll get back with you later in the week."

Before I can answer, he leaves in a rush out the door and jogs down the sidewalk toward the end of the street.

Callie bursts into tears and runs to the back room again.

Emily sniffles and follows her.

Sally stares at us both. "What just happened?"

I'M STANDING on one side of my workbench while Mandy is standing on the other, wrapping the rest of the mangos with brass wire as I attach leaves to the ones she finished.

Once the dust settled, Mandy sent Emily and Callie home, then Sally left once Mandy reassured her she and I could finish the mangos. I texted Zane to let him know I'll be around later this evening if he needs to talk, but he still hasn't replied.

"Zane never told you about her?" The awkwardness between us is still tangible, so this is me trying to deflect and find a way around it.

"Not specifically. Sally mentioned he was seeing someone right after I moved to New York, but then I heard nothing else. I just assumed it had stayed casual."

I nod.

"Did he ever mention anything to you? About Callie?"

Her concern for Zane is thick and twists something inside me.

"No. Never came up."

Mandy checks her phone again.

I recognize that concern. It's the same worry I carry for Shannon and Eliana. For family. "Still no reply?"

"No." Her shoulders slump. "I'm sure he's busy with preparations."

"It'll be okay, Mandy."

"What? Things with Zane or the hurricane?" She says 'hurricane' the same way someone would say 'plague.'

"Both." I can't help but chuckle, but I'm having a hard time not staring at her. No one should look that adorable when they're worried.

And it makes me want to hold her and make all those creases in her forehead go away.

"It's not funny." She puts down the mango she's holding in a very controlled manner before she grabs a rag off the workbench and throws it at me.

"Hey, now. I didn't say it was funny."

"But you laughed."

"Yes, I did. And I'm sorry. But I really couldn't help myself." And now I'm laughing and can't stop.

She rushes around to my side of the workbench. "Stop laughing. This is serious."

"I know." But I still can't stop.

"Stop it." She grabs another rag and tries to swat me with it.

I reach for the rag, catching the end, but when she tries to pull away, I don't let go. Instead, I tug it back, which brings her against me.

She's staring up at me with those shimmering brown eyes that dart to my mouth before she tucks her chin and won't look at me.

I touch my knuckle under her chin and lift her face. "It's going to be okay."

"How do you know?"

"I don't, but that's what I believe."

She blinks and then nods. Her lips part as if she wants to say something, but whatever it is seems trapped within the doubt I see in her eyes.

My need to comfort her draws me closer until I touch my lips to hers. Tentative at first because I don't know where she stands now about us. Soft. Tender. Reassuring.

She makes a soft noise in her throat as she leans into me like she's giving me permission to hold her closer, so I wrap my arms around her and hold her tight, even after the kiss ends. Then she does this thing with her head where she wiggles her face back and forth just so as she settles into the perfect spot between my chin and shoulder.

"Thank you." Her voice reverberates against my chest where she buried her face.

"For what?"

She tilts her head up. "For this. For being so understanding while I figure things out."

"Is that what you're doing here, figuring things out?" I keep my tone light, but my question is dead serious.

"Yes, are you okay with that?"

"Depends."

"On what?"

"If you're still considering the role of girlfriend, because I have to tell you, I've received several applications this week."

"Oh, really?"

"Yes, seems I'm quite in demand lately."

She studies me with this quirky smile that makes me want to kiss her again. "So, are you still taking applications?"

I glance up and pretend to be thinking. "I think today's the last day."

"Then consider this mine." She lifts her head as she tugs mine down for another kiss that stirs something in me to rival any hurricane.

As she leans away, I run my thumb along her perfect cheek. I don't know what changed her mind about us, and I want to ask her if this means she's planning to stay in Sarabella after all.

But right now, this will have to be enough. "I think the position is officially filled now."

She smiles and then snuggles her head into my shoulder again—the perfect spot that feels meant just for her—and everything in me settles into this place of peace and knowing.

Knowing that I'm in love with Amanda Wilde.

CHAPTER 26
Amanda

It goes without saying (yet apparently I'm going to) that Hurricane Phillipe is the hottest topic of discussion today. And the way people talk, and if you didn't have a point of reference and no clue what was brewing in the Gulf of Mexico, you'd think we were talking about some rich, playboy mogul instead of a hurricane forecasters are reporting as a category three now.

So far Phillipe, which when you say it with a French accent sounds almost romantic, is still in his little corner of the ocean below the tip of Florida and seems to be on a path toward Louisiana.

I'm relieved and feeling majorly guilty about it.

My preference, of course, is for this thing to fizzle out before making landfall, but it seems intent to keep going—and growing. I check the weather app on my phone for what must be the fifteenth time since I arrived at my shop this morning. The bands are still doing a dance around the eye, which, according to the latest reports, means it's becoming more defined. Supposedly, that's not a good thing.

I shove my phone under a dust rag on the counter.

In the back room, Emily's nearly completed centerpieces fill the counters, the work area, and the folding table I moved from the front. I've scheduled delivery for Friday for a wedding still planned for Saturday, even though everyone along the coast of Florida up through Louisiana and even Texas is asking the same question.

Where will Hurricane Phillipe land?

"Not in Sarabella." The shop's been way too quiet today, so apparently I'm talking to myself now.

"What's not in Sarabella?"

I whip around. Kade is standing just outside the doorway to the back room, dressed in jeans and a leather jacket, giving him a dangerous, bad boy look that has my pulse pounding so hard I feel almost faint. And he's holding two motorcycle helmets.

"How did I not hear you come in?"

"I'm sneaky that way." His smile holds the promise of mischief.

I check my watch. "Wow, didn't realize it was closing time either."

He holds a helmet up. "Ready to go?"

After a quick grab for my phone, I take the helmet. "Where are we going?"

"It's a surprise."

The temperature is significantly cooler as I walk out the front and lock the door behind us. "Wow, it's actually chilly out."

"Do you have a jacket?"

"No. It wasn't this cool when I left my condo this morning."

"Hurricanes will do that." He slips off his leather jacket and holds it open for me to slip on.

I almost cringe at the reminder. "Won't you get cold?"

"No, I'll have you to warm me up." I feel the heated blush slide up from my neck as I turn around to slip one arm and then another into his jacket that's still warm from his body heat. I'm glad he can't see my face. Or hear my thoughts at the moment.

Kade helps me adjust the strap for my helmet before he puts

his on and then gets on the bike. I slide on behind him, careful to put my feet where he instructs me.

"Keep your arms around my waist, okay?" He says this over his shoulder and starts the engine. His proximity gives me a close-up of that dimple that likes to show up when he grins like that.

I nod and, as he pulls away from the curb, I rest my face against his back. The spicy scent of juniper tickles my nose, filling me with a sense of safety and makes me want to snuggle in closer to him, which I do without thinking about it.

What did I just do?

Before I have time to go into a complete panic, Kade takes one hand off the handlebars to press against mine, where they're overlapped on his abdomen.

I inhale the crispness of the cool air and exhale my fear of what this all means between us, the stress of Emily's wedding, finishing the glass mangos Marnie brought this morning, and, yes, the hurricane, too.

Nothing to worry about. Yet.

Snort.

Tell that to my brain that's filing a complaint against my rebellious heart for breach of contract.

The bike rumbles beneath us with the sun setting ahead of us. And it's glorious. The sky is turning so red, it looks like it's on fire, and as we ride, I realize he's heading for the beach.

After turning into the parking lot, Kade steers the motorcycle to an area near a patch of pines and parks in a spot by the sidewalk.

I slide off the bike and remove my helmet.

Kade does the same, then opens the saddlebag on the back of the seat to pull out a paper bag with a Jack's Seafood restaurant logo and picnic blanket. "I thought we'd have dinner on the beach. I hope you like Italian food."

"I love it." That's when the aroma of garlic sauce and grilled shrimp hit me, putting my stomach on noisy alert. I follow him as we leave the sidewalk to make our way under the pines to one of several picnic tables that face the ocean. We sit next to each other on one side, giving us a view better than most restaurants. Wave after wave rolls over the dark waters, which makes the red sky seem even more ominous.

Instead of putting the blanket on the table, Kade drapes it over us as a shield against a strong breeze hinting at what's yet to come.

He opens one dish after another, revealing shrimp linguini, grilled salmon with rice pilaf and veggies, and a rather generous slice of key lime pie for dessert.

"Wow, so much food!" I'm practically drooling as I claim the shrimp scampi. "That's my favorite."

"I know." He takes the salmon.

"How do you know that?"

He stops and studies me. "I asked Sally."

Of course he did.

A comfortable silence settles between us as we eat and gaze at the ocean. A few brave souls are walking the beach and wading the shallows, looking for shells.

I put my fork down and take a sip of the sparkling water Kade brought for us. "How are Shannon and Eliana doing?"

Kade finishes chewing and wipes his mouth. "They're settled in. Eliana is adjusting to her new school and loves it."

"No more bladder bullies?"

He chuckles. "Not so far."

"That's good."

"It is." His tone is quiet, almost sad.

"I bet you miss that squirt."

His features soften. "Yeah, more than I thought I would."

I lift one shoulder. "How could you not? She's pretty terrific. And a talented painter."

Kade leans in closer and scans my face before dropping his gaze to my lips, which brings mine to his. He's tender and gentle as he touches his lips to mine.

The thought of garlic breath flits through my thoughts, but as he deepens the kiss, my brain checks out, and I'm lost in the moment until the kiss ends.

As the sun finishes its descent, we share the key lime pie and talk about anything and everything, with an emphasis on nothing.

The ride back to my shop is too short. Kade walks me to my car, kisses me again, then gets back on his bike as I get in my car and drive away. I can tell he's waiting to leave until after he knows I'm safe and on my way home.

And I'm sending up prayers, like Aunt Paula taught me, for his safe ride home.

That's when it hits me how invested I've become, something I didn't intend to do, yet it happened anyway.

Everything about this—about Kade—feels right. Meant to be. I should be terrified, but I'm not. Not really…

Aunt Paula once alluded to a time in her life when she loved someone. When I asked what happened, she would only say it didn't work out. I'll never forget the way she described how she felt so much love for this man, but more importantly, she felt truly and deeply loved.

Kade didn't say it, but I suspect it…

And, I suspect…I do, too.

CHAPTER 27
Kade

"If you turn that board horizontally, you'll have plenty of coverage." Zane is holding a drill, ready to make holes in the stucco for the anchors that will hold the screws.

I position the board over the window. "Thanks for the help."

"No problem. That's part of what we're here for." He goes to town with the drill.

"Seriously?"

"Yep, protect Sarabella at all costs."

"Wow, I had no idea."

"A lifeguard is like a storm shelter. You may never need it, but if you do, it can be a lifesaver." He gives a cheeky grin to go with his statement.

I'm shaking my head at this point. "I stepped right into that one, didn't I?"

"Yeah, ya did."

After he drills the rest of the holes, we secure the board over the front window to my studio. Thankfully, the rear door is a heavy-duty garage door without windows.

"They're still saying the hurricane could stay on its path toward the panhandle."

Zane shrugs. "Maybe, but my gut says otherwise."

"Your gut knows hurricane patterns?" I grab the last board for the glass door so we can pre-drill the holes, but I won't install that one until I know we're in the hurricane's path.

"You could say that. I've done a lot of studying on storms and weather patterns. Makes us better prepared as lifeguards. I incorporate it into our training, too."

Once finished, Zane packs up his tools. "I'm heading over to Amanda's shop next."

"I'll lock up and come with you."

He gives me a loaded grin and says, "I figured you would."

"What does that mean?"

He shrugs and shakes his head. "Nothing. Just my gut telling me the obvious."

"Obvious?"

He swats my shoulder with the back of his hand. "Yeah, everyone sees it. You two are really into each other."

His words give me a sense of relief. I guess I wasn't sure where Zane would stand in regard to me dating Mandy. "Then you're okay with it?"

"Yeah, but at the risk of sounding like a corny romance movie, if you break her heart, I'll have to break you." He loads his toolbox into his Jeep parked at the curb.

What if she breaks mine? That's my first thought, which makes me feel like a bit of a wimp, but there it is. Since our date last night, I feel like I'm in this free fall that will either land well or end badly.

Really bad. Losing my brother left a mark in more ways than one and took a long time to recover. The way I feel about Mandy…losing her would feel like a death. Besides, I could never hurt her.

"I care about Mandy a lot." I can't tell him I love her. She needs to hear it first and the right time hasn't presented itself. "I don't intend to hurt her."

Zane gives me a weighted stare. "We never do."

I'm guessing this has something to do with Callie. "Care to unpack that?"

"Not really." He walks to the driver's side and gets in.

We make the short drive to Mandy's shop in silence. I respect Zane and figure he'll talk about it when he needs to.

When we drive up to the back of Mandy's shop, she's already outside wrangling with a piece of plywood about three feet taller than she is.

I jump out of Zane's Jeep and run up the ramp side of the stairs to help her. "What are you doing?"

"I'm trying to get this thing to the front."

Zane takes the other end from her, and we carry it to the front of the shop.

Mandy follows us. "Zane, are you sure this is necessary?"

Zane lowers his end as I push mine up to cover the main front window.

"Am I sure? No, but better to be prepared."

I raise my brows at her. "And his gut says it's likely."

My attempt to lighten the mood only heightens Mandy's growing panic.

"Will the wedding arrangements be okay here? Should I move them?"

Zane stops on his way to get his toolbox. "I seriously doubt there will even be a wedding, so don't worry about them."

Once Zane disappears behind the building, Mandy turns to me. "I wish I knew what to do. I don't know what to expect."

I grip her arms just below the shoulders and give a reassuring squeeze. "None of us do. We'll just have to ride it out."

"But what if my shop is damaged?"

"We'll fix it."

"All those arrangements…we've worked so hard on them. The floor was in terrible shape. What if the rest of the place is, too, and can't withstand a hurricane?"

I pull her into a reassuring hug. "It'll be okay, Mandy."

She pulls away. "You keep saying that, but how do you know?"

"Okay, I don't. I guess I've learned to roll with the punches." She tucks her chin and crosses her arms over her stomach as if to hold herself. "I don't think I can do that. I've worked so hard to get the shop viable, so I can sell it next year, and now I may lose it all."

Her mention of selling the shop feels like a blade in my gut. I guess some part of me thought that her willingness to pursue a relationship with me meant she wanted to stay in Sarabella. She'd hinted at it, but maybe I took that to mean more.

I shove that into the locker along with my heart for now. Right now, Mandy is scared, and I will do whatever I can to make this easier for her.

"Let's not expect the worst when we don't even know for sure." I gesture to the plywood and Zane returning with his toolbox. "All this is just in case, okay?"

She nods, but I can tell she's far from relieved and not at all comforted. I'm at a loss for what else to do. Life has taught me to hold on to things loosely. I've done pretty well in that department.

Until now. I want to hold on to Mandy with a fierceness I've never felt before, but I know I can't do that. She has to choose her own path in this scenario.

So how do I loosen the grip of this need for her to choose me over her dream?

CHAPTER 28
Amanda

My first thoughts as I wake up are, of course, about Kade. After we boarded up most of my shop yesterday, he left with Zane to help with the other shops, including Sally's. By the time they finished, he was too exhausted to do more than send a text saying he was going home to shower and crash.

What a way to start a relationship...I've never had great timing. The crush I carried for my boss was ill-timed, as were most of my romantic interests, come to think of it. I'm just not good at it.

But this feels different. Kade is different...different from anyone I've ever dated. He's solid and real, but there's something there that sits on the edge, like a wild animal waiting to bolt at the first sign of threat.

Until now I haven't really been able to put my finger on it, but now that we've gotten closer, I'm sensing it more and more. I think he's as scared as I am.

An overcast morning greets me as I climb out of bed and open the sliding door. The winds have picked up, rustling the fronds of the nearby palms with a frenzy, and the rain started moving in last night.

The hurricane isn't near us yet, but the outer bands are

letting us know more bad weather is imminent. How much is still somewhat unsure, but as I check the weather app on my phone, I see the predicted path has angled down closer to Sarabella and the news report confirms my fear.

Phillipe has turned and is heading closer. Though still predicted to land north of us, we're now in the edge's path of the storm, which is projected to make landfall tomorrow morning, the day before Emily's wedding.

Since her venue is near the beach, there's no telling what condition the place will be in once the storm moves through. Hopefully, just debris cleanup.

I grab my phone and send a quick text to Emily, asking about the status of the wedding. She replies that she and Aiden plan to make a decision today.

Regardless of what they decide, I make the decision that the centerpieces can't stay at my shop, which is almost as close to the beach as the wedding venue.

I call Kade's cell phone.

"Can't stop thinking of me?"

"You wish." I chuckle.

"Just wake up?"

"Yes, how can you tell?"

"You sound sleepy." His voice is soft and intimate.

My face grows hot and a glance at the dresser mirror confirms my blush. "And you?"

"Couldn't sleep. Been at the shop for hours, getting equipment secured and loading some things in my truck to take to Shannon's after I board my mother's trailer up for her."

"She's not staying there, is she?"

"She would if I let her. I'm taking her over to Shannon's with me. We're going to hunker down there tonight."

"Any chance you could help me get those centerpieces over to Emily's? Her place is more inland."

"Sure, I'll come your way first."

We make plans to meet at my shop in an hour. I text Emily to let her know, and as I grab my keys, Sasha calls.

"Are you someplace safe?"

I've known Sasha for a long time, but her abruptness in times of stress still surprises me at times.

"I'm about to walk out the door to go to my shop."

"Aren't you near the beach? Isn't that dangerous?"

"The hurricane hasn't made landfall yet, and it's still north of us. Plenty of time."

"Are you sure?"

"Yes, I'm sure. Anything else on your mind?" I lock the door to my condo and head down to Aunt Paula's junker, which seems to have a cranky starter in wet weather.

"Actually, yes. I was at an art show last night and you'll never guess who I ran into?"

"Umm, Jeremy?"

Sasha snorts. "Good grief, no. And even if I did, I wouldn't bother to talk about it. He's not worth my time."

She may say that, but I can tell she's still holding a bit of a torch for her old boyfriend. "Okay, then who?"

"Daniel."

"Daniel?"

"Daniel, as in your former boss and the guy you used to pine over."

"Oh, and I didn't pine for him. I just thought he was cute." I take the stairs down so I don't lose cell connection and cut Sasha off.

"Whatever. I ran into him last night. He asked about you. Somehow, word got to him about your shop and those glass mangos you created. He sounded quite impressed."

"Oh, wow, how in the world did he find out?"

"One of his clients is best friends with what's-her-name, the mayor's wife?"

"Bettina Stringer?"

"That sounds right. Anyway, he asked me when you're coming back. I think he wants to offer you a job."

"He said if I ever wanted my old job back, I could have it."

"No, I don't think he meant that. Before his wife dragged him away, he said he regretted not giving you a chance to run your own accounts."

"Really? Wow…I don't know what to do with that."

"Nothing."

"What? But that's what I've worked for the past five years."

"Yes, and he blew it. Now you've proved him wrong and you're doing it on your own terms." She turns her face to the side and raises her brow. "Right?"

I know she's right, but that dream of making it big in the NYC design world is still rather vocal. But isn't the fact that Daniel got wind of my shop and what I'm doing there kind of fulfillment of that dream? I may not be in New York at the moment, but I've somehow still made a mark…

As I step outside, I note of the angry clouds swirling above, matching the turmoil brewing in my stomach. "You're right, Sasha. If you see Daniel again, tell him I'm not interested."

"Good. I'm glad to hear you say that because I kind of said it already."

"You did?"

"Yeah, should I not have?"

"No, it's all good. As long as Phillipe doesn't throw a wrench in the works."

"Who's Phillipe?"

"The hurricane."

"Oh, that's right. Why do they give them names like that?"

I shrug and get into my car. "They always do."

"Has there ever been a Hurricane Sasha?" She gives me a wicked grin.

"I doubt any hurricane could measure up to your level of destruction."

Sasha laughs. "I think our downstairs neighbor would agree with you on that."

I KEEP CHECKING out back for Kade's truck. With the winds and rain, I can't prop open the back door, so I'm inside wrapping the centerpieces in large clear plastic bags to protect them from the rain.

This is turning into a bigger project than I anticipated, as I realize space will be limited because of the rain unless Kade has some way to cover the back of his pickup. I grab my phone to send him a text, asking him to bring a tarp or something when I hear a knock on the back door, which swings open as I grab for the knob.

Next thing I know, I'm tumbling backward with my arms imitating a windmill about to crash and burn, but Kade lunges forward and pulls me against him with an *oomph*.

I only have a moment to stare into his face, to notice the raindrops caught in his eyelashes, and his face and hair are damp, too. A storm crackles between us as he lowers his head and kisses me, tender at first like a query, then he deepens the kiss as if we haven't seen each other in days or weeks instead of less than a day.

He puts his hands on my hips, lifts me onto the workbench, and stands between my knees, running his hands through my hair as he continues to kiss me. And I meet his passion with my own.

Kade's the first to slow the kiss and I'm glad. I'm not sure I could make a life-and-death decision at the moment, even if my life did truly depend upon it.

He leans his forehead against mine while he runs his hand over my shoulders, then my arms, until he reaches my hands and pulls them to his mouth to kiss my fingers. "I missed you."

"I missed you, too." I pull a hand free to run my finger over the scar that runs down his forehead, through his brow, and down his cheek. I stop at the dimple, then do what I've been longing to do—kiss it.

His low growl causes me to lean back. "Does that bother you?"

He swallows as he opens his eyes that match the storm clouds brewing outside. "That bothers me quite a bit."

I get his message clearly. "We better get to work."

He nods and helps me down. I take one of the large clear bags and cut a 'v' in the middle. "Here, slip this over your head. It'll keep us from getting soaked."

I make one for myself as he tugs his over his head. His hair is damp and unruly, giving him a thoroughly roguish look that's making my heart go into overdrive.

We load as many of the centerpieces as we can into my car and lay down the larger pieces for the reception in the truck bed, which has a cover after all.

We make a run back to the shop for one last check of whatever else needs to go, although I'm not sure anything else can fit.

Still wearing a dripping plastic bag to match mine, Kade scans the back area before nodding toward the front of the shop. "What about your inventory?"

"I brought most of it to my condo and stacked the bigger items in that small closet I converted into sales space and the bathroom. Neither one has a window."

He nods. "Any flowers?"

"Jacob is keeping them at his place, so we don't need to worry about those. And adding them the day of the ceremony will be easy and quick, whenever that is." Disappointment drips from my voice.

"Have they canceled the wedding?"

"Not yet. I think Emily is still hoping that this thing will pass through tomorrow with minimal damage."

"Not likely."

I cringe. "I keep praying and hoping this thing will just fizzle out."

"That's not likely either. It's already a category three and growing."

I hope the tears I feel spring up in my eyes and fall down my cheeks mingle with my rain-drenched face, but I should know better. Kade reads me like a book.

He moves closer and pushes back the hair plastered to one side of my face. "You're not alone, Root Beer. I'm here. The town is here, even if parts get blown away. We'll get through this and come back stronger."

"Spoken like a true overcomer. I'm impressed."

"Good." He gives me a satisfied grin. "I think there's a break coming before the next band of rain slams us. Let's take advantage of it."

"Right behind ya, sport."

He frowns at me. "Sport?"

I shrug. "Seemed fitting at the moment."

"Try something different if another moment comes."

"Hey, sport is better than Root Beer."

"I disagree."

"Then I'll use Mav."

He puckers his face and shakes his head. "That's a business nickname. Not meant for girlfriends."

I laugh. "You're serious, aren't you?"

"Dead serious." He opens the back door and gestures for me to go.

As I walk past him, I smile. "How about Ace?"

The rain has waned to a light sprinkle but the sky toward the ocean is blacker than I've ever seen it. I stop at my car with a shudder.

"How about Kade?" He stops next to me and opens the car door that now sounds like a door opening in a haunted mansion, which makes this day feel even more haunting.

"I guess that could work."
"It is my name."
I give him a quick kiss. "So it is."

CHAPTER 29
Kade

I'm glad I'm alone for the drive over to Emily's, so I have some time to get myself together. Mandy does crazy things to my head...and my heart. And I've never felt this level of passion for any woman I've dated in the past. She's like a drug. The good kind.

The healing kind...

With Aiden and Emily helping, we unload the centerpieces into their place in no time. Emily informs us that several people have been notified of canceled flights already, so they made the decision to pull the plug on the wedding. I can tell Emily is heartbroken, and Aiden is like a puppy dog trying to make her feel better.

After we say our goodbyes, I follow Mandy to her car. "Where are you going from here?"

"My condo to change into dry clothes and grab some things, and then Sally's. I'm going to stay with her and Jacob, since they're more inland than my condo."

"Good. Text me when you're settled, okay?"

A light rainfall is starting again.

"You, too. Tell Shannon and Eliana hello for me."

"I will. Or you could come with me and tell them yourself."

I didn't plan to ask Mandy to stay with us through the hurricane, and I'm pretty sure Shannon wouldn't mind, although my mother might be the killjoy in the scenario.

"I already told Sally I'd stay with them. I think she feels better knowing I'll be there."

He nods, then kisses me. "Then I will see you tomorrow after this is over."

I open her door, then head to my truck as she starts her car. The engine starts, sputters, then the whole car shakes before the engine cuts out.

Mandy opens her window as I head back toward her. "It's okay. It does this sometimes. Aunt Paula wasn't big on upkeep."

"I didn't realize this was her car."

She turns the engine over again. It sputters at first, then roars to life. "Yeah, she had it for years, and as long as I can remember, it always acted up when it rained. Something to do with the spark plugs, I think."

Now I'm concerned. "I'll follow you back to your condo and then drive you to Sally's myself."

She waves me off. "No, it'll be fine now." She pats the dashboard. "Old Betsy and I will be just fine."

"Old Betsy?"

"Aunt Paula's nickname for her car."

He shakes his head. "I see."

She lowers her voice to a whisper. "Personally, I would have gone with Clunker or Junk Heap, but I don't want to give her a complex."

I not only love Mandy, but I love her sense of humor, too. She has a way of making me laugh when I least expect it and at the most unexpected times. Like now.

Before she puts her window up again, I steal another kiss and then wave as she drives off before heading to my truck. Once inside, I check the status of the hurricane and see the projected path has shifted yet again and not in a good way. For the first time in close to fifty years, Sarabella will get a direct hit.

I don't know if Mandy knows this yet, and I don't want to tell her until I know she's safe at Sally's, who will probably tell her before I can. Still, I plan to call and check up on her and make sure she's safe.

But for now, I have to make way to my mother's trailer. Even though she's more inland, her mobile home isn't that new, so it won't hold up as well as the newer ones do. I'll do my best to board her place up and then get us both to Shannon's so I can make sure her place is secure, too.

I'm not looking forward to dealing with my mother, but maybe, just maybe, her disappointment in me won't be the topic of discussion for once.

GETTING my mother's place boarded up and secured took longer than I expected. Most of that time, she stayed inside packing a suitcase and gathering irreplaceable items, which of course included every picture she had of Devon. She didn't say much either when I loaded her bags and boxes into my truck. And now it's late afternoon, and we're heading to Shannon's in silence.

If you'd asked me yesterday if I preferred silence over my mother's passive-aggressive comments regarding my life, I would have said the former. But this…I think I'd rather she let her digs rip.

"How's that girlfriend of yours?"

Her sudden words startle me, causing my hands to jerk on the steering wheel. "Amanda is good."

"Is she someplace safe?"

"Uh, yeah, she's staying with some close friends." Frankly, I'm stunned by her concern. And pleased.

"That's good. She seems very nice."

"She is. Amazing, in fact."

I can feel my mother's eyes on me, causing me to cringe

inwardly as I wait for her to tell me how I'm not good enough for Mandy or something like that. "You care for her a lot, don't you?"

My hand running over my mouth makes a sandpaper like sound. "Yes, I do."

"Does she feel the same about you?"

I give her a quick glance. There's no frown, just honest curiosity. "I think so."

Mom nods, then turns her gaze out the windshield but says nothing more.

The sky is what I call grumpy. Not much different from what we see during the usual tropical thunderstorms that move through during rainy season, but it's temporary. In a few hours, the hurricane will be near land and start slamming us with growing winds and rain. That's the angry stage. Once Phillipe hits, that's full rage.

As I pull into Shannon's driveway, she runs out to the passenger side of the truck and opens the door for Mom. "Hi, Jackie. Why don't you go inside with Eliana, and I'll unload your things."

"I can take a bag." Mom slings her purse over her shoulder and gets out of the truck. Her ankle is healed, but she still has a small limp.

"No need. Kade and I have it covered."

Mom hesitates before heading to the front door where Eliana is standing.

Shannon grabs a box, while I grab the suitcase out of the back.

I give her a cursory look and lift my chin. "What's up with you?"

She shrugs. "Just trying to keep the peace. I know how tense things can be between you and your mother."

I follow Shannon up the walk, wheeling the suitcase behind me and carrying a smaller bag. "Mom was actually pleasant today."

Shannon waits for me to get closer. "Pleasant?"

"She asked me about Amanda."

"Asked what about Amanda?" Shannon looks about as stunned as I was.

"About our relationship and if she was someplace safe."

"What did you tell her?"

"That Amanda is staying with some close friends."

"No, about your relationship, you idiot." She gives me this incredulous stare, but I can tell she's trying not to smile.

If Shannon thinks we're going to have a conversation about my relationship with Mandy while a hurricane is bearing down on us, she's crazy.

"Nothing really." I move past her to the house, hoping she'll take the hint that the discussion is closed.

"Hey, I want to know what you told her. Did you tell her you love Amanda?"

I pause for a moment, then keep going.

Shannon's gasp comes from behind me. "You love her, don't you?"

Once inside, I stop and wait for her to come in. "Where do you want to put Mom's bag?"

"In Eliana's room. Elly will sleep with me. Are you going to answer my question?"

"Am I on the couch?"

"Yes. Still waiting." She crosses her arms.

I lug the suitcase into Elly's room and heft it onto the bed.

She puts her hands on her hips after she sets the box on the floor. "Are you ignoring me?"

In a grand gesture, I put my hands on my chest and fake a shocked expression. "Who me? Never. I'm just ignoring *your question*."

I leave the room and stride out the front door back to my truck. Shannon jogs out, which tells me this discussion won't end until I answer her, but I fully intend to make her jump through a few more hoops before I do.

Before she can reach me, I lift a box and stride past her.

Shannon rewards me with a growl but continues her dash to the truck. After depositing the box, I leave Elly's room, fully expecting to see Shannon en route with one of her own, but instead, she's standing in the truck bed, moving the boxes in back toward the tailgate.

As I get closer, she sits on the boxes, blocking me. The woman pulled my bluff.

I reach for a box, but she swats my hands away. "Not until you answer my question."

"No." I stand back and cross my arms. Two can play this game.

"No, won't answer my question, or no, you don't love Amanda?"

"The first one."

She jumps down from the truck with a cheeky grin. "I knew it!"

I growl, grab another box, and make my way back to Elly's room.

Shannon follows close behind and adds her box to the growing stack, then hugs me. "I'm so happy for you, Kade."

"What are you happy about?" My mother is standing in the doorway.

"Kade's in love." Shannon bounces on the front of her feet, looking more like Eliana than a grown woman.

I roll my eyes. So much for telling Mandy first. If it wasn't for a hurricane, I would have told her by now. Lord knows, I've imagined it in my mind at least a hundred times.

My mother gives the barest hint of a smile. "I figured that out the day I met her."

CHAPTER 30
Amanda

We're sitting around Sally's table, playing cards, when the lights flicker.

Sally looks up. "I guess we better get used to that."

I discard a card I know Jacob is just waiting to snatch up, which he does with a satisfied snicker.

"The generator is juiced and ready." He tosses a card onto the discard pile.

There's a bowl of pretzels on the table with my name on it, but I'm trying to resist. Once I start snacking during stressful situations, I turn into a voracious bear leaving hibernation. But bears don't wear bikinis, nor do they frequent the beach.

"Where's Zane?" I haven't seen him since he boarded up my shop and his condo is on the third floor of a building with a beach view. He pays a pretty penny for a place that isn't safe for hurricanes. Just my two cents there.

"He's staying with some friends from work. They're putting together care packages to deliver after the hurricane passes through." Sally takes a card from the deck and discards it.

"Wow, I'm impressed. I didn't know head lifeguards did that." I draw from the deck as well.

I'm one card away from winning Rummy, one gust of wind

away from devouring the bowl of pretzels, and one hurricane update away from hiding under the bed in the guest room. I've lived away from Florida for too long and have lost my devil-may-care attitude when it comes to hurricanes.

"Zane's added a lot of programs to the department."

I study my cards, mulling over which one I can live without the least. There's a stain on my ace of spades that reminds me of a mango. And that's when it hits me.

Where's the box with the rest of the glass mangos that Marnie dropped off? In all the chaos of finishing and delivering the first half of the mango order, and bringing the centerpieces to Emily, I totally lost track of that box.

"Oh, no…" I toss my cards down and run into my temporary bedroom to check the few boxes I brought with me.

Sally calls from the dining room. "What's up, Mandy? Are you okay?"

I return to the table. "I need to check my car for a box I'm missing."

Jacob stares up at me. "Can't it wait until this is over?"

"I don't know, maybe?" Not really, because I need to know. If I left that box at my shop, that's twenty-five glass mangos that could go down in a blaze of disaster. "How close is the hurricane?"

Jacob checks the app he's kept open on his phone. "We have a few hours before the full brunt of the storm hits us, but the winds are definitely picking up. Could be limbs on the roads already."

Sally glares at me. "You aren't seriously thinking about going out in this weather, are you?"

"For twenty-five glass mangos, yes, I am." I grab my cell phone and my keys. "I'll check my car first, but if it's not there, I'll drive over to the shop and come right back. Shouldn't take long."

Jacob pulls a rain jacket out of the coat closet. "It's big, but it'll help."

Sally shoots out of her chair. "Why are you helping her?"

He shrugs. "Because I know there's no talking her out of it."

"And how do you know that?"

He grins, which tugs up the corners of his mustache and beard. "Thirty-five years of marriage to you."

Sally rolls her eyes. "Fine. Get back here as fast as you can, okay?"

I pull on the raincoat and cinch everything as tight as I can and deposit my phone in a cavernous pocket. "Will do."

The rain pelts my hood as I leave the shelter of the house. I hold my hand above my eyes as a shield. The box isn't in my trunk, so I get in the front seat and crane around to look in the back. No box. I remember putting it in a cabinet in the back room when we needed every bit of countertop for the centerpieces.

I stare out the windshield, assessing the rain and the winds. Jacob said we had a few hours before the hurricane makes landfall. After a few more seconds to consider, I insert the key and start the engine. Old Betsy sputters at first but then roars to life.

The streets are mostly empty and covered with some debris already but nothing major. I make it to my shop easier than I expected and pull the car as close to the back steps as I can. Then comes the mustering of courage and the mad dash to the door. I feel like a drowned rat once I get inside and shake the rain off my hands and sleeves.

And step into a puddle of water.

"Oh, no."

Not just a small pool but a stream that's coming from the front. I tip-toe through the water to the front. Water is streaming in under the front door. The wind is blowing that direction and sending it through a small gap that the plywood isn't blocking.

"No, no, no...not my beautiful, new floor." Being careful not to slip, I run to the back and find as many rags as I can and then stuff them into the opening and pile several more behind to try to block it.

By now, a sheen of water covers the entire front of my store—and my brand new floor. I return to the back room in search of something more substantial that I can attach to the door, because the wind and rain are only going to get worse.

That's when I realize the water in the back room isn't actually all coming from the front. There's water dripping down one corner, puddling onto the counter and dripping down to the floor. Good thing I didn't leave those centerpieces here.

I want to cry, but there's no time. Insurance will take care of the damages. There's nothing I can do right now except get the mangos and get back to Sally's.

The box is exactly where I put it. I cover it with a plastic bag and get it into my car without getting too soaked again because of a lull in the downpour and the shop is blocking some of the wind.

At the first turn of the key, Old Betsy sputters. "Come on, girl. Don't let me down."

I try again multiple times, but the engine won't catch.

This can't be happening.

I rest my forehead against my hands on the steering wheel.

The ride over must have saturated the spark plugs. I reach into my oversized raincoat to pull out my cell phone, except it's not in the pocket I thought I put it in, or any of my other pockets. In all the excitement, did it fall out somewhere?

I check the floor of the car, and even the back seat in case it fell out when I leaned over, looking for the box. Then I check the trunk, the stairs up to the back door, and all over the shop.

No phone. It must have fallen out when I ran out to the car at Sally's place.

Landline.

I smack my head as I remember the shop has a landline. Most of the time, I have calls forwarded to my cell because the phone connection isn't very good. Old wiring and right up there with the leaky toilet on my list of things to fix in the place. I pick up the handset and hit the call button to check for a dial tone, but only static comes through.

"Oh, boy…" I'm a firm believer that there is always a solution, some kind of solution, to every problem. The key is to keep looking until you find it. This is no different, right?

I head back out to my car to see it's dried out a little with the lull between bands, but Old Betsy refuses. Maybe there's a patrol car doing a final check of the area. I stay close to the building and make my way against the wind to the front of the shop.

Nothing. Every shop is boarded up. No cars are on the road. Just a bunch of palm fronds and water filling the street. The wind shoves at my back as I return to my car and climb in.

For once in my life, I'm totally at a loss over what to do next.

CHAPTER 31
Kade

Over the last hour, I've texted Mandy several times, but her voicemail picks up every time. I'm trying not to imagine the worst, but it's getting harder not to. Reports have started to pour in about power outages along the coast and moving inland, which explains the power fluctuations here.

Shannon is doing a great job keeping Eliana distracted with coloring and fort building, while my mother keeps a steady stream of snacks going—her way of dealing with the stress of the situation. I don't want to take that relief away from her, so I keep eating even though I'm fuller than a whale in krill season.

I check the map again and see Sarabella is getting slammed by the edge of the hurricane. The storm may have knocked out cell towers, which could explain why she's not replying.

But I can't shake this feeling in my gut that something's wrong. I close the weather app and call Sally.

She picks up after one ring. "Kade, are you safe?"

"Yeah, I'm at Shannon's. We're good here so far. I told Mandy I would call and check on her, but she's not answering her cell phone."

"Hmm, that's not good. She left close to an hour ago to get the box of mangos she forgot at her shop."

"She what?!" My chest is so tight I'm struggling to breathe normally.

"I know. I tried to talk her out of it, but she was determined." Sally's concern amps mine up even more.

Jacob's voice sounds in the background. "I'll drive over and find her."

"Jacob will—"

"I heard. Let me know when she's back safely, okay?"

"I will." Sally ends the connection.

I'm sitting on the couch—aka, my bed for the night—staring at my phone and silently begging for a call or text to let me know Mandy's safe.

"Uncle Kade, are you okay?" Eliana sits and leans against me.

I drape an arm around her and tug her close. "Yeah, squirt, I'm okay. How's the fort?"

"It's amazing! You should come see." She's rubbing her fingers over the two days of whiskers covering my cheeks.

Shannon pads in and sits on the chair, then leans over. "Why are you staring at your phone?"

I let out a noisy breath and rub my face, wishing I'd remembered my shaver. "I'm waiting to hear that Amanda's safe. She went back to her shop to get something she forgot."

"She what? Is she nuts?" Shannon looks as concerned as I feel.

"She forgot the glass mangos. Jacob's driving over to check on her."

Shannon gives me a weak smile. "I'm sure she's fine. There's still time."

As I'm studying the hurricane on my weather app, my phone vibrates and shows Sally's number.

"Did Jacob find her?"

"No, he could only get to the end of our street. There's a tree down so he couldn't get out. And he found her cell phone on the driveway. It must have fallen out of her jacket when she ran out to her car." There's a warble to Sally's voice, like she's trying not to panic.

I run a hand through my hair. "Okay, I'm driving back. I'll get to her."

"Kade, the roads could be worse for you." Now Sally sounds almost frantic.

"I'll keep you posted." I end the call and grab my keys and wallet off the side table.

"Kade, what are you doing?" Shannon stands up in front of me. "You can't drive in this."

"Jacob is blocked in, and Amanda doesn't have her cell. The hurricane isn't near us yet, so I should be fine."

"But you'll be driving right into it when you reach Sarabella." She's standing with her hands on her hips, like a linebacker getting ready to head in for the tackle. "What about Zane? Isn't he closer? Can't you call him?" She's hovering over me as I put my shoes on.

"I'll try calling him from my truck."

"Why not call him first?"

"I need to go, Shannon." I stop and give her a pointed look I hope tells her she can't change my mind. I need to make sure Mandy's okay.

For myself.

She swallows whatever argument she had ready and nods. "Okay."

Since the front door is boarded, I have to go through the garage to the side door, which takes me past Eliana's room.

My mother is standing with her arms crossed as I approach the hallway to the garage. "Where are you going?"

"Amanda may be in trouble. I have to make sure she's okay." I clutch my keys and clench my jaw, waiting for her to tell me how irresponsible I'm being.

She drops her arms and then puts her hand on my cheek, over the scar. "Be careful."

"I will. I promise."

She gives me a tight smile as she drops her hand and pats my shoulder.

Rain pelts me as I run to my truck. The trees and palms turn into green blurs as my windshield wipers struggle to keep up, even at high speed. At this point, the roads are mostly clear. Just an occasional small branch or palm frond.

Yet I know the worst is yet to come as I get closer to Sarabella.

HEAVY WINDS and rain batter my truck as I reach Mango Lane, which is deserted and dark. The power grid must be down, but my headlights cut through the darkness as I make my way to the back of Mandy's shop. A large branch is lying across the hood of her car.

I pull in as close as I can, then make a run for the back door through the heavy downpour. Thankfully, the building is blocking some of the wind. The door is locked, so I start pounding and calling Mandy's name, but I can barely hear my own voice.

As I glance back at her car, I notice movement before the back seat window opens a crack. Mandy's eyes appear first, then more of her face as she opens the window a little more to call out to me.

After pulling my jacket up over my head, I jump down the steps to open her door. I have to get her out of here before more of that nearby oak blows down. "We have to get out of here!"

"The shop is flooded!"

I think she's crying, but it's hard to tell with the downpour.

"Come on, I'll get us someplace safe." I help her into my truck and then race around to the other side. The rain is getting heavier and the winds are picking up.

I'm soaked to the bone and almost shivering when I slide behind the wheel with a grunt.

"Can you get us to Sally's?" Mandy's voice shakes, but I'm unclear if that's because she looked like a drowned cat or she's scared. Maybe both.

And thinking of her being alone and frightened in the back seat of her car does something strange to my insides. The thought of her being in danger brings something primal up that I thought I'd kept secure in its own locker.

I start the engine. "No, they're blocked in by a tree."

"Are they okay?"

"They're fine. Just the street is blocked." I steer the truck toward my studio.

The rain is pelting harder now, making visibility difficult, and the short distance to my studio seems like miles. I park as close to the back as possible to afford some protection. "Stay in the truck until I get the door open enough to go in, okay?"

Mandy shivers and nods.

Once I pull up the door far enough to duck under, Mandy rushes by me, hunkered down. I follow her in and then secure the door again.

We both stand there dripping before I remember stashing a pair of jeans and a couple of shirts in one of the cabinets. I dig them out and pull out the blankets I use to protect pieces when I deliver them.

"These will help." I hand her the bigger of the shirts and a couple of blankets.

"I guess we're stuck here."

"Looks that way." I know I sound angry, but right now I'm barely holding myself together. The less I say, the better.

"I'm sorry. My car wouldn't start, and I lost my cell phone somewhere." She looks so scared and vulnerable.

I want to hold her but can't bring myself to move toward her. "Jacob found it on the driveway when he tried to find you."

"But the tree…"

"Yes, the tree." I shed my jacket and shirt and use a blanket to dry my head and chest while she ducks into the bathroom.

I go behind my workbench and change into the dry jeans, glancing at the bathroom door every so often as I wait for her to come out. I don't know if she's taking her time or hiding out because she's been in there a long time.

She finally comes out, shoulders slumped and sniffling. "I forgot the mangos. They're in the trunk of my car."

My fists are balled at my sides, and I'm clenching my jaw so hard I'm getting a headache. I'm like a pressure cooker that's about to blow. "You risked your life for a box of glass."

"That wasn't my intention." Her eyes are wide, like she's scared of me now.

In the past, when I got like this after Devon…I would walk it off. But there's no place to go at the moment, so I start pacing.

My entire body is wired with near-rage at this point. "I can't believe you thought it was that important."

"Marnie worked hard on those, and I didn't want to let my client down." She whispers this as she tucks her chin.

"She can remake them."

"I said I was sorry. Why are you so mad?"

"Because you could have been hurt. Or worse." I slam my hand down on the workbench as I say this.

She jumps and stares at me like a scared cat ready to bolt.

And I feel like a heel. I've turned into an uncontrollable jerk who's lashing out. "A car is no protection in a hurricane. What if the rest of that tree landed on top of your car before I got there?"

"I didn't think about that."

"I wouldn't have been able to do anything to save you! Just like Devon—all I could do was hold him as he—"

She cringes and I realize I'm yelling. And not only am I yelling, I've blurted out the one detail about Devon's death that I swore never to share.

That I watched him die because I couldn't save him.

Mandy runs into the bathroom and slams the door.

As a clap of thunder makes the building shake, I'm shaking too, because the full reality of what could have happened hits me.

That I could have lost Mandy.

Just like I lost Devon.

CHAPTER 32
Amanda

I'm embarrassed, mortified, and hiding in a bathroom. Kade is right. Going out in a hurricane to rescue a box of glass mangos—idiotic. Putting Jacob at risk in his attempt to find me—thoughtless. Jeopardizing Kade's life as he drove all the way back, directly into a hurricane—irresponsible and senseless.

How could I be so foolish and stupid? I've been so caught up in making the shop a success—making sure I'm a success—that I totally lost sight of what matters.

Really matters.

Sasha's words come flooding back. I did succeed. I did reach my goal. I did everything I set out to do. Yet I still felt like I had to keep proving myself.

Why?

To prove I could make the shop a success? I did that in spades.

To prove I could create something unique that people wanted? The glass mangos more than proved that.

To prove that I wasn't a screwup like my mother, who settled for something that only resembled her dream?

The realization hits me so hard, I can't bring myself to leave the bathroom and face Kade.

What if something happened to him? I would have felt responsible for taking him away from his mother, Shannon, and especially Eliana.

I shed my wet clothes and pull Kade's T-shirt over my head. The spicy scent of juniper mixed with metal floods my senses—things I've come to associate with him. As ashamed as I feel at this moment, I can't stop thinking about how he risked his life.

For me.

The shirt fits me like a short dress, but I wrap myself in the blanket he gave me. Time to face the raging winds and thunder waiting on the other side of the bathroom door.

After a deep breath, I crack open the door and peek out.

Kade is sitting at his workbench, elbows on the table, with his head in his hands.

I pad out, tugging the blanket tighter around me.

When he lifts his head, I'm wrecked. His expression is so heavy, almost tortured, that I can't help but run over to him.

"I'm so sorry. I was foolish and reckless." Something in my heart snaps at the sight of him this way. I hold his head as my thumb swipes over the scar on his cheek.

And he crushes me against him and just holds me. And I hold on to him. He's still shirtless, so I can feel the muscles of his back rippling under my hands. And he's shaking like I am.

He buries his face against my neck as he continues to hold me. Ragged at first, his breathing slows down. "I'm sorry I got upset."

"I deserved it."

His head snaps up. "No, you didn't. I let my fear take over. I'm sorry."

"It's okay. I understand."

He cups my face with his hands. "I don't think I could survive losing you, Mandy."

And I see it in his eyes—the pain he's carried for so long. "Because of Devon."

He swallows and nods.

I touch the scar on his face again. "Tell me what happened."

It's more of a question than a command because I don't want him to feel pressured, but something in my gut says he needs to do this, needs to finally release the trauma of that day.

He tucks his chin. "Not much to tell. The car didn't see us. Hit Devon first and knocked him and his bike into me. He got the worst of it."

"I can't imagine how horrible it must have been."

"I remember waking up and being confused at first. Everything hurt and there was blood in my eyes. Then I saw him lying there. I called out to him but he didn't move." His voice is rough and pained as he lifts his head. "When I got to him, he stared at me with this panicked look in his eyes, but I didn't know what to do to save him. I just held him as he—"

I wrap my arms around Kade and hold him as tears stream down my face for him. The pain emanating from him is almost tangible, but I can't help but think—and hope—that he's feeling some release by sharing it.

His chest expands against me as he takes a deep breath before leaning back. His expression appears more relaxed now, but he looks haggard. "I've never told anyone about that."

"Not even your mother?"

He shakes his head. "Or Shannon. I couldn't put them through that pain."

"But you carried it alone for so long…Kade, I'm so sorry you went through that."

Something fires in his eyes, like the first burst of flame from his blowtorch. He puts his hand behind my head and pulls me closer, staring into my eyes like they hold the answers he's searching for.

And I want to be that answer for him in the worst possible way.

I'm so overwhelmed at the moment that I have to look away.

He uses his other hand to lift my chin. "What's wrong?"

I search his eyes, enchanted by that blasted freckle again. "I can't believe you came for me."

His eyes widen slightly. "How could I not?"

I let myself melt into him as he kisses me. His desire is evident, but there's more. He's gentle, caring…loving.

In all my life, I don't think I've ever felt so cherished and wanted.

Then he moves away from me, silent and contemplative, as he pulls on a T-shirt.

I feel the loss of his arms around me as if I were back out in the hurricane, alone and afraid. But I can tell Kade is still processing—needs space.

He walks the perimeter of the shop, checking who knows what, and studying his cell. "The towers are down now, too. We'll have to wait it out."

Once he finishes the full circuit of the room, he crouches in front of the mini fridge sitting next to the back counter. "I have a few snacks and drinks."

After some rummaging, he stands and brings an armful of items to the workbench, where he sets them down one by one.

He lets out a weak chuckle when he puts down a can of A&W Root Beer.

I pick it up. "I've always wanted to ask you why you called me Root Beer in high school."

His expression appears surprised. "A and W. Amanda Wilde."

I tip my head down and look up at him through my lashes. "My initials? That's how you got that?"

"Yeah, I thought you understood that."

"No, I just thought you were unoriginal."

He grunts at me.

"Seriously, why did you decide to pick on me?"

"I wasn't picking on you."

"Sure felt like it."

He opens two snack packages of sliced cheese and salami and spreads the contents on a paper towel. "I was trying to help."

Suddenly famished, I grab several pieces of food. And the water bottle sitting next to the root beer. I've never been a fan of root beer and since high school, had an aversion to it.

"Help? More like annoy me."

"I was trying to redirect those other idiots making fun of you. I thought maybe if my nickname—"

"Bullying." I'm teasing him at this point and notice the side of his mouth under the dimpled scar go up a tick.

"If my *teasing* you could shift their attention, they'd stop tormenting you about your mother being…"

"A porn star?"

He hesitates, then nods. "Yeah."

My heart is clenching in my chest. He was looking out for me even back then? "You did that for me?"

He shrugs. "Yeah. I'm sorry it backfired and made you think I was bullying you."

Kade's watching me with this uncertain expression that makes me want to smooth my hands over his face and make all the tension, grief, and pain go away. He's fast becoming one of the kindest, most caring men I've ever met.

I open the can of root beer and take a sip. "I think this is my new favorite beverage."

SLEEPING on a bathroom floor is definitely my idea of roughing it. As I wake, the first thing I note is how hard the floor is. The second thing I notice is how quiet things are.

After the raging winds of the hurricane died down some, Kade made a pallet for me on the bathroom floor since, according to him and his past experience in construction, it was under a load-bearing wall. Meanwhile, he slept under his workbench, which he described as being as solid as a rock against anything that may come falling down. I fell asleep watching the rise and fall of his chest slow through the doorway, and now I'm watching him again as he sleeps.

And I'm torn. Torn between my growing feelings for this man, who not only looked out for me in high school—big shocker there to find out the bully I loathed turned out to be a good guy—and braved a hurricane to come find me, and the dream of my future that I've held tight for so long.

That is until Aunt Paula threw a wrench in the works of my plans by dying and leaving me her shop, which after last night, will probably need another new floor and drywall. The furniture inside may have to be replaced as well.

Basically, I'll be starting over.

Again.

I close the door so I can get dressed. My clothes are dry for the most part, but I opt to keep Kade's T-shirt on. When I open the door, he's leaning against the workbench with his arms crossed.

As I walk out, he walks past me, brushing his hand against mine, then heads into the bathroom. I feel a breeze on my cheek and turn toward the roll-up door that's now open.

Debris is everywhere.

Small branches, leaves, and palm fronds cover Kade's truck. Nothing major, just a mess.

I want to check on my shop, but not without Kade. My gut says I may need some protection for that venture, so I go back toward the workbench to see if there's anything suitable left for a makeshift breakfast.

When he walks out, I can tell he's washed his face and tried to tame the mess of dark hair on his head with some success. He hasn't shaved in several days, which just makes him look more rugged. Almost menacing.

A Maverick Menace with a heart of gold that makes me

want to melt on the spot. But I can tell by his expression that he's still processing and somewhat closed off.

"Let's go check on your shop."

I follow him as he walks out the back and rolls the door back down.

He looks at his truck and then studies the surrounding area. "Let's walk."

I can only nod because my nervousness about seeing my shop has stolen my voice.

As we turn the corner, my first view sucks my breath away. The large oak that was behind my shop somehow seems closer than it should be. I walk faster and break into a run. Kade's footsteps sound behind me, which I find comforting to some degree.

But nothing can prepare me for the destruction.

The tree is closer because it's now part of my shop. Or what's left of my shop, because it basically looks like it's crumbled in on itself.

I can't move. I can't speak. I can't even process it all.

Only that my shop—and all the years my Aunt Paula poured into the place—is now a mess of broken wood and mangled shingles.

Kade is heading around to the back, so I follow him again through a blur of tears. As I turn the corner, I see what has him paused and unmoving.

The root ball of the tree is exposed and sits taller than Kade. The top of the tree covers what's left of my shop. And the trunk…the trunk crushed my car.

If Kade hadn't come…

I can't speak, can't think, can't breathe.

Kade holds his hand out. "Do you have your keys?"

"Yeah, why?" With a shaking hand, I dig them out of my pocket and set them in his outstretched hand.

He opens the trunk of my car and lifts out a box.

The glass mangos.

I want to go inside and see if there's anything salvageable, but I'm sure that would just be plain stupid, so I resist. Besides, what the tree didn't destroy, the rain probably did. The furniture inside, the new floor, the rest of my inventory and plants—all destroyed, I'm sure.

Kade puts the box down and holds me as I sob against him. Everything I've worked for is gone.

My shop is gone.

Which means there's nothing to sell.

Which means there's nothing keeping me in Sarabella anymore.

Which means I could go back to New York.

But then there's Kade, who's made it clear he cares about me, but we haven't had time to figure out if this thing between us is built to last or is as fragile as those glass mangos, which made it through the hurricane just fine.

Unlike my car or my shop.

Perhaps the hurricane blew away any possible future with Kade, too.

CHAPTER 33
Kade

After I pull into Shannon's driveway, I cut the engine and sit in my truck. In silence.

On the outside, I look fine, but inside I'm still shaking. From rage, from fear, from almost losing Mandy. I'm not entirely sure, to be honest, because Devon's death is very much a part of the mix.

Right now, that's overshadowing everything I feel for her, which makes me feel very inadequate, and Mandy deserves so much more.

I close my eyes and let my head fall back on the headrest. Until I knew the storm had passed, I kept alert in case anything major happened. But even after the winds died down and the downpour lightened to a steady fall, I only dozed, acutely aware that Mandy slept only a few feet away.

Even though I'm beyond exhausted, I don't think I could sleep because my mind keeps replaying what happened at my shop. The way I acted and the things I said.

I still can't believe I let the part about Devon's death slip out like that. But maybe it was time.

Time to release it and let go of the past. The pain is deep but somehow a relief, too.

But I still can't shake the image of Mandy's car…

I get out of the truck and go back into the garage to find my tools. Once I get the plywood off of Shannon's windows, I'll take Mom to her place to see what condition her trailer is in. I'm not sure what to expect there. I can only hope she has a home still.

As I remove the panel from the front door, Shannon opens it and hands me a cup of coffee. "Figured you might need this."

"Thanks."

She crosses her arms over her FRIENDS T-shirt as she studies me. "We still don't have power, but I'm firing up the grill out back to make eggs and bacon."

"Sounds good."

Her expression is a mix of anger and concern. "You know, you really freaked your mother out last night."

"Add that to my list of failures." I hear the edge to my voice. Yeah, I'm salty today, in more ways than one. I need a shower, a shave, and about twelve hours of sleep, but it's the best I can do at the moment.

"What failures, Kade?"

I drain the cup and hand it back to her. "Never mind."

She follows me to the window. "You didn't fail at anything."

I snort. "My mother would tell you otherwise. I'm sure she gave you an earful after I left last night."

"No, it wasn't like that. She was worried." She pauses. "She cried a lot."

My hand stills and the power wanes in the drill I'm holding as I let up on the trigger. I'm sure I'll get my share of the earful when I take her home. I start the drill again.

"Is Amanda okay?"

"She's fine, but her shop was destroyed." I leave out the part about the tree that destroyed her shop also crushed the car I found Mandy hunkered down in.

As I pull the plywood panel away from the front window,

Eliana's face grins at me through the glass. I wave at her. "Hey, squirt."

Shannon follows me again to the side of the house. "What's she going to do?"

"I don't know."

"Do you think she'll rebuild it?"

"I don't know."

She hesitates. "Do you think she'll go back to New York?"

I drop my arm, knocking the side of the drill against my leg. "I don't know, okay? I don't know what she wants or if it's me she even wants. I haven't a clue what she's going to do."

"Did you even ask her?" Shannon's not one to back off, but I can tell she won't take much more from me.

I pinch the bridge of my nose and force my anger down. "No. She was too upset from seeing that the tree that fell on her shop also crushed her car. Which is where I found her, by the way."

She moves closer and puts her hand on my shoulder. "Then you saved her, Kade."

"Just barely." Emotions I'm not ready to share thicken my voice.

"But you did. And you tried to save Devon. I know you well enough to know you did everything you could."

It's not like this is the first time Shannon's told me this. But it's the first time that it doesn't feel like a dagger hitting me square in the gut. I knew all along she was right, but somehow, now, I can accept it.

I nod. "I did. Just wish I could have done more."

"I know. I miss him, too. Every day and every time I look at his daughter."

Her words make me smile. "She's a terrific kid. A lot like her father."

She hugs me. "And her uncle."

Shannon heads back into the house as I finish removing the plywood from the rest of the windows and sliding doors. The house is small, so it doesn't take long. After we eat, I haul the plywood back into her garage and tuck it into a back corner for the next time a hurricane comes our way. Hopefully not soon.

Before I pack up my tools, I do a walk around the house to assess any damage to the roof and structure, but the house appears solid and weathered the storm well.

I wish I could say the same about Mandy and me.

As we pull into the trailer park, my mother gasps. The sign near the entrance is blown over and several of the homes we pass have sustained various states of battering. The oldest mobile homes show the most damage, with corners of roofs peeled back and carports blown down.

But Mom's seems in pretty good shape. Once I park, she gets out and rushes to her front door and goes inside. I grab my tools from the back and put them by the steps.

She pokes her head out. "Everything seems fine in here. No water damage. No power though."

"That will take a day or two. Do you want me to take you back to Shannon's?"

She scans the rest of her neighborhood. "No, I'll be fine. My neighbors may need help."

I grab her suitcase and bag. "Don't over do. Your ankle is still weak."

After I put her bags in her bedroom and bring in the rest of her boxes, my mother sits on the couch and pats the spot next to her.

"Kade, I need to talk to you."

Inside, I'm groaning, because here it comes. The guilt trip. I'm sure she has lots to say. I stay where I'm standing. "What, Mom?"

She gives me a watery smile. "Please?"

I nod and sit down, staring at my hands clasped and hanging between my knees.

"I'm sorry." Her voice is quiet.

I lift my head to stare at her. That I didn't expect. At all. "For what?"

"For doubting that you did everything you could to save Devon." She sniffs and runs her fingers under her teary eyes. "When you left last night, I was so scared. And then I started to get mad. But then I realized that there was no way you could stay, knowing Amanda was in trouble."

"No, I couldn't."

"You love her, don't you?"

The lump in my throat is as big as my clenched fists. "Yes, I do."

She puts her hand on my forearm. "I know now you did everything you could to save your brother. I'm so sorry I doubted you."

This…this I never expected. And her words release a dam I'd carefully patched over the years. At first, I'm so overwhelmed I can't speak, but as the flood clears, I feel like I can breathe again—I mean, really fill my lungs with the sweet air of freedom I'd imagined for so long.

And then I exhale and give her a shaky grin. "Thank you, Mom. That means a lot."

She smiles and nods. "Good." She takes a deep breath and gives my arm a double pat. "Now, let's get those boards down so you can get back to Sarabella. And Amanda."

I stand and start for the door.

"I really like her, you know. I hope things work out between you two." Mom smiles at me like she used to years ago.

A vise clamps my chest. "Me, too."

CHAPTER 34
Amanda

"It's gone? Completely gone?" Sasha is near tears as I tell her the news. "No more little plants in hand-painted pots...or fall decorations...or cute little bowties and fuzzy collars for puppies and kitties?"

"Only what I managed to pack up and bring to my condo. I'm sure there's not much left to salvage of the rest. I can't go in until they get the tree cut down."

I think I cried out every tear I could against Kade's chest before we went back to free his truck of debris and find a way to Sally's. Jacob, bless his big heart and his bushy beard, dried my phone carefully and made sure there was no damage. Thank goodness for water-resistant cell phones and durable cases.

People must have started cleaning up at the break of dawn because there were already piles of branches forming along the street and the sounds of chainsaws grinding away came from every direction.

Jacob started tackling the tree that blocked their street at the first light of dawn, so we were able to get by. Once Kade knew I was safe with Sally, he gave me a hug and left to go check on his mother, Shannon, and Eliana.

I know he had to go and make sure they were safe, since cell service is still spotty, and he wasn't able to get through to them this far from the inland. But I'm like a sailboat without a keel, listing from side to side.

But no kiss? Just a hug…

I feel lost…directionless. I'm not sure what to do now that my shop is totaled, and now that things with Kade have turned more serious, I'm not sure how objective I can be.

"Yep. Pretty much. I'll know more over the next few days."

"What are you going to do?"

I hear the hesitation in Sasha's voice. Her way of being delicate, which is so not her norm.

"I have no idea. I'll have to wait and see if the insurance will cover rebuilding the shop, I guess. I've never had to deal with a hurricane like this before. It may take a while."

"How about I come down and help you? I can catch the next flight out—"

I hold my hand up. "As much as I'd love to have you here, Sasha, I don't even know what help I need yet. But thank you."

"Well, in that case, why don't you come back here and take a break? Give yourself some time to think and reorganize."

My first reaction is that I can't do that, but the more I think about it, the more the possibility grows. "I'll think about it."

"Good. The trees are still changing colors, so we could take a trip upstate like we used to." She's so hopeful looking I may start crying again.

Just the thought of seeing all those colors is a salve to my broken spirit. "Let me get the ball rolling here, and I'll let you know."

Sasha claps her hands softly. "Great. Talk soon!"

I slump back on the guest room bed and drop my phone, then pick it up again to call Kade. But I stop myself. He has enough on his hands right now, making sure his family is safe. And I'm sure his mother will want to check on her trailer. I say a silent prayer that it's still there.

Should I send a quick text to tell him I'm thinking about

him? Or will that make me appear clingy? I already carry the titles of thoughtless and reckless at this point. I really don't need another one.

A knock on the door halts my texting thoughts.

"Come in."

Sally pokes her head in. "Are you hungry? I'm trying to open the fridge as little as possible until the power is back, so tell me if you need something from that department. Pantry is up for grabs."

I shake my head. "Thanks, but I'm not hungry. I'll stick with room temp if I need something."

She studies me through her slow nod before stepping into the room. "Everything's going to be okay."

I try to smile. "Kade said that, too."

"He's a smart guy."

I give her a wry grin. "He said that before the hurricane demolished my shop. And my car."

She holds her hands out to her sides. "Then he has a heart of gold and the best of intentions."

"That he does. He saved my life." I glance to the side as my thoughts fill with his image. The way he showed up at my shop last night. The way he huddled me into his truck and brought me to safety. The way he looked shirtless and angry…

If only I could harness the electricity that memory shoots through me to cook us all a hot meal. As if…

"And I will forever love that man for doing so."

I want to say, 'Me too,' but that would make it way too real, and I'm not ready for that…yet.

Sally sits on the bed in front of me and takes my hand. "Whatever you need, Jacob and I are here. And Zane. We'll help you rebuild and get back on your feet in no time."

I nod and shrug. "I love that, but I'm not sure I can do it."

"Hey, you're not in this alone, remember?"

"I know. It's just that…" I pause, searching for the right

words. "I'm tired, Sally. I worked so hard to get that place going, and going well. Despite raccoons and cockroaches."

She blurts out a short laugh as I snort.

"But I don't know if I have it in me to start all over. This wasn't my dream. It was Aunt Paula's."

A brief flash of pain in her expression gives me a glimpse of how much she misses Aunt Paula, too. "I know. She only ever wanted what was best for you."

"I know, but I *don't* know if I'm meant to be in Sarabella. I feel like everything—the universe, God, whatever—is trying to tell me I don't belong here. I never felt like I did, to be honest."

"Why?"

I give her a look that screams, 'You know why.'

Sally exhales noisily. "Don't let your mother's past determine yours. Or your future, for that matter. Mandy, you are your own person. The past only has as much control over your future as you let it."

Wise words, for sure. I drop my gaze as I contemplate what they mean.

For me.

She releases my hand. "What about Kade?"

"What about him?"

"I thought you two were really hitting it off."

"We are. At least, we did." Hunched over, I tuck my chin. "I don't know now. He was pretty mad at me for risking my life for a box of mangos."

"Now there's a line you don't hear every day."

"I'm serious. He was livid." I sit up straight with my hands out as if to push away her disbelief.

Sally rolls her eyes, which almost makes me laugh because she always hated when I did that as a teenager. "Because he's in love with you, hon."

"Maybe. But I don't know if that's enough." I peek up through hooded eyes to gauge Sally's reaction.

"I know. Your dream is in New York."

"Right."

She tilts her head and squints her eyes. "But is it?"

Her question startles me, mainly because she's not Sasha. "What do you mean?"

She looks thoughtful for a moment. "Sometimes dreams change and that's okay. They're not set in stone. Dreams have a life of their own and if we hold on too tight, we run the risk of missing an opportunity that could reveal an even better dream than the one we're so determined to keep."

Her words remind me of what Sasha said, but I still feel some resistance deep in my heart. "My roommate suggested I go back and take a break while things get sorted out with my shop."

"That might be a good idea."

"Might?"

"Just think about it first. Maybe let the dust settle for a few days. You and Kade could spend some time together, too."

I nod but stay silent as Sally leaves the room.

As much as I want to spend time with Kade, I'm afraid to. What if my feelings for him influence my decision about going back to New York?

Aunt Paula did fine as a single woman. She ran her shop and had a full—albeit brief—life. She was happy—at least, I think she was. And she lived every day the way she thought best without having to compromise.

I know I love Kade, but I can't give up my dream because that would be settling for something less, like my mother did.

Wouldn't it?

CHAPTER 35
Amanda

I wake up at dawn the next morning and all I can think about is my shop. The gnawing in my gut wakes me faster than the coffee I'm craving, so I throw off the covers and get dressed. Surely by now, I can get a closer look at what's left. The rains have stopped and the streets are mostly cleared.

The house is quiet as I leave and drive over to Mango Lane. Sally graciously loaned me her car to do whatever I need. Even though I've already seen my shop demolished under that huge oak, I'm still not prepared for the gut punch of seeing it again.

Or seeing Kade there, taking down the plywood from the front door.

I stop at the bottom of the steps and holler over the sound of his drill. "Hi!"

The drill stops as he whips around. "Hey there."

The temperature is still cooler than normal from the residual clouds left over from the hurricane, so I tuck my hands into the pockets of my hoodie. "What are you doing?"

He lifts the drill. "Un-boarding your shop." He says this like it should be obvious to me.

"I know that, but why?"

"So you can get a better look at what you're dealing with."

I hunch my shoulders to my ears as I tuck my chin. My eyes are burning and I really don't want to subject Kade to more of my tears. "It really doesn't matter."

He puts the drill down and comes down the stairs. "Sure it does. Once your insurance kicks in, you can rebuild and start fresh."

I love his positivity, but right now, it feels more like a crushing weight of discouragement. "What if I don't want to, Kade?"

"But I thought you couldn't sell it unless you ran it for a year."

I hold my hand out at the mess behind him, unable to contain my sarcasm. "In case you didn't notice, there's nothing left to sell."

"Not yet, but there will be after you rebuild and get things going again. You still have plenty of time."

My shoulders drop as I exhale the last of my strength. I close the gap between us and put my hand on his chest. "I love that you think it's that simple, but for me…for me, it's just not worth it. I have a call in with my aunt's lawyer to find out what the legal requirements are."

He puts his hand over mine. "Don't give up, Mandy. What you did with the shop in such a short time was amazing. And how you helped other artists get their work seen. You can do this."

I give him a watery smile. "But I don't know if I want to."

He nods, but I don't miss the way the muscle in his jaw pulses.

Or the coolness settling between us, and I'm not talking about the air.

"Once the airport is up and running again, I think I'm going back to New York for a while so I can think and clear my head." I'm literally making this decision as I share it with Kade. Part of me feels relieved that I'm leaving, yet another part feels like I'm tucking my tail and making a run for it.

"How long will you be gone?"

"I don't know yet. I'm sure I can deal with a lot of this from up there, but I'll have to fly back at some point to deal with Aunt Paula's condo."

The way he drops his chin and makes his mouth this flat line chips at the numbness that's been seeping in since last night. I put my hand against his cheek with my thumb over his scar. More than anything, I want to see him smile and flash that dimple again.

"I'm not leaving yet."

He lifts his head, green eyes flashing with a mix of longing and disappointment, then it's as if the light fades from his gaze. "I think you've already left, Mandy."

My heart twists into a knot so tight I can hardly breathe.

Kade vaults up the steps, puts his drill away, and picks up his toolbox. As he's about to pass me, he stops and kisses me on the cheek.

"Take care of yourself up there, Root Beer." He strides to his truck and drives off.

The air feels colder now. I walk up the steps, ready to unlock the door and inspect what's left inside.

"I wouldn't do that if I were you." Zane's walking up the path to my shop with Sarabella Lifeguard emblazoned across his shirt.

"You're not actually on beach duty, are you?"

"You'd be surprised how many people want to head out to the beach and see what it looks like. Lots of big shells get washed up."

"Is the beach open again?"

"No, but they still try." Zane chuckles dryly.

I glance back at my shop. "I was curious if there was anything left that was salvageable."

"You should wait until the structural engineers assess the area. Even Mom's shop sustained some damage."

Now I feel like a major heel. "I didn't even ask her about her shop." I wave back at mine. "I was too preoccupied with my own misery."

Zane draws me in for a hug. "I'm sure she understands."

I step back. "I told Kade I'm going back to New York for a while. I need to clear my head and figure out what to do."

He lifts his chin, then drops it. "That explains the way he drove off."

"You saw that, huh?"

"Yeah. He's hurt."

I can't stop the tears now. "I know. I never meant to cause him pain, but I never planned to stay, Zane."

"I know. He knows it, too. Doesn't make it any less difficult. Trust me, I know."

"Is that what happened between you and Callie?"

"Something like that."

We both sigh.

He holds out his hand. "Give me your keys. I'll look after things here for you, so you can think or do whatever you need."

I take the shop key off the ring and drop it into his hand.

"Hey, do you recognize what this key might go to?" I hold up that key I've yet to find a home for.

Zane leans in closer. "Nope, doesn't look familiar."

I tuck my hand back and study it again for myself. "I searched the shop and Aunt Paula's condo twice, but I can't find what it belongs to."

"Any thoughts about what you'll do with the condo?"

"You interested?" I laugh for the first time in what feels like days.

He smiles, flashing me a set of perfect white teeth offset by his lifeguard tan. If Zane were a player, he'd have an unlimited supply of dates, but in all the years I've known him, he's never dated that much. I'm guessing that may have a lot to do with Callie. Part of me wants to stay in Sarabella just to see that play out.

"No, just wondering."

"I don't really know. I'm not sure about anything at the moment." I pocket the rest of the keys.

He rests his hand on my shoulder. "You'll figure it out, Mandy. You always do."

Maybe.

I just know I can't do that here right now.

After Zane leaves, I pull out my phone to call Sasha. As soon as her face shows on the screen, she blurts out, "When are you arriving?"

My best friend/roommate knows me well. "I'll let you know as soon as I can book a flight."

"Good." Sasha tilts her head. "Should I ask if you're okay?"

"Not yet."

"Understood. See you soon."

I end the call and walk back to Sally's car. Part of me wants to drive over to Kade's shop and try to smooth things over between us, but being as I'm unsure what's really between us, I don't see the point.

And I don't want to hurt him any more than I already have. So, hello again, my old friend New York.

And goodbye Sarabella. For now…

CHAPTER 36
Kade

The hurricane stalled much of the construction in the area, including the builder I've been doing metalwork for. With those projects on hold for now, I've wound up with free time on my hands. So I volunteered with the team Zane spearheaded to help with clean up. Seeing several of our old construction friends has been great, too.

Because I need a distraction.

Knowing Mandy is in New York is killing me. I can't stand the idea of not having her in my life, so I've chosen not to think about it. Yeah, it's a pathetic solution, but it's the only one I have at the moment.

Except for today.

Today Shannon and Eliana are coming to spend the day with me. And they're bringing my mother so she can see my shop. She's never once even asked about what I do, and now she wants to see my work for herself.

They say every storm cloud has a silver lining. For me, it seems Hurricane Phillipe's was my mother's shift in attitude.

I'm not complaining. Quite the opposite. I'm still trying to wrap my brain around it though. Even Shannon has noticed the change in her.

When they arrive, I show Mom around my shop, giving her some brief explanations of what a metalsmith does, and the work I'm doing under contract for the builder I'm working with.

She seems impressed and surprised at the same time.

"Your work is beautiful, Kade. I didn't realize…" Her voice trails off and she gives me a hopeful smile as if to apologize but also to say, 'Let's not fight about it.'

Not that I would. Although, I will admit, my first thought was a retort. Glad I kept that one to myself. This whole getting along thing will take time, but our relationship is healing. Finally.

"Uncle Kade, what's this box for?"

I turn around to where Elly is standing by the back counter. She pokes at the metal box I found during the clean-up around Bloomed to Be Wilde.

Mandy's shop…

"That belongs to Amanda. The tree that blew over onto her roof collapsed the ceiling. It must have been in the attic."

Shannon touches the lock. "Does she know you found it?"

"No, not yet."

"Why don't you go to New York and take it to her?"

Shannon must be nuts.

I shake my head. "Not a good idea."

"Why?"

"It's just not. She'll be back at some point, most likely to sell her condo, I'm sure. I'll give it to Zane, and he can get it to her." For me, the subject is closed, but I can see by Shannon's expression that the discussion is far from over.

But what I don't expect is pushback from my mother.

"Kade, why are you running away?" She's questioning me with her eyes, too.

I hold my hands out to my sides. "I'm not the one running away."

"Yes, I agree. Amanda is running back to New York, but that doesn't mean you have to run away from your feelings for her."

I send a pleading glance for rescue Shannon's way, but she's standing there with this expression of agreement on her face as she watches Mom and me volley back and forth. At least we're not arguing.

"Mom, we said our goodbyes. It's done. She'd rather be in New York and my life is here." Besides, Eliana is my priority now. She needs a father figure in her life—full-time, not long-distance.

"Then move to New York." Mom holds her hands up, showing her frustration.

"I can't."

"Why not?"

I cross my arms and lean against the workbench. Time to be honest and lay my cards on the table. "I need to be around for you guys." I lower my voice so the squirt won't hear where she's coloring at her miniature worktable. "Especially for Eliana."

Shannon jumps in. "Kade, we're fine. And New York is a short flight."

"It's not the same." I push away from the bench and turn around.

"You're right, it's not the same as having her father here."

"That's not what I meant." I spin back around. This discussion is getting way too deep.

"Isn't it though? It's like you've locked yourself away from the world to keep punishing yourself for Devon's death. It's time you start living again, Kade."

Her locker analogy hits so close to home it hurts. The welds on those doors are growing weaker and weaker.

Mom pulls my head down to kiss my scarred cheek. "Go after her, son. You deserve to be happy."

CHAPTER 37
Amanda

Being back in New York is...familiar. Don't get me wrong. It feels great to be back, but something's different. In the short time I've been here, Sasha and I have spent three days exploring upstate New York and I have close to a hundred new pictures on my phone of mountainsides covered in shades of red, orange, and yellow; hay bales and cornstalks arranged with pumpkins in various shapes and sizes; and stops for hot cider and an unexpected yet brief snow flurry.

All in all, a great visit so far...

But that's what it feels like—a visit.

The roots I planted here over ten years ago seem to have meandered their way to Sarabella, and it's just today that I'm realizing this.

But I could be wrong, couldn't I?

"What has you so knotted up today?" Sasha somehow slipped into the chair across from me at our tiny kitchen parlor set without me noticing.

I blink and shake my head. The coffee cup I'm holding is noticeably cool and so is my mood, it seems.

"Nothing. Just nervous about this job interview."

"It's not an interview. You're just going to see your old boss, who made it clear you have a job there anytime you want. And I can tell you firsthand he's very interested."

I shrug. "I know. But that art show was weeks ago. You know this business. Something could have changed since then."

Sasha gives me this incredulous look. "Amanda, if he was that positive about having something for you even after you'd been gone for two months, I'm sure he still feels the same after a few more weeks."

"True." But then there's my lack of excitement. Sure, this could wind up being the same assistant job as before, or it could be an accounts manager position where I'll get to call the shots.

Much like I did in my shop…

Maybe once I get there and talk to Daniel, walk around the place, and hear what he has to say, my creative juices will start marching again, and I'll know my next step for my future.

Which may or may not include Kade…

That's the other weight hanging around my heart at the moment. He hasn't texted me at all since I left, but I haven't texted him either.

I think he made his goodbye pretty clear during our last encounter, and perhaps that's part of what's driving me to go to this interview—despite what Sasha says, I know Daniel and this will most definitely still be a job interview—to help me decide if I really want to rebuild my life in New York.

Because the thought of being in Sarabella holds all kinds of appeal, but if Kade's not part of it, I'm not sure I could stand being there with the constant reminders of what we shared.

I'm not sure about much right now, except that I have to do something. At least in New York, I have a potential job, a decent place to live, and my best friend.

What more do I really need?

"And this would be your office." Daniel gestures to the tiny space that used to be the copier/break room. A decent desk sits in the middle, and two bookshelves bracket a small window that looks out over an alley. At least there's some natural light.

I step in and try to imagine myself here.

"I know it's small, but we just negotiated a lease for the floor above us, so as soon as that's completed, my plan is to put our creative team upstairs."

I slide around one side of what I realize is an adjustable desk and sit in the ergonomic chair that I'm sure costs more than my rent. An iMac sits on one side and a large monitor sits next to it, something I asked Daniel for over and over again before I left. I wiggle the mouse and see the thing is loaded with all the Adobe software I used and more.

"Wow, that's quite the setup."

"Business is good. We need to grow to keep up." Daniel crosses his arms and leans against the doorjamb, revealing the wedding band on his left hand. Marriage seems to agree with him. I don't recall Daniel ever looking relaxed in the office.

"So, what do you think? I'll start you off with a couple of small accounts of your own. Then once we know you're ready, I'll hire us both entry-level assistants." He finishes this with a chuckle.

The job is pretty much everything I wanted and had been working toward before I left. With that kind of salary increase, Sasha and I could upgrade to a larger apartment by the time our lease comes up for renewal next year.

But something still isn't clicking. "Can I have a couple of days to think it over? I still have to get things settled with my shop and decide if I'm selling my aunt's condo."

He drops his arms as he straightens. "Of course. Take as long as you need, Amanda. You're worth the wait. I know my clients agree. Several expressed their disappointment when you left."

"Really?" I sound like a bumbling newbie. Not a professional designer in New York City about to have her own accounts. "I mean, that's nice to hear."

"It's the truth." He gives me a pointed look.

I push out of the chair, which is so comfortable I could nap in it, and walk toward the doorway to follow Daniel through a sea of secretary cubicles.

He pauses at the reception desk. "Are you free for dinner later? Samantha and I would love to take you to this Moroccan restaurant that just opened up. That is, if she's feeling up to it."

"Is she sick?" Concern makes me frown. Trouble in paradise already?

A sheepish expression replaces his typical confidence. "No, pregnant. We just found out."

"Wow, that's great." I'm happy for him. Really and truly, I am. But I'm also a little envious. Just being real…

"I'll text you the details, okay?"

"Sure, sounds great." I hold my hand out to shake Daniel's. "And thank you. I appreciate this opportunity more than you know."

Once the elevator doors close, I let out a quiet squeal and jump up and down. This is everything I hoped for and the potential for more.

But doubts tinge my excitement. I try to unearth and identify them the entire trip back to the apartment but to no avail.

As I approach the steps leading to our walk-up, a man sitting on the steps stands up.

I pause in front of him, staring and speechless, lost again in his sexy green gaze.

What is Kade doing in New York?

He smiles, letting his dimple finish the job on my heart. "Hey there, Root Beer."

I lift my hands from my sides. "What are you doing here?"

He steps down to the sidewalk. "I found something in your shop after they removed the tree."

"You were at my shop?"

BLOOMED TO BE MESSY

"Yeah…" He drops his chin for a moment. "Zane put together a team of us who have construction experience to help with cleanup and rebuilding. There's a lot to be done, and not enough construction workers. He's amazing."

"Yes, he is." And sneaky. The guy's supposed to be like my brother, yet he's told me nothing about this. "What about your contract with that builder?" I hadn't even thought about how the hurricane could have affected Kade's work.

He runs a hand through his hair. "That's on hold until they get repairs done first, which is complicated since there's—"

"A shortage of workers." I nod and smile as I speak.

"Right. Anyway, I wanted to bring you this." He opens his duffel bag and lifts out a metal box. "I think this may be what that key goes to."

I take the box from him like it's a long-lost treasure unearthed from the depths of some legendary tomb. "I investigated every nook and cranny in that place and never saw it."

"It was probably in the attic. The tree pretty much demolished that part of the roof."

"I have the key upstairs. Want to come up and open it with me?"

He hesitates, then checks his watch.

As much as I want to know what's in the box, I want this time with Kade even more.

He grabs his duffel by the handles, and I'm expecting him to say he has to go.

"Sure, I can spare a few minutes."

Something akin to hope sparks in my heart. "Great."

We walk up the flights of steps in silence until we reach my door. Once inside, I put my purse down and set the box on the small dinette table.

"I'll go get the key." I dash into my bedroom and grab the key from my dresser before returning to the main living area.

Kade stands at the window where the escape ladder runs down the building. "It's very…colorful out there."

I laugh. "Sasha likes to paint in natural light, and that's the closest thing we have to a balcony."

"What about the rooftop?"

"She does that on occasion, but it's a lot of work to haul all her stuff back and forth."

"I can imagine."

I put the key into the lock on the box and it turns. "You're right. It works."

At first glance, the box seems to be filled with old letters, but as I sift through I find a necklace with a glass pendant wrapped in a delicate wire that complements the shape of the glass and picks up the metallic flecks of color running through the pendant.

I hold it up to the light. "Wow, it reminds me of—"

"The glass mangos. Do you think Marnie made it?"

"I don't know. I'll have to ask her when I see her again."

Kade's gaze is penetrating. "Are you coming back to Sarabella?"

"Well, I kind of have to. I'm still waiting to hear from the insurance company about what they're going to cover. Plus, there's the condo…"

He drops his gaze. "Right."

The door to the apartment opens. Sasha starts to rush toward me but stops when she notices Kade. "I rushed home to find out how things went, but who are you?"

I hold out my hand. "Sasha, this is Kade."

She tucks her chin and looks up at me. "Sarabella Kade?"

"Yes." I laugh softly.

"Nice to meet you, Kade." Sasha holds out her hand as she examines every inch of him. Like I said, Sasha doesn't hold back.

"And you, Sasha." Kade glances at me as he shakes her hand, as if to ask what the deal was.

I lift the necklace up again. "Kade found what that mystery key belongs to. Seems my Aunt Paula had a box hidden in the attic of the shop. This was in it, along with some old letters."

Sasha takes the necklace from me. "It's beautiful. I love the colors." She sets her attention fully on Kade. "How long are you staying?"

Kade rubs a hand over his mouth. "I fly back in the morning."

"Then you can join us for dinner," Sasha says as if it's a done deal.

One I have to break. "I have plans already." I shoot a glance at Kade before focusing back on Sasha. "Daniel invited me to dinner."

Her eyes grow round. "Right! That's why I rushed back. How'd it go?"

I'm feeling super awkward now. How do I tell Sasha that I basically had my dream job handed to me on a mostly silver platter while Kade is standing there?

"It went great. I'll tell you all about it later." I widen my eyes, hoping she'll take the hint.

"Oh...then I'll look forward to hearing about it *later*. I better get back to work." She faces Kade. "Again, it was nice to meet you." Sasha waggles her fingers at me, then rushes out the door.

Silence fills the place, heaviest in the span between us. I put the necklace back in the box.

Kade grabs his duffel. "I should probably get going so you can get ready for your date with Daniel."

He thinks I have a date with Daniel...I could let him leave, thinking that I've moved on and that he should, too, but something in me hates the idea of him thinking I'd do that.

Because I haven't. At all.

"Daniel is my old boss, who is married and pregnant. Well, his wife is, I mean."

"Your old boss?" Kade looks visibly relieved, but the line between his brows is still there.

I want so much to smooth that concern away and kiss every

part of his face. Especially that dimple. More than anything, I want to feel his arms around me again.

"Yes, he, um…he offered me a job." I clasp my hands in front of me as I lift one shoulder. I may as well be a shy teenager standing in front of her first crush.

"That's great." His expression shifts, letting me know he's retreating, which breaks my heart at the same time.

But I owe him the full truth. "It's the job I was working toward before Aunt Paula died."

He nods and attempts a tight smile. "I'm happy for you."

"I haven't accepted it yet. I told him I wanted to think about it." I drop my hands and take a step closer to him. "I could cancel dinner tonight so we can talk."

"No, you should go. Sounds important." He picks up his duffel again. "I need to get going, anyway."

I start to say something but end up just nodding.

Kade moves close enough for me to smell his spicy scent, and as he kisses my forehead, I lean in only to lose his warmth when he steps around me and heads out the door.

And then I'm alone again.

But I'm back in New York with everything I've wanted and worked so hard for, sitting at my feet, waiting for me to jump in.

Except…I'm not jumping.

And all I can think about is a set of green eyes and a sexy dimple.

CHAPTER 38
Kade

Seeing Mandy in New York made her leaving Sarabella seem more real. She has a life there, and now her dream job is finally a reality. I admit, finding that out hit me harder than I expected.

I had a plan laid out and wanted to surprise her. A plan to rebuild her shop and get her inventory restocked, thanks to help from Jacob and Sally, who organized getting new inventory from all the vendors Mandy connected with in the past. Even Marnie commissioned several local artists to create new pieces for Bloomed to Be Wilde.

That was my plan to convince Mandy to stay in Sarabella, but if she wants to stay in New York, I have to make a choice.

Let her go.

Or make my life fit hers by moving to New York.

In the short time I've known Mandy, one thing is clear. She's incredibly talented, and amazing, and deserves to have the best future possible.

I plan to do whatever I can to be part of that, even if it means moving.

Because she's worth it. I just hope she thinks I am.

So I expanded my plan. Mandy isn't the only one with

connections in New York. An old friend has a spare room he's offered me for however long I need it, and I found studio space not far away from there.

The builder I contracted with still wants to work with me remotely and work out a schedule for me to make installations one week of the month until the subdivision is completed. That means regular work and income until I get established in New York.

Plus, it turns out they have projects all along the East Coast, so this could be a test run for more work down the road, depending upon the architectural designs for future subdivisions.

But right now, all my time and energy are being spent on rebuilding Amanda's shop.

Because I want her to have a choice. Just like I do.

I know she'll be great in New York, but what she did with her shop, and how so many people rallied right away to help with the effort to bring her shop back to life, is a testimony to her potential to do even more than she thinks she can.

And I intend to prove that to her.

In a week's time, we cleared the remaining debris after the tree removal, reframed the walls, and hired a company to handle the roof. Today, Zane and I are working on drywall.

I don't know if Mandy decided to accept the job—I'm guessing she did. Zane said she's coming back tomorrow to 'settle things.' I've shared none of my plans with him. Only Shannon and my mother know what I've been up to. And I plan to keep it that way because I want Mandy to hear from me first and not the rumor mill.

"The paint's coming tomorrow." Zane may not build houses anymore, but he hasn't lost his knack for mudding drywall.

"Good. We should be able to start painting in a couple of days."

Zane pauses. "Shouldn't Amanda pick the colors?"

"I think she'll like what I picked." Working with her on those mangos gave me a lot of proximity to the artist in her and her love of fall colors. "She can always change it if she wants to."

"Won't really matter if she sells it, I guess."

I grunt but say nothing more. I'm busy replacing the rest of the flooring damaged by the rain.

"Sorry. You probably don't want to talk about it."

"I'll talk about Mandy if you talk about Callie." I've been trying to get Zane to open up ever since they had their run-in, but the guy is closed up tighter than a tomb.

"And consider the topic dropped." He chuckles, but I hear the edge to his voice.

"How's it going in there? I brought food." Sally's voice brings a halt to our work.

Because rebuilding a shop is hard work and builds an appetite. All I can say is the food Sally brought won't last fifteen minutes. Twenty tops.

As Zane and I inhale the food, Sally walks around the shop. "This place hasn't looked this good in years."

Zane nods as he inhales half of a hamburger in one bite, then takes a long draw from a can of soda to wash it down. "Agreed. I think Amanda will be pleasantly surprised."

Sally directs her gaze at me. "Hopefully enough to change her mind about leaving."

I feign interest in my french fries. "It's her choice."

She smiles, nods, and gives me a thumbs up, which I'm guessing means she has done her part.

Oh, did I forget to mention I let Sally in on my plans, too? Because she's helping me with a contingency plan.

One where I hope Mandy decides she's all in.

CHAPTER 39
Amanda

"How does it feel to be back?" The video call does nothing to hide Sasha's squirmy expression. She's trying to be delicate, which is so out of character for her.

But I get it. She knows what's at stake.

"Weird but good. Unsettling yet…homey." Almost three months ago, I rushed back to Sarabella when I received word of my Aunt Paula's unexpected death. I can barely remember the flight that day. Most of that first week is a blur.

And now I'm back in what feels like similar circumstances. Almost like saying goodbye to Aunt Paula all over again.

Goodbye to what's left of her—my shop.

And it feels like her death all over again. I've been sitting in her favorite chair in the condo all morning, trying to feel closer to her. And in a way, I do.

Sasha nods. "Everything in place for the wedding?"

"Yes. And everything looks amazing." I had to hit the ground running when I arrived two days ago to finish Emily's centerpieces and help her arrange them at the venue yesterday. Right now, a wedding feels like a breath of life in what's turned into a sad ending. I just hope I can hold myself together during the ceremony.

I'm thrilled that Emily will get her very own happily ever after, and...a little melancholy over it as well. Because I can't help but wonder...

Sasha's voice brings me back, front and center. "I know, I saw the pictures you sent."

"That's right, I did."

I can't help but wonder if I'll ever have the kind of happiness I see Daniel experiencing with his new wife and a baby on the way. And Emily and Aiden—a romance birthed from banana bread, of all things.

I've made my whole life's goal about not being my mother, about not settling for some warped version of my dream. But maybe I'm not meant to have that kind of happiness. Maybe it's impossible to have the career I want and a romance that resembles a fairy tale. Maybe my career will have to be enough, and that's not settling.

Or is it?

"Amanda, I know I've asked you this a lot lately, but are you okay? I mean, really okay?"

Her question makes me realize I drifted off again. "Yeah, I guess. Aunt Paula's letters really have me rethinking some things."

"Rethinking is good. So is reframing." Sasha gives me one of her authoritative expressions. The woman is a master at reframing any situation.

I giggle. "Yes, so you've told me many-a-time."

"Then what exactly are you rethinking?" Her brows lift as she waits for my answer.

I pick up the stack of letters that I just read again and hold them up to my phone screen. "These letters are filled with declarations of love from a man named Julius and his reminders of their time together. I had no idea my aunt was so passionate about life, art, and the world."

According to the letters, Aunt Paula had a dream to fulfill, and she put that above everything.

Much like I have…

I put my arm down and stare at the scrawling handwriting filled with declarations of his love for her and reminders of their time together. "He wanted a life with her, but she turned him down."

"Why?"

I shrug. "I'm not entirely sure. It all happened after I left for college."

"And she never mentioned him?"

"Not really. She mentioned a relationship not working out once, but I assumed it happened before I was born."

"What do the letters say, exactly?"

"He talks about understanding how important her shop is, and her life in Sarabella, but he wanted to take her to see the world. He sent her the necklace from Greece with a plea for her to join him. He had everything arranged. All she had to do was say yes."

But it's the last letter that's left me undone.…he met someone and was engaged.

Sasha tilts her head. "I wonder if she was afraid."

"Maybe. Or maybe she didn't feel she could leave the shop behind. She always called it her dream place."

But was it enough for her?

I remember Shannon saying that Kade was an all-or-nothing kind of guy when it came to those he loved. Part of me wants to grab hold of that—of him—more than the new job waiting for me when I return to New York.

And that terrifies me.

What if I take the chance and the shop fails? What about the dream that sent me to New York in the first place? Do I just set that aside for Kade? And what if I do and things don't work out between us?

I'll have lost everything I worked for, right?

Sasha lets out a breathy sigh that blows her bangs around. "Okay, I want you to try something. Do you trust me?"

"Always."

"Close your eyes and picture yourself working for Daniel. You have your office set up just the way you imagined and you're sitting in that fancy chair, talking to clients about their products and your exciting plans to help them take things to the next level."

I sit back and do as she says.

"Can you see it all?"

"Yes, even the fuzzy giraffe you gave me is sitting on the side of the desk." Eyes still closed, I laugh. That giraffe is hilarious with its buggy eyes and pink and black coloring instead of brown and tan.

"Okay, now tell me how you feel."

I lift one shoulder. "Good. Seems pretty exciting. A lot of work, but it's good." I open my eyes.

"Keep your eyes closed." Sasha sounds like a drill sergeant.

I slam my lids down. "Sorry."

"Okay, now picture your shop rebuilt just the way you want it. All brand new inside, filled with all those wonderful items you found from the local vendors you connected with, the glass mangos you and Kade and what's her name—"

"Marnie."

"Such a weird name," she mumbles. "And Marnie created together. Imagine opening your shop each day, helping customers. What it will look like through Thanksgiving and Christmas…"

I can picture it. All of it. New displays for the store and the front window, garlands of fall leaves, and then little Christmas trees with twinkle lights. I'm overwhelmed by this cozy sense of comfort and peace.

And home.

And Kade.

And us…

An excitement I didn't feel when I thought about the job in

New York is bubbling up more and more as I think about all these things.

My eyes pop open.

Sasha studies me. "Well?"

"Well, what?"

She rolls her eyes and makes that clicking sound. "How does it make you feel?"

"You sure you want to know?"

She sighs. "Just tell me what I already suspect."

"Amazing." My voice sounds breathless as I say it. And I know.

I knoooooow…

"Sasha, I have to go. I have a wedding to get to!"

And a shop to visit and figure out what needs to be done to get it up and running again. I launch out of Aunt Paula's chair but stop and spin around to look at the colorful paisley fabric and her books sitting on the side table.

"Pray for me, Aunt Paula. I have a shop to fix."

And maybe, just maybe, find a guy who likes to call me Root Beer.

CHAPTER 40
Kade

Everything is ready to go. I even had signs made—one for the front door of Mandy's shop and one directing people where to go.

But first I have to attend Emily and Aiden's wedding. I say 'have to' as in Eliana insisted we had to go. Seems she won Emily's heart that day at the festival and received her own invitation to the wedding. As did Shannon, of course.

I think I actually saw my mother pout when she found out we had a wedding to go to instead of having lunch together, which has become our routine since the hurricane. Breakfast at her place on Saturday mornings.

And it's been good. Really great to reconnect and rebuild our relationship without the shadows of the past hanging over us.

Knowing I'll see Mandy today has me twisted in knots. I haven't seen her in what feels like weeks, because, well, it's been weeks. Three to be exact since I saw her in New York.

And if things go according to my plan, Emily's wedding isn't the only life-changing event planned for the day.

The thought makes my insides twist tighter. Because in the end, it's still going to be Mandy's choice. That's the way it needs to be so that whatever she chooses, she'll know that's what she wants.

No doubts. Just all in. Like me.

"Uncle Kade, which side do we sit on?"

"Huh?" I realize I'm still standing off to the side, staring but not seeing rows of white chairs arranged in front of a platform.

The original venue wound up with water damage so Emily and Aiden decided to hold the ceremony at the same place they're doing the reception. And they enlisted me to help break down chairs and set up tables after the ceremony while the wedding party poses for pictures and guests enjoy complimentary drinks and hors d'oeuvres while they wait for the reception to start.

Shannon takes Eliana's hand. "She means, are we sitting on the bride's side or the groom's?"

I pop my brows up. "Good question. I know them both."

"Which side will Amanda be sitting on?" Shannon leers at me.

"Team Emily it is."

As Shannon and Eliana walk down the aisle to find seats, I scan the room for Mandy but don't see her yet. But as I turn to follow Shannon and Elly, a splash of green catches my eye.

Mandy looks stunning in her dress, and she has her hair swept up, revealing the soft and delicate curve of her neck. My fingers are itching to brush over that line, studying the smoothness like I do when I'm molding metal into intricate shapes.

Her eyes meet mine as she waves at me from across the room.

I'm so glued to the floor as she walks over to me, making me fall in love with her even more with every step. I close my eyes and run a hand over my mouth to break the spell before I make a complete and utter fool of myself in front of the wedding attendees here to see someone else's romance culminate.

And I realize I want that with Mandy more than anything.

I'll live anywhere in the country she wants to, as long as we're together. Building a life…together.

"Hi, there." She tilts her head. One curled tendril of hair hanging down around her face falls in front of her mouth.

Before I can think, I brush it away, running my thumb across her mouth as I do, which causes her lips to part just so. "It's good to see you."

So good that I wish the wedding and reception were over already so I can get on with my big reveal.

"Are you here alone?" She glances away, but not before I catch a glimmer of doubt in her eyes.

"No, actually."

"Oh." Her smile falters.

"Shannon and Eliana are here, too."

Her smile returns wider than ever. "I was hoping I'd get to see them. Can I sit with you?"

"Of course." I put my elbow out as an invitation to guide her to where Shannon and Eliana have settled.

Mandy rewards me with the warmth of her hand on my arm, which I cover with my other hand. As we walk down the aisle, I notice Aiden nod at me and smile. I get the distinct sense that if he could say something to me right now, it would be, 'This is going to be you one day.'

We sit but not for long. The music shifts to the wedding chorus, and we all stand in a rustle of fabric and excited breaths at seeing the bride enter the room. And Emily makes a stunning bride indeed, but not as beautiful as I imagine Mandy would be.

During the exchange of vows, Mandy inserts her hand in mine. I study how our fingers entwine before searching out her face.

She won't look at me, but she smiles and squeezes my hand.

After the ceremony ends and the wedding party and attendees leave the room, I kick into high gear to get the chairs folded and loaded onto the waiting carts.

Zane and I make a silent competition of it, but I'm certain

I'd get the medal if there was one. The sooner we get things moving, the sooner I can get my plan into place. I think Zane knows what I'm thinking because he keeps giving me this goofy grin like he's excited for me.

For us.

I want an 'us' so much, it's making me impatient. Waiting for the reception to end is sweet agony as I anticipate and play out potential scenarios in my head.

Once the guests return, I find Mandy and grab her hand. "Come with me."

Her heels tap on the floor behind me as I tug her along. "Where are we going?"

I stop and turn around, which causes her to bump into me. "Do you trust me?"

She nods as she leans in, tilting her head up.

I can read her mind, and her lips, that are asking to be kissed, but anticipation will only make that inevitable kiss sweeter.

"Of course."

I lead her out of the building and down the sidewalk to where I parked my truck.

She pauses as I open the passenger door. "I told Emily I would help after the reception ends."

"We'll be back in time."

The drive to her shop is brief. We could have walked, but I don't want to waste time or make her walk in heels. As we pull up in front of her shop, she gasps and beats me in opening her door.

"Kade, what…did you…wow." She covers her face with her hands so I can only see her eyes, which are round with shock.

We're standing on the sidewalk, side-by-side, staring at her shop that is nearly finished. "We've been working round the clock."

"We?"

"Zane and the team he put together."

"I don't know what to say." Her voice is soft. Unsure.

"There's still a fair bit of work to do inside." I lead her up the steps to the front door, which still needs to be painted, along with most of the trim work that was replaced.

She reads the sign on the door. "A temporary location?" She faces me. "Isn't that your studio?"

"Come on. I'll show you." This time we walk because I want her to see the signs pointing to my studio.

As we approach my door, she gasps. "Temporary home of Bloomed to Be Wilde."

I unlock the door and let her go in first.

Not an easy feat to move a workbench and all my tools and equipment, but with Zane's help, we cleared a workable space to create a temporary shop for Mandy.

She stands near the breakfront I salvaged from her shop. Sally set up a couple of tables as temporary solutions to display the items we saved from the shop, plus new ones. Eliana painted more pots for the succulents Jacob donated, and Marnie and I created twenty more glass mangos to add to Mandy's inventory.

"I know it's not the same, but this will keep you going until your shop is finished."

She picks up one of the pots Eliana painted as she holds her hand over her mouth. I think she's trying not to cry.

But she still isn't saying anything and the range of emotions on her face is too fast for me to follow. But the final one makes me think I miscalculated everything because I can see it clearly now.

Mandy's not sure.

CHAPTER 41
Amanda

"This is...amazing, Kade. I can't believe you did this for me."

He's asking me to stay in Sarabella. I know he is.

This morning I thought I was sure this was what I wanted. So why am I doubting now?

"It's just temporary. This way you can get things rolling faster and at the end of the year, sell your shop."

Sell...

He thinks I still want to sell my shop and go back to New York.

Okay...maybe I misunderstood. Is he only looking for something casual? But Shannon described Kade as an all-or-nothing kind of guy. And in my book, nothing does not include hand-holding at a wedding.

So what gives?

I drop my hands and turn my back to him as I walk over to the table displaying more mangos—my attempt to hide the tears threatening to burst out and ruin my make-up. I know we never declared our feelings for each other, yet I was so sure. But that was weeks ago.

Did I make the same mistake Aunt Paula did and wait too long?

"And I move to New York."

His words snap me around faster than a bungee cord. "Wait…what? Why?"

"So we can be together." He's studying me again.

"What about your studio? What about Eliana?" I know how important it is for him to be here for them. Especially the squirt—now he has me calling her that.

"I can work anywhere, and flights between here and New York are easy."

"But I thought you felt like you needed to be around for her? You know, be here so you can help Shannon raise her." I brave a step closer, daring to believe this could be real and not some weird post-wedding hallucination I'm having from drinking too much champagne.

"And I will. I need to be in Sarabella about one week out of the month to install the pieces I'm still doing for the builder." He moves closer. "And I already have a space on hold for my studio and a friend there has a room I can lease."

That's when I realize he's already done the legwork to figure this all out. "You'd really do all that for me?"

His green eyes smolder as he pushes that errant tendril back behind my ear again. "I'd do anything for you, Root Beer."

My heart is pounding so hard I can barely speak, because the entire paradigm of my life is shifting. I want to stay in Sarabella with my makeshift family. I want to make Bloomed to Be Wilde something special in this town. And I want a future with Kade.

I'm not settling.

This is my dream now.

"What if I don't want to sell my shop? What if I want to stay here in Sarabella…with you?"

Kade lowers his head toward mine. "Is that your choice?"

I feel lost in the sparkle of his green eyes, yet at the same time, feel as if I've found myself. Found where I belong in Sarabella. Found home…

If this were the last day of my life, I'd die a happy woman and tell Aunt Paula all about it in heaven.

"Yes."

His eyes drop to my lips as he leans in. "As long as you're sure."

I moisten my lips as I anticipate the first touch of his to mine. "I'm all in."

CHAPTER 42
Amanda

EPILOGUE

ONE YEAR LATER

"Are you ready?" Kade hollers from the top step, ready to connect power to the Christmas lights lining the walkway to my shop and the cluster of trees of various sizes standing to the right of the door. We've worked all day creating a kind of winter wonderland Florida-style.

And yes, that means the palm trees are decorated, too. I promised Sasha when she comes to visit that she'd get to see a tropical Christmas.

"Ready!"

He plugs the main cord into the outlet and warm light bursts out from everywhere.

"It's beautiful!" I clap my hands and jump up and down like a kid.

Kade saunters down the steps with a sly grin on his face.

"What are you up to?" I've learned to recognize that grin, which usually signals he has a surprise for me. And our last year together has been full of them.

My shop wound up fully restored and more beautiful than I imagined. Kade even picked paint colors I absolutely adored.

And Bloomed to Be Wilde was just featured in a travel magazine as one of the best boutiques in the area for one-of-a-kind items and pieces of art.

And flowers, of course.

"Just a little something I made for you." He pulls something from his pocket.

I try not to gasp when I recognize the box. Yes, it's a ring box, and I can't stop staring at the red velvet as I wait to see what I suspect is inside.

But he's not opening it, so I shoot my gaze upward. "Are you going to show me what it is?"

"That depends."

"On what?"

"Well, it's been over a year. Any plans to sell your shop?"

I pull my head back. "You're kidding, right?"

"No, just making sure." He chuckles.

I put my hand on his chest. "I'm all in, remember?"

He opens the box in what almost feels like slow motion.

I bend over to see the ring. Okay, not a diamond, but a piece of glass that looks like it came from one of the mangos, which continue to be my best-selling item.

"Is that glass like the mangos?" I pick up the ring to take in the vine that twines around a delicate piece of rounded glass in shades of green, orange, and red and the delicate leaves on the sides. It's exquisite, and I love it, but I don't know if it's just a ring he made me or if it's THE RING.

"I created the setting. Marnie did the glass, which I can replace with a diamond, if that's your choice."

I gasp. "Then you're asking me—"

Kade goes down on one knee in the middle of my Christmas wonderland of lights. He couldn't have picked a more perfect moment. "Yes, I'm asking you to marry me, Mandy."

I lift my eyes to his green ones that are so filled with love I'm dizzy. "I want to keep the glass."

He lifts his brows in surprise and grins with delight. "Are you sure?"

We started with mangos. It seems only fitting we keep the trend going. And the green reminds me of his eyes.

"Yes, I'm more than sure." I hold my hand out, ring finger lifted just so.

Grinning, he takes the ring and slips it on my finger, then stands as he pulls me against him. "I'm glad you chose to keep the glass."

"Why?" I know 'my' why, but I want to hear his.

His eyes dart back and forth for a moment as he studies my face. And for me, regarding Kade, it will always be about those smoking green eyes and that sexy dimple that comes out to play regularly now.

"Because it's us."

I bring my face up to meet his kiss. "It will always be us."

Want to find out what happens with Zane and Callie?
He thought they'd be together forever. When the tide brings her back into his life, will love throw them a lifeline?
Start reading Rescued to Be Messy today!

Did you enjoy *Bloomed to Be Messy?* You can read about Emily and Aiden free!

She could be the girl of his dreams. Too bad he just made a fool of himself asking her out....

Tap here to download a free copy of "Brewed to be Messy." You'll also be signed up for my newsletter, where you'll receive sneak previews, exclusive content, and all my thoughts on sweet romantic comedy.

Before You Wilt...

Dear friend,

If you enjoyed *Bloomed to Be Messy*, please share it with your friends and leave a review on Amazon so other readers can enjoy Amanda and Kade's story, too.

And thank you for reading!

~*Dineen*

Follow me on Amazon to get book alerts as they happen!

Join My Facebook Reader Group!

ABOUT ME

Dineen Miller is an Amazon bestselling and award-winning author of both fiction and nonfiction, but only recently discovered she has a sublime addiction to writing and reading romantic comedies. In addition to these, she's been known to write romantic suspense and has dabbled with thrillers and fantasy.

Needing additional outlets for her creativity, she's designed several coloring books under her own name and under Hue Manatee Art, and has crocheted too many afghans to count. No, she does not have cats, but she is a dog-mom to two furry rescues that answer to wiggle butt and snuggle boy. And she's married to a punny guy, who thinks she's unique.

Visit my website at DineenMiller.com for more information about me and my books. And please connect with me on these social media platforms:

Acknowledgments

First and foremost, the story behind the story. During a conversation with my oldest daughter, she told me about her plans to visit a close friend. As we chatted, my daughter shared some of her friend's story of taking over her grandmother's flower shop and how she transformed it into a vital hub in a small town.

I knew right away I needed to chat with this amazing young woman because I was so inspired by her story. So, a very special thank you goes to Corinne Nelson for sharing her incredible journey with me, and especially for being so courageous and inspiring in her true life story. You are an amazing force of nature, my young friend. And thank you for doing a video interview to boot! I know my readers will love it and you!

Special thanks to my beta readers Trisha Ontiveros, Charity Henico, and Sally Silva. Thank you for giving your time and input so generously. And to Author Ad School coach, Jen Lassalle, for her help brainstorming the theme and title soft this series, and for her ongoing encouragement. I am so very grateful to all of you.

I want to thank my Facebook group, Dineen's Rockstar Readers, and my email subscribers for taking this journey with me. *Bloomed to Be Messy* is a brand new adventure for me in storytelling, one I didn't see coming and am so thrilled to be on! I feel like I finally found my true voice. So thank you, my friends, for all your support and for reading Amanda and Kade's story. So fun!

As always, thank you to my editors, Alice Shepherd and Judy DeVries for helping me make this story (and so many others!) shine. You ladies are the best.

And to you, dear reader, thank you for diving into the Messy Love on Mango Lane stories. I know this one touched on the grief of losing someone dear in our lives and the aftermath that comes with it. If you are in that place, my friend, I pray you have others to walk with you through the healing journey. I have found that the ones who do so are oftentimes the most unexpected.

Live authentically, love fully, and laugh often.

~Dineen

Printed in Great Britain
by Amazon

45192906R00199